Charlie Higson started writing when he was ten years old. After university he was a singer and painter and decorator before he started writing for television. He went on to create and star in the hugely successful comedy series *The Fast Show*. He is the author of the bestselling Young Bond books and the incredibly successful horror series, The Enemy.

Charlie doesn't do Facebook, but you can tweet him @monstroso.

Also by Charlie Higson

FULL WHACK

CHARLIE HIGSON

ABACUS

ABACUS

First published in Great Britain in 1995
Reissued in 2022 by Abacus

1 3 5 7 9 10 8 6 4 2

A CIP catalogue record for this book
is available from the British Library.

ISBN 978-03491-4486-3

Typeset in Garamond by M Rules
Printed and bound in Great Britain by
Clays Ltd, Elcograf S.p.A.

Papers used by Abacus are from well-managed forests
and other responsible sources.

Abacus
An imprint of
Little, Brown Book Group
Carmelite House
50 Victoria Embankment
London EC4Y 0DZ

An Hachette UK Company
www.hachette.co.uk

www.littlebrown.co.uk

For Vicky and Frank

Thanks to my brother, Dan Higson, for helping research parts of this book.

ONE

Dennis Pike had picked the wrong day to give up smoking. There was frost on the windows in the morning. The bread was stale, the milk was sour, there was a dead junkie in the lift and now two kids were breaking into his car.

It wasn't an expensive car, a pale yellow two-door 1982 Ford Escort. There was nothing valuable in it and the radio was locked in the boot. But there was no point explaining this to the two boys, they'd already smashed the passenger window and were reaching in to unlock the door.

'Oi! What are you doing?' he shouted, and furiously wheeled his shopping trolley towards them, bouncing and bumping down the ramp from Dalston Cross.

They looked at him disinterestedly. They were probably only sixteen, maybe less. They wore big, loose, zip-up designer jackets, baggy jeans and trainers.

After a moment they turned their attention back to the car.

'I said what are you doing?'

They didn't reply, just opened the door.

'That's my car.'

'It's a crap car,' the taller of the two boys said and turned back round to Pike, brandishing a baseball bat.

Pike sighed. Everybody wanted to be an American.

The boy had small eyes set wide apart in a dull, flat face. He took

1

a couple of paces towards Pike, slapping the bat into his open palm. 'Piss off,' he said.

What a day.

It had started when he'd poured the milk onto his corn flakes and it had come out in cheesy lumps. He'd forgotten to put the bread away the night before and it was hard and dry. So he'd gone out to the corner shop and that was when he'd discovered the dead junkie in the lift. A young white guy in jeans and sweat shirt. Long hair in a style like people didn't have any more. He looked like a smack-head and Pike felt almost nostalgic. These days it was all crack. A proper old-fashioned junkie was something you didn't see that often. He lay curled up in the corner and at first Pike had thought he was asleep or passed out, so he'd kicked him. His skin prickled when he realized he was dead.

It was bound to happen sooner or later – a dead man in the lift. Ever since the police had opened up a dinky little designer police station on Sandringham Road to try and deter the dealers, the dealers had all moved round the corner to the flats. They hung about in the doorway of the betting shop opposite, trying to look flash and inconspicuous at the same time. Pike was sick of finding people passing over wads of money on the walkways and shaking rock-filled hands in the stairwells.

After getting the bread and milk he'd got a tape out of Mammoth Video to cheer himself up. *Southern Comfort*. He'd eaten breakfast, then settled down in his leather recliner with a cup of tea and pressed start on the remote control. The machine made a horrible, rasping, churning type of a sound. The picture juddered and everything went dead.

When he'd tried eject it wouldn't give him the tape back. He'd lifted the flap and tried to tug it out but it was stuck fast.

So his video was fucked. He'd checked the paper for the television, but there were no films on till later, only dreary daytime programmes about dogs and family problems and cheery Australians.

2

What a fucking day.

'Go on, piss off.' The kid with the baseball bat came closer.

There was no chance that the guard, way down the other end of the car park in his little hut was going to see them, or even do anything if he did. It was a wet night and there was no one else around; five other cars at most. The car park felt vast and isolated. One side was bordered by a great mass of factories and warehouses, one by a train line and one by the backside of the Dalston Cross shopping mall.

Baseball Bat's friend, whose black Naf Naf jacket was two sizes too big for him, nodded his head rhythmically and muttered 'Yeah, yeah, yeah . . .' under his breath. Over and over.

Pike wished he hadn't decided to give up smoking last night, but it was part of his new order. Quit work, quit fags and get ready for the future. He didn't need this.

'Come on, just leave it,' he said, but they weren't impressed. He knew what he looked like to them. An old geezer with glasses and a shopping trolley.

He glanced down into the trolley for a possible weapon. A French loaf, not much use. A bottle of vinegar, too small, liable to smash and cut his hand.

'Did you really have to break the window?' he said, buying time. 'That is such a pain in the arse.'

'Well, I really care about that, don't I?' Baseball Bat said sarcastically. Naf Naf laughed. That was when Pike noticed the frozen chicken.

'Okay,' he said. 'Why don't you just walk away? Huh? We'll say no more about the window. Because I've just given up smoking and I don't need this shit.'

'Why don't you just walk away, mate?' the boy raised the bat in a challenge.

Bloody kids.

Pike always went to the supermarket at Dalston Cross on

3

Tuesdays. He'd tried all times, all days, but Tuesday evening at seven-thirty was when it was least busy. Pike hated crowds.

He knew that the market on Ridley Road, right next door, was half the price, but it made no odds to him. Pike liked to go in, load up a trolley with a week's supplies, pay for it quick and get out. What's more, Dalston Cross had this huge car park out the back so he didn't have to carry any heavy bags.

Dalston Cross was the area's premier indoor shopping precinct, with its very own campanile. Pike knew it was a campanile because someone had told him while he was waiting in a queue at the checkout one day. Well, of course, it made sense, north-east London was famous for its Italian-style bell-towers.

Inside, there was piped Christmas music playing and a Santa's grotto had been set up. Around the grotto was a pen enclosing a Christmas scene with moving models; elves and gnomes and woodland creatures dressed in Victorian clothing. There was something vaguely sinister about the repetitive nodding heads and waving arms in the empty mall. More creatures were hung from the ceiling like in some kind of sick Xmas abattoir.

It was pleasant wandering the deserted, brightly lit aisles of the huge supermarket. Pike positively enjoyed shopping under these conditions. He found himself looking forward to his weekly ritual and after the problems of the morning it had been quite relaxing.

And then this had happened.

Baseball Bat walked towards Pike and put on his best hard-nut expression.

'Okay,' said Pike. 'It's your choice.'

With one hand he pushed the trolley at the boy, distracting him. With the other he picked out the frozen chicken. As the boy's hands went to stop the trolley and he looked down, Pike launched the chicken shot-put style and it smacked into his forehead with a thwack. At the same time a train roared past on the North London Line, and Pike was vaguely aware of a smear of lights and faces.

Stunned, Baseball Bat tottered back and sat down heavily on the wet tarmac dropping the bat. Pike ran round and picked it up. He wondered if anyone on the train had witnessed the little scene, some budding Agatha Christie type who might try and work out what was going on with the trolley, the bat and the frozen chicken. Naf Naf was too surprised by the turn of events to do anything more than gawp, and Pike pushed him back against the car with the end of the bat.

Naf Naf's eyes widened and he said 'shit' quietly.

'It's a bugger, isn't it?' said Pike. 'Now, turn your pockets out. You're going to pay for this window.'

It was no use, though. They had a pathetic four pounds thirty-eight pence between them. Pike didn't have the heart to take it. He kept the bat instead.

He went home, let himself into his flat and rang a twenty-four-hour window replacement service. Then he sat down to watch the television and wait.

He'd furnished the flat almost exclusively from a secondhand office equipment suppliers under the railway arches by Hackney Downs station. There were beige, industrial-strength carpet tiles on all the floors and dark green metal shelving units around most of the walls. He didn't have cupboards, he had filing cabinets. The chairs were all office chairs, with wheels and tilting backs. Instead of tables he had mostly metal desks. His only nod to comfort was his prized leather reclining seat from where he watched the TV. And what a TV. The latest wide-screen affair, thirty-six inches, with Nicam, built-in stereo speakers and a state of the art VCR wired in below.

A fucked state of the art VCR.

He looked ruefully at the packet of Silk Cut he'd left on the mantelpiece as a test. Well, he'd survived all this without caving in and the first day was bound to be the worst. At least there was some decent telly on this evening. A couple of films and a thing about crocodiles that looked interesting.

An hour or so later he was feeling pretty mellow and he decided he might as well chuck the cigarettes away. He picked up the packet and aimed it at the metal bin, but before he could throw it, the doorbell went.

It was the window guy. Pike went down with him as he fixed the door, paid him in cash what seemed like a ridiculously large figure, then went back up to his flat.

As he got out of the now junkie-free lift he saw two blokes standing outside his flat peering in the window.

'Hello?' he said, cautiously moving down the walkway towards them.

They turned round and his heart sank.

It was the Bishop brothers, Chas and Noel. Ten years had changed them, but they still looked like bad luck.

He fished the packet of Silk Cut out of his pocket and took out a cigarette.

'Hello, Noel,' he said. 'Got a light?'

TWO

The Bishop brothers. Pike remembered the first time he'd met them. In The Cock in Tottenham.

Noel had come over to where Pike was drinking at the bar and introduced himself. 'I'm Noel and this is Chas. We're brothers. Twins. Identical.' He laughed. That was his joke. Brothers they may have been, but twins they were not. Two people couldn't have looked more unlike. Chas had been short and stocky with slicked-back hair, Noel, tall and skinny with a curly perm. They looked awful.

'Identical to what?' Pike had asked. 'Certainly nothing human.'

It had been one of those moments that could have gone either way. He'd seen their brains turning over, considering – 'Is he having a go? Do we start a fight? Or do we treat it as a joke?' It was to Pike's eternal regret that they both laughed. If only they could have all clobbered each other for a few minutes that would have been that and he'd not have been burdened with having Noel and his stupid brother as friends for the rest of his life.

'You gonna ask us in, then?' Noel asked, handing Pike a Bic lighter.

'Nope.' Pike lit his cigarette and handed the lighter back.

'Come on, Pikey. It's been ten years.'

'What do you want, Noel?' said Pike, unlocking the door.

'Have a heart,' said Chas. 'It's freezing out here.'

7

Pike realized there was no point in arguing. They'd tracked him down, there had to be a reason and they were unlikely to give up now and just go away.

He opened the door and nodded for them to follow him in.

Chas had always fancied himself as the more stylish of the two. Tonight he was wearing a grey suit of some sparkly material with the sleeves rolled up, a black shirt open at the neck, a lot of gold, and expensive burgundy loafers with tassels. He had a deep tan and a drinker's coarsened features. He'd bleached his hair, a sort of silvery blond, in an elaborate blow-dried hairstyle. Pike couldn't understand why anyone would want to have their hair done up to look so much like a wig. Noel was something else again. His body had filled out, it had become round and egglike, but his long arms and legs were still skinny. He wore high-waisted jeans pulled up over his gut, a white shirt and a colourful nylon jacket which in Pike's day would have been called an anorak. He had a small round head the top of which was completely bald, but he'd made up for it by growing his hair very long round the back and sides. It hung down, straight and lank, to his collar.

Pike was unused to having anyone in his sitting room. It wasn't designed for visitors. The recliner was the only comfortable chair and Noel had already grabbed that.

'Nice,' he said, putting his hands behind his head and leaning back. 'That's a big telly.'

Chas was looking at the metal shelving unit stacked to the ceiling with videos.

'That's a lot of videos,' he said. 'You watched them all?'

'What do you two want?'

'You got anything to drink, Pikey?' said Noel.

'There's some beers in the fridge.'

Noel smiled and winked at him. 'Good lad.'

Pike went and fetched a four-pack of Fosters, handed them round.

'Almost didn't recognize you, Dennis,' Chas said, popping a can. 'What happened to you?'

'I got older.'

'You're completely grey,' said Noel. 'What's that all about?'

'It runs in the family,' Pike said. 'My dad was white before he was forty, but at least he's still got a full head of hair.'

Noel stroked his bald pate. 'Disgusting, innit?'

'And what's with the glasses?' said Chas, turning over a metal waste bin and sitting on it. 'Dennis Pike, the wild man of Tottenham, in specs? Times have changed.'

'All right. I've gone grey. I wear glasses. I've got a big telly. You didn't come here to tell me that.'

'We need your help, Dennis,' Chas said earnestly.

'Yeah. Goodnight,' Pike replied.

'Hear us out Dennis.'

'I'm not interested in any of your schemes, Chas.'

'No, no. It's not like that.'

'What you been doing the last ten years, Pikey?' said Noel, turning on the TV set and muting the sound.

'Nothing,'

'You must have been doing something.'

Pike looked at the TV screen. *Against All Odds* was on. He'd been looking forward to watching it. He was a big fan of the original with Robert Mitchum and had never seen the Jeff Bridges version.

'I've been keeping myself to myself,' he said. 'I aim to keep it that way.'

'We're gonna rob Patterson,' said Chas with a big grin. 'Shit's got it coming to him.'

Pike shook his head. 'You guys are morons, aren't you?'

'Patterson's gone up in the world,' said Noel. 'He's a big cheese now. Got his own business. Electronics.'

'So you're going to rob him?'

'It's a perfect plan,' said Chas.

'I doubt it, if it's one of yours.'

'Listen.' Chas lit a cigarette, Benson and Hedges. 'Even if he knows it's us, he can't go to the law, can he? Couldn't take us to court. It'd all come out, wouldn't it? He'd be sunk. It's beautiful – rob the robbers.'

'We'd all be fucking sunk, Chas. The fuck d'you think I've been keeping my head down these last ten years?'

'We just need a bit of muscle, Pikey. That's all,' said Noel.

'Forget it. I'm out of that.'

'He's loaded,' said Chas. 'Millionaire more than likely.'

'I'm not interested. I've got money. I worked. I saved up. I'm going away. Last thing I need right now is for you two muppets to drag me back into the shit. Jesus, I bet you don't even have a plan, do you?'

'We've got a concept,' said Chas.

'A fucking concept.'

'All right,' said Noel. 'It's true. We haven't exactly sorted out the mechanics. We're still at the planning stage, putting together a team, but ...'

'Oh, fuck off. Get out of here.'

'It's a beautiful concept,' said Noel. 'Ripping off Patterson.'

'Why me, Noel? Why couldn't you have gone to one of the others? Chrissie, or Colin or Mick?'

'They're all dead.'

Pike sat down on a desk top. 'Shit, I forgot,' he said. 'Mick got stuffed in Florida, didn't he?'

'Drugs.'

'He couldn't keep out of it, could he? I didn't know about Colin and Chrissie, though.'

'Colin come off his bike,' said Chas.

'Figures. And Chrissie? Drunk himself to death, I bet.'

'Choked,' said Noel. 'Vomit. Silly sod was supposed to be on the wagon. He'd been dry three years.'

'The lads are dying, Dennis,' said Chas, tipping ash on to the floor. 'We're the only ones left.'

'We were losers, Chas. All of us. We were all due to take an early bath.'

'You're a wanker, Pikey,' said Noel sadly. 'You've lost it.'

'Maybe I have.' On the screen Rachel Ward was flouncing about in some skimpy outfit somewhere hot, Mexico it looked like. 'Maybe I am a wanker. But I'll tell you this, Noel. I used to think civilians were wankers, people who worked for a living, but I found out it's a lot more hard work being a bad man, a fucking hooligan. I was a mug. But not any more. I've got enough money stashed in a high-interest account that I can live off until I'm out of here. Canada. Six weeks and bye, bye.'

'Jesus, Pikey,' said Noel. 'What a sad story. You used to be Dennis the Menace, north London's very own berserker, the wild man of Tottenham. You used to be Pike, for fuck's sake. Look at you now with your grey hair and your glasses and your high-interest account.'

'It won't work, Noel. I'm not having anything to do with it. What did you expect? You'd tell me your half-baked "concept" and I'd go on the rampage? Fuck over Ian Patterson? Pretend nothing had changed?'

'Where's your bog, Dennis?' said Chas. 'This beer's gone right through me.'

'Out in the hall. By the front door.'

Chas grunted as he hauled himself up off the bin. Then he belched, adjusted his trousers and went out, closing the door behind him.

Noel flicked through the channels. 'You got Sky?' he asked.

'No.'

'Rubbish, innit?'

'How did you find me, Noel?'

'Herman the German.'

'Who's he when he's at home?'

'Chas met him in the nick.'

'I didn't know Chas was inside.'

'Two years, cheque cards.'

'Silly bastard.'

'Herman's a hacker, computers and that. Genius. When Chas got out he looked him up. He's a useful lad to know in this day and age. They've pulled a couple of scams together, him and Chas. Herman's not really a bad man, you know, he just loves the work. Anything to do with computers. Computer junkie.'

'Yeah, so how did you find me?'

'Mammoth Video.'

'You what?'

'You were always mad for the films, weren't you? Stood to reason you'd be a member somewhere. Well, all the big video chains are computerized, linked up. Herman just went though them till he found you. Took about twenty minutes, apparently.'

'Jesus.'

'It's a funny old world, hackers and that. Like a sort of club. They communicate with each other all round the world and they've all got daft nicknames, like ... Oh, Christ, what's Herman call himself? No, it's gone. I told Chas he should call him Adolf Hacker. Adolf ... You get it?'

Pike did get it, but he didn't bother to laugh.

They heard the toilet flush and Chas came back in.

'Nice bathroom, that,' he said. 'They look like original tiles. Worth a few bob, they are.'

'Please, Chas, I don't want to have to check that the bathroom's still tiled when you leave.'

'All right, keep your hair on. I was only commenting.'

'Here, Chas?' said Noel. 'What's Herman's nickname? When he's hacking? What is it again?'

'Pike ain't interested in that,' said Chas, curtly.

'I remember now.' Noel grinned. 'The Red Baron. That's it. The Red Baron.'

'Come on, Noel,' said Chas. 'Let's split. It's obvious Dennis doesn't want to know.'

Noel looked surprised. 'You're not going to give up, Chas? Jesus, you've been going on about this for weeks. He wouldn't shut up about you, Pikey, said you were the only man for the job, sort out Patterson. Christ, he was even going to mention Marti.'

'What about Marti?'

'It doesn't matter now, Dennis,' said Chas. 'I can see we're wasting our time.'

'What about Marti? What's she got to do with all this.'

'She's still with Patterson. Chas just thought you might still be sore at him.'

'Christ, Noel. It's ten years. I'm not suddenly going to get cut up all over again and go gunning for the wanker. He's welcome to her. It's finished.'

'Yeah, I can see that,' said Noel. 'It's finished, you're finished.'

'Let's go, Noel,' said Chas.

'It's been a pleasure seeing you again,' said Pike as Noel struggled up out of the recliner.

'Mutual, I'm sure,' said Noel. 'Listen, Pikey, if you should change your mind, here's my card.'

'Your card?'

'He don't want that, Noel,' said Chas putting a hand on Noel's arm. 'Don't bother.'

But Noel had already got his wallet out. A battered old plastic affair held together by an elastic band.

'Leave it, Noel,' said Chas.

'Just in case.' Noel handed Pike a card. Pike read it.

'Noel Bishop. Independent financial advice?'

'It's an old card. But me number's the same.'

'Independent financial advice?'

'Gambling and that, you know, horses, what to put your money on.'

'You're the worst gambler I ever met, Noel.'

'Yeah, well the punters weren't to know that.'

'They soon found out,' said Chas.

'Yeah,' said Noel ruefully. 'Lost a lot of money on that little enterprise. Still, the cards come in useful.'

They were by the front door now. Pike glanced into the bathroom. There was a dog-end floating in the toilet bowl.

'See you, then,' said Chas.

'I sincerely hope not.' Pike opened the front door and the Bishops went out.

'You must give me the name of your hairdresser, Chas,' said Pike.

Chas smiled and put a hand to his hair. He was halfway to the lift before he realized that Pike was taking the piss.

THREE

Wednesday afternoon Pike drove up to Dalston and parked in a busy side street. Then he walked up to Kingsland Road where his building society was.

It had been raining and the pavement was black and greasy. It was unusually warm and Pike felt overdressed in his sheepskin jacket. The traffic was hardly moving and people strolled across the road, dodging in and out of the cars and buses.

There were a couple of young African women getting money out of the machine and he waited for them. They were chatting away about something, Pike didn't listen. Finally they finished and it was his turn. He took his card out of his wallet, slipped it into the machine and punched in the number, then the regulation hundred quid for the week. He waited, looking around at the busy street. A surge of people came out of the overground station and fought their way through a knot of losers selling *Socialist Worker* newspapers. When he looked back at the machine there was a message for him.

'We are sorry we are unable to deal with your request at present. Please refer to your branch.'

He took the card out and tried again. The same thing happened.

It was a nuisance, but nothing more. He went inside the building. There were several people waiting patiently in the brightly lit interior. Pike joined the back of the line and idly looked at the posters on the walls advertising special accounts with stupid names.

15

He looked up at a TV monitor, it showed him standing looking up. He looked old. A stranger. He turned away.

A window became free and Pike went over to it. A young girl in a uniform smiled at him.

'Good morning.'

'Hello.' Pike slid his card beneath the glass. 'I've got some kind of a problem with this,' he explained. 'Machine won't accept it.'

'Yes, sir.'

'It may be damaged, or something, I suppose.' Pike watched as the girl swiped the card through a slot on her computer.

They both waited. The girl tapped a button repeatedly, then took the card out and tried it again.

She smiled at Pike, then turned and called towards the back of the office. 'Doreen? Doreen, can you help a moment?'

A slightly older woman with glasses came over. The two of them talked quietly to each other, the young girl occasionally pointing at her screen. They tried the card one more time.

Doreen leaned over towards the glass partition.

'Is this your card, sir?'

'Of course it's my card. Why? What's the problem?'

Doreen smiled, as if to say there wasn't a problem. 'What name is the account in, please?'

'My name. Pike. Dennis Pike.'

Doreen frowned and tapped some keys on the computer. 'Is that Pike with an "i"?'

'Yes.'

'Well . . .'

'What is it?'

'There doesn't seem to be any record of your account.'

'What?'

'There doesn't seem to be any record of your account on the computer.'

'That's nonsense. I've got a card haven't I?'

16

'Yes . . .' They asked him to spell his whole name for them. Then for his address. But it was no good.

'We'll have to look into this, Mr Pike. In the meantime, do you have another account with us, at all?'

'I've got a deposit account, yes.'

'Were you just wanting to withdraw some money?'

'A hundred quid.'

'If you have the passbook with you . . .'

Pike sighed. The passbook was at home, in the filing cabinet next to his bed where he kept all his documents. What a pisser. Well, he'd just have to go back and get it.

'Doreen?' said the original girl. 'Surely that account would show up here? But there's no record of either account.'

'Brilliant.' Pike looked round at the row of dispassionate people waiting to be served. He angrily tapped his wallet on the counter.

'Do you know the account number?' Doreen asked.

'Not off by heart, no.'

'The problem is, we're just a small branch, the accounts are handled in . . .'

'I don't want to know,' said Pike. 'I just want to get some money out.'

'There's definitely something wrong here,' said Doreen, still fiddling with the keyboard. 'It keeps saying "Refer to R. Baron".'

'Baron?'

'Yes, It could be a problem with the account, could be a computer error, or it might be blah-di-blah-yacketty-yak . . .'

Pike wasn't listening.

R. Baron.

Rob the robbers.

I've got a scheme.

Herman the German.

The Red Baron.

Had he had time? When Chas had gone to the bog last night.

17

Had he had time to nip into the bedroom and go through the filing cabinet? Get the information he needed? The information Herman needed. After all, you could do that sort of thing these days, couldn't you? Nick money with a computer. If you knew how to do it. Where to look. If you knew that your victim couldn't come after you. And Chas knew that well enough. He knew Pike could never go to the law.

Rob the robbers.

That was why Chas and Herman had left the message, 'Refer to R. Baron'. It meant 'Keep off'.

He should never have told them about the money. No wonder Chas changed his tune and left so quickly ...

Doreen was asking him something.

'I beg your pardon?'

'I said, do you want us to follow this up.'

'No, no. It's all right. I know what it means. I talked to Mr Baron the other day. I'd forgotten. It's ... You know. Don't worry.'

'We can ring this Mr Baron if you like. He's probably the ...'

'No, no,' Pike took his card and backed away, smiling. 'It's quite all right ...'

He went back outside. The crowds were confusing, it was like coming out into a changed world. Some religious nutter was preaching through a loud-hailer and two or three people were dancing around and singing and shouting halleluiah.

Halle-fucking-luiah.

Pike stood there in a daze for a while.

Ten years of going down a one-way street, and now someone had dug up the road.

Chas.

Pike took a hold of himself. He'd just have to find the bastard. Jesus, no wonder he'd changed his tack so quickly when he'd come back in from the the toilet. No wonder he'd been so reluctant for Noel to give him his card.

Of course. The card.

Pike went through the rubbish in his pockets and found the slip of printed cardboard. There was a public phone outside the station. He doubted that Noel would be at home, of course, if he and his brother had just ripped him off, but it was the only thing he had to go on.

He put ten pence into the phone and dialled the number on the card. After a few rings it was answered.

'Noel Bishop.'

'This is Pike.'

'Pikey! Hello, mate.' Noel sounded genuinely pleased to hear from him. 'You changed your mind?'

'Don't come it with me, Noel. What the fuck are you up to?'

'Er, good question. You've lost me, mate. What's the matter?'

'You know what the matter is.'

'No, 'fraid not.'

Pike looked down at his trainers. Noel was never a good bluffer and he sounded genuinely confused now. Perhaps he really didn't know what was going on.

'Is Chas there?'

'Haven't seen him since yours.'

'Where's he live?'

'Whitechapel. Slumland. Why?'

'What's the address?'

'What's up?'

'Just give me the address, Noel. Maybe this doesn't concern you. For your sake you'd better fucking hope so. Now are you going to give me the address, or what?'

'Not until you tell me what you want it for.'

'I want to see Chas. I want to see your brother.'

'You don't sound very happy, Pikey.'

'Oh, I'm happy. Delirious.'

'Listen. Why don't we go together, eh?'

'This doesn't concern you, Noel.'

19

'He's my brother, Dennis. I wouldn't want anything to happen to him. I know what you're like.'

'Jesus, Noel. Just tell me where he fucking lives, will you?'

'Listen, meet me at Bethnal Green tube, twenty minutes. I'll take you there.'

'Noel . . .'

'Park down the way a bit, on the left.'

'Noel!'

But Noel hung up.

Pike swore. He really didn't want Noel tagging along. He should have handled it better. Should have been more cool with him. But he wasn't used to this sort of thing any more. It had been too long.

He lit a cigarette and walked back to his car.

Ten years. He'd thought he was clear. But Chas had turned up and dragged him back into it. The shit life. The hard life.

Pike didn't like to think about the past. The bad old days at the Alma. Days of football, senseless drinking and senseless violence. Different things had been important in those days. Things like front, territory, respect, and the ability to smack somebody into casualty with minimum effort and maximum effect. Then, they'd been the Lads, the Team, the Firm, the Regiment. Seven of them. Seven young hooligans without a care in the world. Chrissie Boyd, Colin Shakespeare, Mick Beadle, the Bishop brothers, Dennis 'the Menace' Pike and Patterson.

Ian Patterson the skinny Jock. Come down out of Edinburgh. Took it on himself to be the bossman, organize them into a proper fucking and fighting unit. Fill them full of dreams of gangsters and big money. The lads from the Alma were going to be next in line to be Kings of the Castle. The Alma became 'the office'. They held 'committee meetings'. Patterson was managing director. Noel was chairman. Colin, who worked in a City bank, was treasurer. Chrissie, the landlord, was facilities officer and in charge of office supplies. Chas was secretary, Mick was tea boy, and Dennis?

Dennis was security.

They had calling cards. 'The Business. For all office cleaning'. And they had 'receptionists', a string of girls who would service them on request. Dreams and schemes. At all-night drinking sessions they plotted to rule the world, but it was just beer talking. Nothing came to nothing, everything turned to shit.

The Alma crew were never going to amount to anything. They were just yobs. Grown-up boys who should have joined the Scouts. Their forays into paying crime yielded chicken shit. They didn't have the heart for it, really. The ambition.

Except Patterson. Patterson was different. He had drive, and he had brains. The others were just losers, piss-artists, scallywags. They liked the football, and lager. They liked shagging as many women as they could get their hands on, and the sheer exhilaration of fighting other young men with similar aspirations.

Most of all they liked the comfort and comradeship of being a gang. Though none of them would ever have called it that. Sure, they thought they were the bollocks. Hard men. Bad men. Desperadoes. They thought London belonged to them, and in the bars and clubs of north London, from Tottenham down to Hackney, they reigned supreme.

And it was the best life. The best fucking life in the world.

The best.

Until that night ten years ago.

FOUR

Pike got into his car and manoeuvred out of his space. Some tit had parked right up his arse and he had to bump him a couple of times to get clear.

It had started to rain again so he turned on the wipers. They needed replacing, they left a smear right across his field of vision. He had to crouch slightly in his seat to get a good view.

Ten years since the team broke up for their own safety.

Pike had stayed underground, but from time to time he heard about the others. One way or another they'd stuck with it; the other life, outside the law, apart from normal society. They were soldiers not civilians.

Mick had gone full time into dealing. Colin became a bike courier, boasted he'd deliver anything, anywhere, anytime. Did a lot of work for Mick. Roaring around town on a huge Yamaha. Chrissie lost the pub, slipped into small-time crime, burglary, shoplifting, mugging, and slipped further and further into big-time alcoholism. The Bishops, they probably didn't even think of what they did as criminal. Not really criminal, not hurting people, not guns and knives. Just drugs and porn and credit cards. Dodgy goods, dodgy schemes, dodgy dreams.

Yes. Only two of them had left the life. Patterson and Pike.

So he'd gone into computers had he? The devious Jock. Well, something like that had always been on the cards. He was smarter than the others. Not just a numskull. He had his head screwed on.

But what had been on the cards for Pike? The worst of all of them. The man without fear, the berserker, crazy Dennis. The one-man barmy army.

Probably an early death in some heroic battle against fearsome odds. Cut down by gunfire. Executed by the law when they brought back hanging. A Viking's funeral . . .

But it hadn't gone like that, had it?

Dennis had bottled it.

With his head down, out of sight, the sweats had come, the panic, bad nights . . .

Dennis had lost it.

He drove past Bethnal Green station and pulled over to the side of the road. Single yellow line. He left the engine running and sat back in his seat, listening to the rain fall on the car.

When the sickness had left him he'd stayed where he was, in his burrow. And the old life had become just a bad dream. All but one part of it. The last part. July the fourth 1982. A Thursday.

A hot night with a full moon. Striding into 'the office' in his grey suit, his eighty-quid shoes, his French shirt, and his smart tie. Paco Rabanne aftershave. Gold cuff links. Jet black hair, gelled and immaculate. The dog's bollocks. The bees knees. The cock. Arms raised above his head, he punches the air, triumphant. And what is the triumph? Simple. The triumph is his arrival. Just that.

He is there.

It's the start of another night of drinking, of chasing the little black triangle and whatever else might turn up. The triumph of being young and careless and with your mates. The triumph of belonging. The triumph of knowing that in two or three hours you'll be roaring drunk and on some crazy adventure. And nothing else matters. That's why Pike punches the air as he comes into the pub.

23

The Bishops are already there. Standing at the bar in their best suits. Chas's out of date, too flash. Noel's just bad. No clothes looked good on Noel. Little Mick Beadle is with them. Mick the speed freak, pupils big, eyes red, teeth grinding, mouth dry, spinning his keys round and back, round and back. Talking too quick and jabbing the air rhythmically.

'Pikey!' Noel yells as he sees Dennis. Dennis struts over. Back slapping, drink buying, name calling, laughter. They stand there, glasses in hands, their backs to the bar, surveying their kingdom.

'We're going into drugs,' says Mick, grinning with his rotten teeth.

'Who says?' asks Pike, taking his first big pull of lager.

'I do,' says Mick. 'It's the thing. Easy money.'

'Easy as selling smack to a schoolkid,' says Chas, laughing too loud at his little joke.

'I've got the contacts,' says Mick.

'I bet you have,' says Noel, who still had a bit of hair left on top of his head in those days. 'You must be personal friends with every dealer in north London. They've got mortgages paid for by you.'

'What about Patterson?' says Chas. 'What's he got to say about this?'

'Fuck Patterson.'

'Mick, you're too much of a case to pull this off by yourself,' says Noel.

'No. All of us.'

'And Patterson?'

'Fuck Patterson. What d'you say, Dennis? What d'you think . . . ?'

Pike looks at him, shrugs. He thinks Mick is a tit, but says nothing. What's it to him? What's any of it to him?

The doors bash open and there's Colin. Colin in bike leathers. There are jeers, shouts of poof, shouts of arse bandit.

'Leave it out,' he says. 'I'm on me bike.'

'Bike boy!'

'Boy racer.'

'Poof.'

'Hard men don't wear leather,' says Mick.

'Hard men don't ride bikes.'

Colin pushes Mick back playfully and takes his leather jacket off. Underneath there's a shirt and tie. He chucks the jacket over the bar to Chrissie, with his helmet.

'Look after these for us, Chrissie.'

Chrissie giggles. Already pissed. His eyes unfocused, cruising. He'll be like this all night, drinking steadily, dead on his feet. You'd think he couldn't last, that at any moment he'd crash to the floor, unconscious, but he never did. He could outlast the rest of them, no problem, always be the last one standing. Always lock up, check the till and get to bed after the mayhem.

'We're going into drugs, Colin,' says Mick.

'What about Patterson?'

'Fuck Patterson.'

Then he's there. Last to arrive. Making an entrance. Patterson. Shorter hair than the others, cropped, but not pooffy like a skinhead. Raw-boned, tiny eyes, tiny, devious, little black eyes. Big hands. Raw silk suit. Church's brogues. And looking right in it. But then, they'd only ever known him dress like this, he hadn't been around with them in the seventies, in the days of shoulder-length curly perms, loons, stack-heeled boots, cheesecloth shirts, tank tops, huge round collars. The wild days of the seventies, travelling Europe like some mercenary army, teenage mobsters with an utter contempt for everything. The days before they learnt to dress down for a kicking, became, first casual, incognito, revelling in their ordinariness, then one better, smart. And that coincided with the arrival from Scotland of Patterson.

Patterson, clapping his hands and approaching the bar with a hungry look.

'All right, Patterson?' Mick shouts. 'We're going into drugs.'

25

'No we're not,' says Patterson, and he smiles and nods his head like some wise and kindly old uncle.

'Oh,' says Mick. 'Right.' And the others laugh.

'Mugs' game,' says the Jock. 'Sooner or later you're taking more drugs than you're selling. Like Chrissie, here, and this pub. Drinks more than he serves. The economics go to fuck, and you go soft. Wind up dead or in the can. No. I'll tell you the thing...'

And Patterson spins another yarn, another crazy scheme, another unattainable dream, and they all listen. All except Pike.

Pike stands apart, drinking, the shutters down, unreadable. He knows it's all lies, all bullshit. Pike and Patterson both. But the others, they want to believe. To believe for a moment that they already have it all, the untold wealth, the flashest German motor, the big house, the top-model girlfriend...

For Pike there's no tomorrow. Just this. The only thing that matters is now, focusing in, going into the target, turning on the juice. This is it. The crystal moment. When the drinks are starting to kick in and the night is young.

Anything can happen.

Standing there like heroes. Seven of them at the bar. Ready for anything.

Anything except what they got...

There was a bang on the roof and Pike jumped.

Shit. There. It was back, the old fear. The Bishops had brought it in with them. In with the cold December air.

Shit.

Noel opened the passenger door and stuck his head in.

'All right?' he said. 'Nice car.'

'Shut up and get in,' said Pike, putting the Escort into gear.

Noel clambered in and Pike pulled out into the traffic.

'Well, here we are again,' said Noel. 'You going to tell me what this is all about, or what?'

'Your brother's ripped me off, Noel.'

'Chas?'

'Yes, dear old Chas.'

Pike told Noel about the missing building society account, the message on the computer, the German Herman connection. At the end of it, Noel laughed.

'It must be some other R. Baron,' he said. 'Chas wouldn't shit on you. Chas wouldn't have the suss to even think of it.'

'Listen, Noel. This Herman geezer, the Red fucking Baron, could have filled him in about computer scams. Chas finds the passbook ... Maybe doesn't even need to do that, just takes down the account details ...'

'Nah. Not Chas. We come round to get you to help us, not rip you off.'

'But once I told him about the money. Once he saw how much was in there ... He knew I wouldn't get the law onto him.'

'Yeah, and he knows that you're worse than the law.'

'That's what doesn't figure. How did he ever expect to get away with it?'

'So, there we are. *Voilà*,' Noel beamed at him. 'Chas would be too scared to do a thing like that.'

'Come on, Noel. It's too much of a coincidence – refer to R. Baron.'

'We'll see.'

'Where's this Herman bloke hang out?' Pike asked.

'Haven't got a clue.'

Pike twisted in his seat to get a good look at Noel, make sure he wasn't bullshitting him.

'I've never met him, Pikey. He's Chas's pet. Keeps him secret.'

'Someone must know where he lives.'

'I guess so,' Noel thought about it. 'There's Patterson, I suppose.'

'You what?'

'Patterson. Herman works for him. Or at least he did. I mean, still does as far as I know.'

'Herman works for Patterson?'

'Yeah. That's how Chas got to know him. In Wandsworth. Turned out they both had a mutual acquaintance in Ian Patterson.'

'I think you'd better tell me about this, Noel.'

'All right. Well, you know Patterson's gone into electronics?'

'So you say.'

'Yeah. He's got his own company, computers, and that, games. At first Herman's on board, like, I don't know, inventing things, whatever you do in a set-up like that. He's a whizz kid, lives for computers, apparently, and when Patterson finds out what he's capable of, he uses him to get an edge on the competition.'

'How do you mean?'

'Hacking, getting into other people's systems, spying, nicking stuff down a wire, fucking things up. I don't know the first thing about it, but Chas'd go on and on about it. I mean, that's what Herman does. That's what Patterson used him for. Only something went wrong and Herman got caught. Patterson must have had a chat with him, because Herman takes the fall. Claims he was flying solo. Keeps Patterson's name out of it. Result – Patterson's in the clear, spotless reputation and Herman gets three years. He's on remand in Wandsworth and who should he meet there?'

'Chas,' Pike said wearily.

'Yup.'

'Jesus, I wish somebody had told me all this yesterday.'

'You go underground for ten years, Pikey, you're bound to get out of touch.'

'Yeah. Well I'm getting back in touch bloody quick, Noel.'

FIVE

'Canada? You're going to Canada?'

They were stopped at the lights at the junction of Cambridge Heath and the Mile End Road and Noel hadn't stopped talking since Pike had picked him up at Bethnal Green.

'What the bloody hell are you going to do in Canada?'

'Whatever I like, Noel. That's just the point, I'm getting out. I'm starting over.'

'But you belong here, Pikey,' said Noel.

'I've had enough.'

'It's important to have a sense of history, tradition.'

'That's what I'm getting away from.'

The lights changed and they turned right towards the city. Pike looked out at the dreary stores and the sweat-shop factories with names like 'Zhanco Exports' and 'Goldpower Ltd', like they were out of some cheesy old spy story of the thirties. *Bulldog Drummond*, or something. Sad businesses that changed their names every couple of months to keep one step ahead of the law.

This part of London was the dumper. The poorest of the poor traditionally ended up here. The Chinese, the Russians, the Jews, the Irish, and now the desperate from the Indian subcontinent, all rubbing right up against the unimaginable wealth of the City, with its glass towers and surveillance cameras.

They passed the London Hospital and turned right into the narrow streets of dark Victorian buildings around Brick Lane.

'What's Chas doing living round here, then?' Pike asked, watching two old Bengali men plodding through the cold in big black overcoats.

'He's staying with this bird. It's not his place. Just kips there, and that. He hasn't got a place of his own at the moment.'

'Your brother's a waste of time, Noel.'

'Leave it out, Pikey. He does his best.'

They pulled into a street of high, gloomy terraces. Hundred-year-old slums, with washing strung up between the buildings, cobbled streets, broken windows, skinny kids hanging out, staring at you. Only these were all brown faces. Asians, Bangladeshi, Bengali, looking cold and miserable and in the wrong place.

'Here we are,' said Noel, stopping the car. 'Monte Carlo.'

'You forget there's any of this left in London,' said Pike.

'Make the most of it,' Noel turned off the engine. 'It's all changing. The money's moving in.'

'I suppose you'd keep it like this, would you? A fucking slum. For the sake of heritage?'

'We-ell . . . It's all change nowadays, innit?'

'Is it? I thought it was the same old shit.'

'You've got to know where you stand, Pikey. Got to know where you belong.'

'I don't know,' said Pike, opening his door. 'Sometimes, living in London, it's like living in one huge fucking museum.'

It was four o'clock and already dark. The day had turned and there was a bitter chill in the damp air. Despite his sheepskin, Pike shivered as he got out of the warm car and locked the stereo in the boot.

Noel was up some steps at a door, speaking into an entry phone. Pike looked at him huddled there, like an Easter egg on stilts. Presently there was a buzz and the door opened.

Inside, the old building smelled of cats and cooking and piss. There was a dim bulb in the hallway and no carpets on the bare boards.

'I see Chas still likes to live in style,' said Pike.

'It's only temporary, till he finds his own place.'

'You'd stick up for him whatever, wouldn't you, Noel?'

'He's my brother. I look out for him.'

'Who's this bird, then?' Pike asked as they tramped up the narrow dark stairway.

'Christine. Young bird. She'd be a bit tasty if she got her shit together.'

They went up three floors to the top of the building and Noel knocked on a scratched and battered door. They waited a minute or so, then Noel knocked again.

'Christine!'

At last the door was opened by a skinny, sick-looking girl. She must have only been about twenty, though it was hard to tell. She had long, greasy black hair and pale olive skin covered in acne. She was wearing trousers with vertical black and white stripes, they might once have been skin-tight, but now her bones were showing and they hung limp and loose. She looked sullen and slightly cross-eyed. There was nothing behind her face; no lights on.

Pike could tell at once she was a junkie.

'Hello, Christine,' said Noel. 'Chas in?'

'Nah.'

'He gone out?'

Christine shrugged.

'Jesus, Noel,' said Pike, pushing past Christine into the flat. 'If he's not in stands to reason he's gone out. Do you know where he is, love?'

Christine shrugged again and closed the door.

'Or when he'll be back?'

'Nah.'

31

'All right. Try this one. When did he go out?'

Christine sniffed and sat down in an armchair that looked as undernourished and sickly as her. There was a three-bar electric fire in front of it, with only two bars working. She curled herself up and stared sullenly at the heater.

'When did you see him last?'

Christine looked out of the curtainless window at the building opposite and sucked a strand of hair, 'Dunno. Yesterday.'

'When yesterday?' said Pike. 'When was it exactly?'

She went quiet and completely blank. Pike assumed she was thinking, but it was just a guess.

The room depressed him. There was a poster on the wall for a rock concert, it was three years old. There was a threadbare carpet, a television, two armchairs, the fire, and that was about it. Except for a stack of boxes along one wall.

'When yesterday?' he asked again. 'Morning? Night?'

'Night.' She picked up a packet of Jaffa cakes and began to eat them.

'He left last night?'

'S'pose so, yeah.'

'What time?'

'Late. He's gone out, come back, then gone out again, late ... I think.'

'And you've not seen him since then?' Noel asked.

Christine shook her head. 'Listen, I've got to go out,' she said, but made no effort to move, just carried on nibbling at the Jaffa cakes.

'In a minute,' said Pike.

Christine scowled at the floor like a sulky schoolgirl.

'What's in all these boxes?' said Noel, lifting the flap of one of them.

'Porn,' said Christine.

Noel frowned and took out a handful of flat, plastic cartridges.

'They're floppy discs,' Christine explained. 'Computer porn. Some kraut Chas knows gets it from the Continent for him. Comes down a wire, or something. He puts it onto them discs, Chas flogs 'em.'

'There you are,' said Noel triumphantly. 'He can't have gone far. Wouldn't leave these behind.'

'You want some?' Christine asked.

'I wouldn't know what to do with it,' said Noel.

'What about a microwave? I've got a couple of microwaves. Half price. Brand new ...'

'Nah.'

'Chas didn't say where he was going?' Pike asked.

'Just went. I thought he was with you, Noel.'

'When we left yours he dropped me off at the tube,' Noel told Pike. 'About half nine, ten. Me car's knackered and ...'

'You sure he hasn't been back?' Pike asked the girl.

'Listen. He just went. He didn't say where he was going, how long he'd be, he didn't say anything, all right? Now just fuck off. Jesus, what is it with you lot and Chas?'

'What do you mean, "us lot"?' said Pike.

'You and the other bloke.'

'What other bloke? There been someone else asking after him?'

'Yeah, some mad fucker was here. Terry.'

'Terry? I don't know any Terries,' said Noel.

'He knew Chas. Said he owed him money.'

'That doesn't surprise me,' Noel chuckled.

'I thought that was maybe why Chas'd gone,' said Christine.

'What do you mean?'

'To hide from this Terry. He said something about Wandsworth.'

'Who did?' said Pike. 'Chas?'

'No. Terry.'

'Oh, shit,' said Noel. 'Terry Nugent.'

'You know him, then?' Pike looked at Noel.

'Know of him. Chas was inside with him. Chas fixed up some kind of a protection deal with him.'

'How d'you mean?' asked Pike.

'Chas is in Wanno for two weeks,' said Chas. 'Decides it's not for him. He tries to cut a deal with the Governor. Grouses up a couple of guys to try and get moved somewhere swankier. But the Governor doesn't go for it, and Chas is back on the floor, only now every cunt in the place wants his head on a pole. Chas gets Nugent to look after him, probably told him he had millions stashed away after some blag. So now, Terry's out and Chas is skint.'

'Listen,' said Pike to the girl. 'If Chas turns up, get him to give Noel a ring. Urgent.'

Christine shrugged.

'This is important,' said Pike.

'Yeah,' said Christine sarcastically. 'Sure.'

'Come on,' said Pike. 'Let's go.'

They left Christine sitting in the chair in front of the fire, playing with her hair and eating Jaffa cakes.

'Nice girl,' said Pike as they started down the stairs. 'Chas landed on his feet there.'

'Lay off him, Pike.'

Halfway down they heard someone coming up. The stairs were barely wide enough to pass on so they waited on the landing.

Out of the shadows came a squat man wearing a knitted cap. He was solidly built, like a brick with arms and legs stuck on the corners and a little head on top. No neck, just a head. He loomed out of the darkness and stared at the two of them. This was a disconcerting experience as he had a glass eye. He looked slowly from Noel to Pike then back to Noel.

'You're his brother, aren't you?'

'Eh?'

'Noel Bishop.'

'If you're looking for Chas, he's not there,' said Pike.

'Who asked you?' said the squat man, switching his look to Pike.

He was shorter than Pike, with stocky bowed legs. Despite the cold he was wearing just a T-shirt and loose jogging pants.

Pike shrugged. The squat man went back to looking at Noel.

'Where is he?' he asked.

'You Terry Nugent?' said Noel. 'Chas speaks very highly of you.'

'Where is he?'

'He owe you money, does he?'

'Something like that.'

Noel laughed. 'He hasn't got any bloody money.'

Nugent stepped closer to Noel. Stared up into his pasty round face. The tiny landing suddenly felt even smaller. Noel backed away. The thing was, the glass eye looked more alive than the real one.

'I looked after him inside,' said Terry. 'He owes me. So where is he?'

'I honestly don't know. We were looking for him, too.'

'I've seen you come in,' said Terry quietly. 'I'm watching the place. I've seen you come in. I know who you are. You're the brother. I see things, right?' He tapped his glass eye. 'This eye, it sees things. It sees you. Don't think you can hide from me if you're covering for him.'

'We're not covering for him. I told you, Terry, we're looking for him, too.'

'If you're lying to me, I'll kill you.'

'Come on,' said Pike. 'We were just on our way out.'

'Who do you think you are, anyway?'

'Just a family friend.'

'If you're lying to me . . .'

'Yeah, I know, you'll kill me. Come on, Noel, let's go.'

'Wait a minute.' Terry Nugent put a stubby hand which was wider than it was long on Pike's shoulder. 'I know you, right?'

'No you don't. Don't make that mistake, Terry.'

'I know both of you, now. All right? I've seen you. Don't mess me around.'

'I won't mess you around, Terry,' said Pike. 'Why would I want to do a thing like that?'

'You wouldn't.'

'There you are, then. Ta-taa. Nice to have met you. It's been real.'

'If we find Chas,' said Noel, keeping as close to Pike as he could on the way down. 'We'll be sure to let you know.'

Outside in the street, Pike saw that Noel was sweating. He wiped the bald top of his head and let out his breath noisily. 'Woah,' he said. 'Trust Chas.'

'Professional hard-nuts,' said Pike. 'They're so fucking boring.' He unlocked the car.

'What d'you make of it, then?' said Noel.

'How about Chas made some stupid promises to Nugent?' said Pike. 'Needs to pay him off quick. How about Chas is more scared of Cyclops than he is of me?'

'I still don't think he'd rip you off, Pikey.'

'No. An honest, decent, upstanding bloke like your brother would never do an underhand thing like that, would he?'

Noel looked pissed off. He sullenly got in the car and slammed the door.

'Listen, Noel,' said Pike, getting into the driver's seat. 'Let's just say, for argument's sake, that Chas *has* tampered with my account.'

'All right. For argument's sake.'

'We know he scarpered right after you came to see me. Where did he go?'

'Herman?'

'Right. And who knows where Herman lives?'

'Patterson.'

'Very good. I'm glad to see you're keeping up.' Pike started the engine and turned on the lights. 'You know where Patterson lives?'

'Yeah.'

'Right. Then let's pay old Jock a visit. It'll be just like old times.'

SIX

Basil Smallbone sat in the car and waited for Terry Nugent to come out of the house. He was used to waiting. It didn't bother him. For whatever reasons, Terry had decided to be his friend, and Basil would do anything for a friend.

Basil Smallbone didn't have any other friends. Never had done. He put it down to his name. You'd have thought with a surname like Smallbone his parents would have gone out of their way to give him an innocuous Christian name. Something that wouldn't give offence – John, or Peter, or Chris, or something. But Basil? He could never escape from the fact that Basil was a comedy name. He'd very early on in life come to the conclusion that his parents hated him. And he was probably right.

It seemed that there was always some joke figure around called Basil. When he was a kid it was Basil Brush, the irritating puppet fox. Then there was Basil Fawlty, the insane hotel owner. Then there was Basil the Great, fucking mouse detective. To his knowledge there was only one Basil who wasn't a total tosser. Basil D'Olivera, the cricketer, and he was a coon. Coons could get away with having comedy names. It wasn't as if he could change it, shorten it. Let's face it, Baz was worse. And nicknames? Well, he'd never been very lucky with nicknames. At school he was Shitface, on account of the strawberry birthmark down one side of his face. Actually, not everyone called him Shitface – some people called him Smallbone, which they considered just as funny. Inside he'd been called Shorteyes, or Dolly-dick, or Baby Fucker, or just 'that pervert'.

But not Terry. Terry had been nice to him from the start. Terry always called him just Smallbone. And he managed to do it without any hint of a sneer. There was no superiority in it. Which wasn't to say that he wasn't superior, of course.

He was. In every way.

It had been Basil's third stretch. Not counting the time when he was fifteen and he'd attacked one of his tormentors. He'd jumped him coming home from school. Battered him half to death with a brick before he even knew Basil was there. He'd spent six months in care when it had come out what hopeless cases his parents were.

But that didn't count. Everyone did a stint in care. Prison was different. First two times were for abuse of a minor. A girl the first time, a boy the second. On those occasions he'd been kept separated. The other inmates didn't like child molesters. But the third time he was in for assault. Never mind that it was self-defence. He'd been working on the estate. They ran a scheme for entertaining the kids in the holidays. He had to supervise them in the community hall, take them on trips, organize activities for them. The thing was he'd been good at it. The kids liked him, he liked the kids. That was what nobody could ever understand. He liked the company of children. He preferred them to adults. Sure, they were cruel sometimes, insensitive, but they didn't know any better. Not like adults. When they were cruel they meant it.

It had been a lovely summer, and he'd behaved. He hadn't so much as touched any of the kids, hadn't even thought about them. If he ever felt like he was losing it, he had his books, his pictures. He'd shut himself away with them until he felt safe again.

That was the best time, that summer. He'd really felt like he was becoming whole again, a useful part of society. Then one day one of the parents came to visit. A huge fat man with bad breath. Norman Manners. He'd found out, somehow he'd found out about Basil.

Basil had never seen anyone so angry. Manners pushed the door of Basil's flat in as soon as he opened it, shoved him about. Yelled at him ... 'You fucking pervert! You keep away from my kids. I'll break every bone in your fucking body, you sick pervert ...'

Basil had been terrified, he thought Norman was going to kill him. He fell into the kitchen and remembered the boiling saucepan of vegetable soup on the cooker. He threw it full in Norman's face.

They gave him two years. It was so unfair. The fact that he was a child molester wasn't admissible, but it obviously came out, Manners made sure of that. And nobody liked child molesters. Two fucking years for trying to save his own life.

This time on remand in Wandsworth he wasn't segregated. He'd hated Wandsworth. He should have been processed and moved on, in and out, but it never worked like that. He was there for nearly a year before they moved him to Highpoint. For the first few months he'd crept about in terror, waiting for the day when somebody would find out about his past. He hadn't wanted to go on the rule, and the kangas didn't encourage it. He was trying to be a normal inmate. A normal person.

But it couldn't last. One evening he was in the washroom when two blokes he hadn't seen before came in. Two blokes like Norman Manners. They were all the same. They bounced his head off the wall a couple of times, then forced him to confess to what he'd done. Then one of them held him and the other began to beat him with a bar of soap in a long sock. Slowly and methodically.

Then Terry Nugent came in.

Basil wasn't quite sure what he did to the first bloke, the one behind him, but it was something quick and painful. He fell to the ground like someone had hit him with a sledgehammer, taking Basil down with him onto the pissy floor. The bully lay there, curled up, clutching his sides and moaning. That was enough for the second bloke. He sauntered off with as much dignity as he could muster.

Basil picked himself up and thanked Terry.

'It's all right.' That was it. Terry said nothing else. Just walked away and left him there.

After that they left Basil alone. It was understood that Terry was looking out for him. Nobody had the balls to cross Terry Nugent.

But why had he done it? Basil was curious, and over the weeks his curiosity grew, until one day he found himself next to him at the basin, slopping out, and he plucked up the courage to speak to him.

'I never properly thanked you for what you did,' he said.

'It doesn't matter.'

'It's just, you helped me, and I don't know why.'

'Why not?'

'You know everyone else here hates me. For what – what I done.'

'Little girls, and that?'

'Yes. And they hate me for it.'

'They're stupid people.'

Terry went to the sink to wash his hands. Basil followed. 'You're not – I mean, you never . . . ?' Basil trailed off, not knowing how to say it.

'If you're going to ask me have I ever raped a little girl, the answer's no. It is disgusting. It is against God.'

'Oh.'

'But, everyone in here is disgusting.' Terry sniffed, no expression on his face. 'They are foolish. They just want to feel better than someone. But they're no different to you. See, Smallbone, you can kill someone, you can rip their ears off, you can fornicate with their children, it doesn't make any difference. It's just what you do, isn't it?'

Basil began to carefully brush his fine hair, trying to block out the stink of the slops basin.

'Nobody wants to think they're bottom of the cess pit,' said Terry. 'The white collars feel superior to the common thieves, the killers feel superior to the rapists, the rapists feel superior to the child molesters, the child molesters . . . Who do you feel superior to, Smallbone? Maybe someone who fornicated with a child younger than you did. And the bottom line? What have you got to do to a baby to be on the bottom line? Rape it and eat it? See, we're all in the cess pit, Smallbone, and if you ask me, excrement is excrement. They beat it out of you to feel good about theirselves, then what do they do? They go to Thailand for their holidays, go straight to the red-light district in Bangkok and come back boasting that they had fornication with a thirteen-year-old virgin. See? Fools. Excrement is excrement. They beat it out of you, I beat it out of them.'

'Why?'

'Because the wicked people must not be allowed to forget their sins. They must not be allowed to think that they are better because they abuse someone like you. I seen you. You read books. You're smart. Most in here are ignorant. They do not know what they are doing. But I'm in charge, see? Nobody does a thing without my word. And it works both ways. We are all in the same boat.'

'What do you mean?'

'What I mean, Smallbone, is that one day maybe you can do something for me.'

And Basil did. He became Terry's 'secretary'. His dog. Sorting out all the little hassles for him; writing his letters, researching legal matters, looking things up for him in the library. Terry took some kind of perverse pride in having a leper as his fetchit, an outcast.

But they couldn't stay in Wandsworth together for ever, and in Highpoint Basil was alone again. Mercifully he was out after a couple of months, good behaviour, but there was a hole in his life, now; an emptiness. His wife, Margaret, she'd left him long ago, after it came out about what he did. They'd never really got on anyway. She didn't like sex, and after the first two or three times they'd given up. It suited him. He didn't like Margaret. He'd only married her because that was what you did. You fucked someone, you got engaged and you got married.

41

And then you split up.

So when he came home from prison he stayed in a lot. Couldn't face going out, knowing he might hunt down a child out of loneliness and rage. He took up drinking, though he wasn't very good at it, hated the taste. Had to make himself sweet cocktails to get the stuff down. It didn't always stay down. He was sick most nights.

But when Terry got out he looked Basil up and it was like the old days. The dead period was over. He was Terry's man again. He chauffeured him, he sorted out his bills and letters. He looked after him.

So he was happy to wait for him now. Even in this part of town. Jesus, it was like Bombay, or something. The black hole of Calcutta. Dark slums crawling with Pakis. But Pakis were all right. He was safe here. They kept themselves to themselves. Didn't give you a hard time.

He looked across the road at a shop. Lit by a bright yellow light. Tins on the shelves. Boxes of strange-looking vegetables out front. A little man in a sort of round hat and long apron thing stood in the doorway staring out. There were no customers.

Then the back door of the car opened and Terry got in. Basil hadn't seen him coming. 'All right?' he asked. 'Was it him? The brother?'

'Yes,' said Terry.

'Any use?'

'No. He's covering for Chas.'

'Who was the old geezer with glasses?'

'I don't know. He's not important.'

'Do we follow them?'

'Yes, we do. If nothing shakes out we'll have to put a bit of pressure on.'

Basil felt a little surge of excitement, a tingling wash across his chest. He'd like to watch Terry go into action. Since the time in the toilets at Wandsworth he'd never actually seen Terry commit any violence on anyone. He never needed to, people were scared enough of him without that. But he knew what Terry was capable of.

He remembered when he'd first got up the courage to ask him why he was inside. As it turned out he hadn't needed to be nervous, Terry was more than happy to tell him all about it.

'See, Smallbone, you know me. I am not one to take things lying down. I know what's right. There are rules that must be obeyed. If someone shows me disrespect they must be taught a lesson. You've got to have discipline. I was working on a site, as a roofer. I had never done roofing before. I was helping a friend. As a rule I don't do labouring. It is not dignified. There was an architect, see? And he's on my case right from the start. Mouthing off, talking too much, showing off – "You're doing it wrong. Do it like this. Do it like that. Yap, yap, yap." He was giving me a headache. So one day I was on my lunchbreak, just sitting there having a sandwich and a mug of tea. Minding my own business. And he comes in screaming the place down . . . "What the f are you playing at? That f-ing felt's on upside down, you stupid moron." Bad language, unnecessary behaviour, this I can put up with, but when he turns round and calls me stupid, I have to draw the line. So I get up, calmly, and I pull my hat down and I just look at him. Just that. Calm. And I say to him, politely, "Are you going to take that back? Calling me stupid?" And he says, "No." I'm off the site. I'm stupid and there's no two ways about it.'

'So what did you do?'

'I'll tell you Smallbone, what could I do? I crucified him.'

'Right. You sorted him out. How exactly did you do it, then?'

'I just told you, I crucified him. I fastened him to a door with a nail gun.'

'Christ.'

SEVEN

Ropes of white bulbs were strung out along the Embankment like
fairy lights and Pike remembered that it would soon be Christmas.
It was as if the whole river was some festive tableau. The sky was
pink with burning street lights, the water reflecting it back, shot
through with black and silver. A tour boat chugged downstream
towards Greenwich sending out gleaming ripples. Across the other
side the great concrete slabs of the South Bank looked almost pretty
under their night-time illumination.

'Ah,' said Noel. 'You can never get too much of the river at night.'

'Very picturesque,' said Pike flatly.

'You've got no room for sentiment, have you?' said Noel and Pike
laughed at him.

'Let's get some music on, eh?' said Noel. 'It's no fucking fun
trying to talk to you.'

'There's some tapes and shit in the glove compartment.'

Noel pulled the door down and rummaged around before bring-
ing out a handful of cassettes.

'What have we here, then? Ennio Macaroni . . .'

'Morricone.'

'Italian, yeah? What is it, rave music?'

'Film music. He did all the spaghetti westerns, *Good, the Bad
and the Ugly*, and that.'

Noel whistled the theme then slung the tape back in the

compartment. 'It's good, that, but I wouldn't want to listen to a whole bleeding tape of it. What's this? John Barry. Never heard of him.'

'He did the James Bond music, *Born Free*, all the great sixties stuff.'

'More film music? Haven't you got any dance music, any black stuff?'

'No. Don't really keep up, these days. Just listen to film music.'

Noel peered at another tape. '*Kottsy-Squattsy*? What the bleeding hell's that when it's at home?'

'*Koyanisquattsi.*'

'You what?'

'It's a film.'

'What sort of a film would be called *Kottsy-Squattsy*?'

'A documentary film.'

'Oh, hold me back.'

'No, it's okay. Right up your street, I would have thought. All about how everything's changing for the worse. How mankind is destroying the planet.'

'Oh, so it's a comedy, then?'

'No. It's just a lot of nice pictures set to music. I used to get the video out and get stoned.'

Noel read the box. 'Philip Glass?'

'That's the fellow. There's this one bit where it's really speeded up; cars, planes, people, night and day, the whole city, like a machine. It's wild. Does you in, just goes on and on, faster and faster . . .'

'Oh, yeah?' said Noel. 'Pikey, you've got to get your shit together. Fancy sitting at home watching documentaries about speeded-up traffic all day. You've gone soft.'

'Look, if you don't want to play any of my music, don't. Doesn't bother me.' Pike grabbed the tape off Noel and chucked it back in the glove compartment. 'Put it away. You wouldn't like it.'

'I'll be the judge of that.' Noel got the cassette out again and opened the box. 'No one can say Noel Bishop isn't open to new ideas.' He pushed the tape into the stereo and turned the volume up. Arpeggios blasted out from the speakers, up and down, up and down, unchanging.

Noel turned to Pike.

'What the bloody hell is this? Diddly-diddly-diddly-diddly. You listen to this, do you?'

'Yup.'

'You must be barmy.'

'Wait till you hear the speeded-up bit, "The Grid". That's where they really go for it.'

'No thanks.' Noel pressed the eject. 'I'm worried about you, Pikey. Look at this shit . . .' He flipped through the rest of the cassettes. '*The Cook, The Thief, His Wife* and the blah, blah, blah, *Star Wars, Paris Texas, Apocalypse Now, Taxi Driver* – liked the film, don't remember the music – *Opera Goes to the Movies.* Come off it, Pikey, opera?'

'Put the fucking radio on, then. I don't care.'

Noel fiddled with the dial till he found some obscure pirate station pumping out heavy ragamuffin music, then he settled back in his seat to enjoy the view of the river.

'How can you listen to this stuff?' Pike asked. 'All this rave stuff? House, bloody madhouse reggae . . .'

'Ragga, this is.'

'Whatever it is. It's unlistenable.'

Noel laughed. 'All right, dad, I'll get the Val Doonican out. Christ. Listen to you.'

'No, honestly, Noel. Is this stuff music, or what?'

'Course it is.'

'It makes me feel old.'

'That's 'cos you are old. Me, I've kept in touch.'

'And you like it do you? Seriously? Rave music – all that duh-duh-duh-duh-duh-duh-duh . . .'

'Got into it back in the summer of love.'

'Nineteen sixty-seven?' said Pike.

'That was the old summer of love. This was the new one, the re-mix. Couple of years back. "E" had just hit in a big way, and the kids just wanted to stay up all night dancing to robot music and thinking how nice everyone was. Any fool could see there was big money to be made.'

'And you were that fool,' said Pike.

'One of them. Jesus, you could hold a rave anywhere, all you needed was a bit of space and a gargantuan sound system. 'Cos once the "E" came on, the poxiest old public bog looked like heaven. Me and Chas and a guy called Handsome started organizing it.'

'You're joking? Handsome?'

Noel chuckled.

'He actually had the front to tell people he was called Handsome?' said Pike.

'Yeah,' said Noel. 'He had a lot of front, looked like a heavy metal type, all black leather and long hair.'

'What was it we used to say?' Pike asked. 'Real men don't wear leather?'

'Hard men don't wear leather,' said Noel.

'Yeah,' said Pike. 'If you've got to dress up to look hard, you're not hard at all.'

'All right, it was all front,' said Noel. 'But he had a source of wicked "E". That was his function, really, to supply the gear. He used to arse about claiming he was in charge of security and all, but first sign of any trouble and old Handsome was nowhere to be found. And trouble we had. It was wild at first, we were making a fucking fortune, then the big gangs woke up and muscled in on it. Scared people like us off. Handsome disappeared. Me and Chas escaped by the skin of our teeth, and that was that. Got too dangerous. Still, we made a few bob, had us a few laughs. Spent it all, of course. Chas lost his gambling. Mine ... well, I must have enjoyed getting rid of it, 'cos I don't remember a thing about it. But I really got into the music. It wasn't just the drugs, you know? It was the whole scene. It was fun. Fun like I hadn't had for years. I was beginning to think an old sod like me was past it, all the good times had gone, but you'd meet all sorts there, young, old, black, white, pensioners, schoolkids, it was magic . . . I got hooked on the vibe . . .'

'The vibe?' said Pike scornfully.

'Yeah, too right, the fucking vibe. Don't mock. It was like being a lad again and going to the clubs. Only this time it wasn't all so fucking heavy. No violence. Jesus, I began to understand what they meant by peace and love and understanding.'

'You became a hippie.'

'Near as dammit. Even went down to Glastonbury last summer. Me and Chas.'

'What's at Glastonbury?' Pike asked.

'Wake up, Pike, where have you been? There's this massive festival down there every year, loadsa music, loadsa sex, stacks of drugs, stalls selling every kind of shit you can imagine. It's like a little city of tents, with shopping streets, bars, restaurants, you name it. Fucking mad. And guess who we bumped into?'

'The King of the Elves?'

'Near as dammit. It was good old Handsome and his pals. He and these other two guys were running a nice tight little operation down there. Had it well sussed. Selling gear to the beautiful people. The crusties had their own little encampment – wigwams and everything – and Handsome and co. had set up shop right in the middle of it. They were doing all the festivals, using the travellers as cover. Best source of "E" ever. They wouldn't let on where they got it from but they had to be making it themselves. The guy behind it all was a bloke called Doctor Fun.'

'Fuck's sake, Noel, how many drugs do these people take? Haven't they got any shame?'

'You had to be there, it all kind of made sense. The Doc was older than the others, in his forties. Really tall and thin, long pointy beard and the poshest voice you ever heard. He was at Oxford in the sixties, chemist. Got turned on to the drug culture. Decided he could make the stuff himself. Been doing it ever since. He claimed he didn't keep any of the profits, claimed he's doing it to change the world, to turn the youth on to alternative possibilities.'

'Bullshit,' said Pike.

'My sentiments entirely. But, you see, there was this whole new thing, the raves, the festivals, there really was a feeling of, I don't know, being nice to people. It was weird.'

Pike snorted. 'Give us a break, Noel.'

'You always were a cynical git.'

'Cynicism's not in it.'

'Well whatever you think. They had a sweet deal going. Me and Chas tried to get in on it, but they wouldn't have it. Wanted to keep it small, keep it manageable. Don't think they trusted us.'

'Why ever not?'

'They did say that if we ever came up with enough cash we could buy in on a shipment, act as middlemen.'

'Dealers, you mean,' said Pike.

'Yeah, but that's a risky business these days. What with the yardies, and that. You've got to be young and tough to hack it in that world. I'm past it. I just fancied setting up my wigwam in some remote area, enjoying the countryside, kicking back and letting the Doc get on with the cooking. Turn up, drop out, fuck off – or whatever that slogan was.'

'Tune in, turn off, drop out,' said Pike.

'No, it's turn in, tune up and drop off.'

'Bollocks, it definitely starts "turn on",' said Pike.

'You sure?'

'Not really, no, but it doesn't make any difference. Simple fact of the matter is, you wouldn't last five minutes in the countryside,

Noel. You're a good city boy. What would you do with yourself in compost land?'

'Take dangerous drugs, shag sheep, fucking enjoy myself. I don't have to check into the Sunnyside Home for the terminally confused just yet. Not like you.'

'I'm thirty-four, Noel,' said Pike. 'I'm not a lad any more. I've moved on. You can't hold onto the good shit for ever. Can't be the oldest teenager in town. It's undignified.'

'Fuck that. You're as young as you feel. I mean, what have you done in the last ten years?'

'Watched videos.'

'And that's it, is it?'

'Yup.'

'You must have worked, to get all that dosh together.'

'Yeah, I worked,' said Pike. 'But that doesn't count. Right up till last week I worked. Minicabs. Bar work. Carpet showroom. Van driver. Gym instructor. Anything. Day. Night. Two jobs at a time, sometimes. I was even manager of a cinema for a couple of years.'

'You're joking.'

'Best job I ever had.'

'So why'd you quit?'

'Closed the cinema, redeveloped it. Turned it into offices.'

'Dennis the Menace selling carpets, and ripping people's tickets in half ...? You were the wild man. You were the beast of Tottenham.'

'I needed money, Noel. I didn't care what I did. I needed money so I could get out. Get away from here. And I did it. Had all I needed. Then your fucking brother turns up and the last ten years have been for nothing. Might just as well not have happened. All that shit for nothing.'

'You don't know he's took it.'

'No, but I'm gonna find out. I don't want to have wasted my life, Noel.'

50

'Well, I'm sorry, but whichever way you look at it, you have.'

'Yeah? So what have you done that's been so fucking exciting? You've run some discos, gone to a pop concert, hung out with people called Handsome and Doctor Fun ...'

'I've enjoyed myself,' said Noel. 'D'you understand that word, "enjoy"? Do you remember it? It means "to have a good time". It's something you used to do. I know you don't have much respect for me, Pike, but I've done things. I've lived in the fast lane. Not like you, you're not even in the slow lane – you're on the hard shoulder, broken down, and the AA aren't on the way. Jesus, remember the dream, Pikey? Dangerous drugs, dangerous sex, fast cars and fat wads ... I've dreamt it.'

'Yeah, and look at you now. I'd say you've woken up, Noel.'

'All right. So now I'm skint, but I've had money. More money than you, Pike, in my hands. Cash.'

'And what have you done with it?'

'I told you, I've spent it. What else can you do with money? And now I'm fucked up. My liver's dodgy, my kidneys have taken a hammering, my lungs are shit, my eyes are red. I've got spots, I'm bald, fat and I've got fallen arches. So what? I've had a laugh, Pikey.'

The black DJ, in his impenetrable London-Jamaican patois, was excitedly rabbiting on about something or other and Pike turned the volume down.

'What you doing?' said Noel.

'It was giving me a headache.'

'Nah. Full whack. Maximum damage.' Noel turned it back up again.

'Suit yourself.'

'What's the matter with you? You won't even put up a fight anymore. Jesus, in the old days, someone like Terry Nugent gives you some lip, you'd have smacked him one. Where's the old fighting spirit?'

'What's to fight? What's to prove? I don't have any turf to

protect. I don't have to stare people down anymore. Don't have to size everyone up. What's the point? It's all just a waste of time.'

'It doesn't change, though, Pike. It may get more refined, more subtle, but it's all the same. All your life. You wind up in some home and there's some old cunt eyeing you up over the last bit of angel cake. What you gonna do?'

'Noel?'

'Yes, Dennis?'

'What would you say if I told you we were being followed?'

'I'd say Terry Nugent.'

'Yeah. So would I.'

Noel twisted round in his seat. 'What's that nutter want?'

'Chas. Same as me.'

'Which car?'

'The Vauxhall. Astra, or a Nova . . .'

'I see it,' said Noel. 'Brown Astra. There's two of them in it. What you gonna do?'

'I'll easily get shot of them around Victoria, but we'd better keep on our toes. I don't want Terry Nugent fucking things up. We've got to get to my money before he does.'

'If it's even been stolen.'

'Let's just hope for Chas's sake that it hasn't. Eh?'

EIGHT

At Westminster Bridge they pulled off the Embankment onto Parliament Square and Pike raced up into the network of streets around Victoria. He knew the area well from his van and minicab days and by jumping a couple of lights and making a few illegal turns it wasn't too difficult to lose the Astra. It was just one more hassle, really. One more headache he could do without.

With a bit more jiggery-pokery they ended up down on Chelsea Embankment and back on course for Patterson. Pike looked at his watch, it was gone six-thirty. This was all taking too long. Noel had persuaded him to stop for a cup of tea and a sandwich earlier, justifying it by saying that Patterson was unlikely to get in from work much before seven, and now this. Pike was impatient to get it over and done with.

Traffic was heavy, it was bad timing to get stuck in the rush hour, but at least it had made losing Nugent a bit easier. Noel kept a lookout in the back, and they saw nothing else of the brown Astra. The rest of the drive to Chelsea Harbour was uneventful, if slow.

When they got there they parked in an underground car park. They got lost finding their way out and when they reached ground level they were completely disoriented. They wandered around for a while before they found a map and after a few minutes' bickering they realized that Patterson lived in the Belvedere, a jagged, pyramid-topped tower which seemed to be the central feature of the area.

'Trust Patterson,' said Noel as they walked through the cold night towards the brightly lit tower. 'He always did have too much front for his own good.'

'I don't know,' said Pike, 'look at this place, it's like a ghost town.'

True enough, the Harbour was half-deserted. An enclave of luxury in the middle of nowhere. A fantasy. A few years back, in the boom time of the eighties, this must have seemed like a good idea, a spanking new top-class development in Chelsea, right on the river. Only Chelsea proper was up the road past the abandoned warehouses and factories.

There was a variety of elaborate new buildings, a swanky hotel, even a marina with a few luxury yachts sitting in it, wrapped up for the winter. But time and the economy had moved on and there was a lonely, stranded feel about the place.

They went down some steps and into the reception area for the Belvedere. It was like the lobby of a posh hotel, with discreet lighting, expensive carpets and a uniformed security guard sat at a desk.

'We've come to visit Ian Patterson,' said Noel self-consciously.

'Certainly, sir,' said the guard politely, and he picked up a telephone.

'Who shall I say it is?'

'Tell him Noel Bishop and Dennis Pike.'

'Yes, sir.' He pressed a button and looked amiably at the two of them, standing there embarrassed. Pike studied the abstract paintings on the walls. Noel sucked his teeth and rocked on his feet.

The guard had a brief conversation, then smiled at them again.

'If you'd like to go on up. Seventh floor.'

'Ta.' A lift door opened for them. They stepped in and pressed the button for the seventh floor.

The lift had glass walls and climbed slowly up the outside of the building.

'Jesus Christ,' said Noel, looking out at the river. 'Chas told me about this place, but I didn't believe him. You know how he exaggerates.'

'Chas has been here?'

'Yeah. Tried to get Patterson interested in some scheme of his. That's what gave him the idea to knock him off.'

'When was this? How recent?'

'Couple of months back.'

'Chas has been touting his schemes all round town of late, then?' said Pike.

'Yeah. 'Fraid so.'

The lift stopped and they stepped out. There was only one door here; Patterson's door. And Patterson was there waiting for them.

He looked exactly as he had done ten years ago. Lean, tidy and devious. He shook Dennis's hand and winked. 'Pike. It's been too long.'

'Has it?'

'Oh, you charmer, you.' He led them into his flat.

They passed through a small hallway with fitted cupboards down one side into the sitting room.

The first thing Pike noticed was the view out across the river.

The second thing he noticed was Marti.

If anything she was more beautiful. She'd matured. There'd always been something of the kid about her before, something gauche, the smell of jail-bait. But now she was all grown-up, and she could obviously afford to make herself look the part. She was still small and doll-like but her hair was big, in a completely unnatural style that only a hairdresser's constant attentions could maintain. Her skin was smooth and evenly tanned, her make-up immaculate and understated, her clothes expensive. It was designer stuff, restrained for Marti. She had on some kind of elegant, silky, black top with a gold brooch, and a short black skirt with sheer tights. She stood up from the sofa as they came in, her legs swishing.

'Hello, Noel. Hello, Dennis.' She smiled at them, like the perfect dutiful wife when the husband has important clients round.

'Hello, Marti.'

Marti of Tottenham. The face that launched a thousand scraps.

'Drinks?' said Patterson, putting an arm round Marti's shoulders.

'Got any Scotch?' asked Noel, sitting himself down in an uncomfortable-looking, formal armchair.

'Of course. Pike?'

'Just a glass of water for me.'

'Water?'

'I'm driving,' said Pike with a straight face.

Patterson grinned at him. 'I've got some mineral water in the fridge.' He left the room.

Dennis looked around. The decor was incongruous for a swanky, super-modern apartment block. It was fussy and cluttered; all antiques, reproduction furniture, Victorian rugs and glass-fronted bookcases with matching leather-bound books. It had an unlived-in feel, like a show flat. There were tastefully arranged dried flowers, little statuettes on occasional tables, there was even an elaborate glass chandelier hanging from the low ceiling.

'How do you like our little nest?' asked Marti, settling back down on the sofa and tucking her long legs under her.

'Very nice,' said Pike. 'Very chic. Very *Homes and Garden*.'

'Yes, well, we don't have a garden, obviously.' Marti's voice had changed, lost its common touch, its adenoidal north London twang. It was now sort of neutral, lost somewhere in middle England, classless and characterless.

'Michael Caine's got a flat here, you know?'

'You don't say.'

'I've never seen him, though. There's a lot of famous people live here. Lot of rich people.'

'I can imagine.'

'Nice view,' said Noel. 'You can never get too much of the river at night.'

'It is lovely, isn't it?'

Patterson came back in with a tray of drinks. He was wearing smart, pale blue jeans which looked like they'd never been worn before, and a light, woollen, V-necked sweater with no shirt.

Pike realized he was sweating. The central heating was turned way up.

'Scotch for you, Noel,' said Patterson, handing round the drinks. 'And a glass of water for you, Pike.'

Patterson's voice had changed as well. It was still noticeably Scottish, but, whereas before he had deliberately exaggerated his accent and used obscure Edinburgh slang to confuse people, now it sounded like he was leaning the other way.

'We were just admiring the view,' said Noel.

'Knock-out, isn't it?' Patterson said automatically, without looking round to the window. He gave Marti a glass of red wine and sat down next to her.

Pike was the only one still standing. He decided he'd better sit, and picked the matching armchair to Noel's. He was right. It was uncomfortable. He thought of his leather recliner at home, his big TV and his rows of videos, and he sighed, rubbing his eyes which were dry from the central heating.

'Well, this is jolly, isn't it?' said Patterson. 'Just like old times.'

'Not really,' said Pike, looking round the room.

'Well, the scenery might have changed, but us boys are the same, eh?' He put a hand on Marti's leg and beamed at Pike. 'There's not many of us left. Mick assassinated in Miami, Colin falling off his bike, Chrissie drinking himself to death. Where are the hooligans of yesteryear, eh?'

'Living in Chelsea Harbour by the looks of it,' said Noel. 'You're doing all right for yourself.'

'I was in the right place at the right time, Noel. I saw which way the wind was turning. Computers, microchips, micro-technology. I saw the future and I invested in it.'

'What is it you do, exactly?' Noel asked.

'I sell the buggers. Got a string of stores. IP Electronics. Cheap hardware. People used to think computers were out of their reach, great big things with spools of tape and flashing lights, like in James Bond films. Billion-dollar babies made by IBM. Then, in the seventies, while you were busy kicking the shite out of people at football matches, a bunch of American hippies started to get into computers and nobody noticed. Nobody noticed that they were about to change the fucking world.'

'Well, give me football any day,' said Noel.

'Forget it. Forget football. Forget rock and roll. When they come to write the history books and they look back on this century, look back at who really changed people's lives, it won't be Jimi Hendrix and Mick Jagger, forget Clint Eastwood and big Arnie, forget Ghandi, Martin Luther King and Pele, the names written in stone will be Nakiyama at Sega, Nintendo, Bill Gates, Steve Wozniak and the Mac guys . . .'

'Never heard of them,' said Noel.

'That's because you're still living in the Stone Age, Noel. Everyone wants computers, now, and I'm the man to sell 'em to them. IBM are going down the plug, but Ian Patterson is on the up.'

He winked at them and poured himself a drink from the wine bottle.

'Plus, I'm getting into software; games. I'm telling you Sonic the Hedgehog is bigger than Elvis. The Super Mario Brothers are the new Beatles.'

'There's only two of them,' said Noel. 'That, I do know.'

'What?'

'There's only two Mario Brothers. There were four Beatles.'

'I was speaking metaphorically.'

'Well it don't work. You'd have to say, I don't know, the Everlys, or the Righteous Brothers.'

'Fine.'

'Maybe Sam and Dave.'

'Yeah, all right, Noel. Point taken. But what can I do for you, anyway? I'm sure you didn't come here just to talk about the Super Mario Brothers.'

'We need a favour,' said Pike.

'Any way I can oblige, boys. I'm at your service.'

'We need an address.'

'Fire away,' Patterson sipped his drink and replaced the glass on the little coffee table.

'Herman,' said Pike. 'Don't know his other name.'

'Herman Muller?' Patterson raised an eyebrow.

'Herman the German,' said Noel.

Patterson spread his hands in an empty gesture. 'No can do, guys. Sorry.'

NINE

Pike looked at Patterson, sitting there with his big fake grin and his expensive clothes, so at home on the leather sofa, and he remembered all those times in the Alma, when Patterson had told some outrageous lie, or made some insupportable claim and expected everyone to believe him. Knew that most of the cretins there would. But he'd never look Pike in the eye. Like he wasn't looking at him, now. He was looking at Noel.

Pike was looking at him, though. 'Nice of you to be so obliging,' he said.

'It's not that simple, Pike,' said Patterson with a patronizing edge to his voice.

'Yes, it is. You give us Herman's address. We go away. What could be simpler?'

'He's not for public consumption.'

'We just want to talk to him.'

'I have to protect my workforce, Pike. Herman's a very delicate flower, very highly strung. I can't just let all and sundry go barging in on him. I have to handle him with kid gloves, have to look after him.'

'Is that why you let him go down for two years?'

'He only did eighteen months.'

'Oh, that's all right, then.'

'He understood. Business is business. Besides, that's why I look

60

after him now, so it doesn't happen again. He's like a child. Needs a lot of supervision.'

'You're all heart, Patterson.'

'I made it up to him, afterwards. He's doing very nicely, now. I set him up in style. Far from the madding crowd. He has all the resources he needs.' Patterson took another sip of wine.

'And that makes up for doing time for you, does it?'

'He enjoyed himself in there, Pike.'

'Sure he did.'

'He completely rebuilt their computer system.' Patterson laughed. 'Why are you interested in him, anyway?' Trying to sound casual.

'It's not really him. We're looking for Chas. We think he might be hanging out with Herman.'

'Yes, I think they do know each other. But I doubt if Chas is there. Have you lost your big brother, then, Noel?'

Noel shrugged. 'He's gone AWOL.'

'The Super Bishop brothers, Noel and Chas, always up to something.' Patterson chuckled. 'Chas came here, you know?'

'We know.'

'Tell you what I'll do,' said Patterson. 'I'll look into it. I'll speak to Herman, see if Chas has been there. I can't say fairer than that. If I find anything out I'll give you a call. But it's best I don't see you in person. As you can see, those days are behind me. I'm a legitimate businessman now, boys. A pillar of the community. I'm a big name.'

'Ian's not a very big name,' said Pike, swirling the ice around in his glass.

'No,' said Noel. 'But arsehole is.'

'Bravo,' said Patterson. 'Very droll. But I've told you my bottom line. Herman is off limits. For my eyes only. Now, guys, I don't want to appear rude, but the less dealings we have with each other the better. I'd rather you hadn't come here in the first place. Let's face it, I stand to lose more than the rest of you, if certain facts were ever to come to light.' He winked at Noel. 'If you know what I mean.'

'We all stand to lose the same,' said Pike. 'We're all in the same boat.'

'Look, I run an important business. I've built it up from nothing into a major going concern. I've got a stake in the future. You get me? And I don't want the past interfering. Now give me your number and I'll see what I can do.'

Noel gave him one of his cards, and Patterson slipped it into his pocket without looking at it.

Pike stood up. 'If Chas does something stupid. If Chas is with Herman, this could all blow up in your face.'

'That's precisely why I'm going to handle it, not a couple of thugs like you two. Herman is a very valuable employee, I don't want you near him. I don't want you near me.'

'The feeling's mutual.'

'Goodbye, now, boys. Be good.'

'Ian,' said Marti, who'd been listening to the conversation with undisguised boredom. 'We ain't seen them in ten years. Let's have a drink and chat about something else.'

'It's all right, Marti,' said Pike. 'We're going.'

She shrugged. 'I'll see you to the door, then.'

She got up and swished across the carpet towards them. Then led the way into the little hallway. Noel walked out of the flat to the lift, but as Dennis stepped out the door Marti held onto his arm and pulled him back.

'How are you, Dennis?'

'Not so bad.'

'You look old.'

'It's my hair.'

She ran a hand through it. 'You always had nice hair. I dunno, it suits you, grey.'

'Ta.'

'Not sure about the glasses, though. You should get contact lenses, like me.'

'I was wondering why your eyes had gone green.'

Noel, who was holding the lift, called out for Pike to get his arse in gear. Pike made to move, but Marti stopped him again.

'Don't worry about Ian,' she said. 'It was nice to see you again. I don't see anyone from the old days. To tell you the truth it's bloody boring here.' She kissed him quickly and smiled. 'Give me a ring. He's out during the day.'

'Come off it, Marti.'

'I'm serious. For old time's sake.'

Pike could smell the drink on Marti's breath. She was half gone, that look in her eyes like she was capable of anything, like nothing mattered. He remembered how she tasted when she'd been drinking; the sweetness, the sloppiness of it.

He shook his head and stepped into the corridor.

Marti shrugged, 'Suit yourself.'

As he walked away he heard her call out behind him. 'I remember why I left you now, anyway. You got boring.'

Pike got into the lift and the doors slid shut.

'She giving you a hard time again?' Noel asked.

Pike said nothing.

'She always did know how to get to you. You were a right sucker for her, you know. We all knew she was slipping around with Patterson long before you did.'

'I knew,' said Pike.

'So why didn't you slap her?'

'What difference does it make?'

'Well, you know, a man's got to have his pride.'

'We all fucked around,' said Pike. 'None of us was loyal.'

'Yeah, but girls are different. Girls have to behave. Men are men.'

'I am sick to death of trying to be a man, Noel.'

'Listen to you. You've got some twisted ideas into your head watching all them videos. You're like one of them born again Open University wankers who get banged up for life and then get degrees in Latin, or Chemistry, or something and end up on all the TV chat shows. You haven't just gone soft, you've rotted away.'

'Oh, shut up, Noel.'

The lift came to a halt and they got out. The security guard nodded and wished them goodnight as they went out into the icy December night.

It felt especially cold outside after the over-heated apartment. Pike had to stamp his feet to keep warm.

'What now, then?' Noel asked, buttoning his jacket against the chill. 'Sit at home and wait for Patterson to call?'

'He won't call.'

'You're probably right. What, then?'

'Think, Noel. Is there anyone else who might know? Anywhere else Chas might have gone?'

'I dunno.'

'Family, friends, girlfriends . . . ?'

'I could try dad, I suppose. Chas sometimes goes there, but it's a long shot.'

'Where's he live?'

'Swindon.'

'Give him a bell, then.'

'What's the time?'

Pike looked at his watch. 'Just gone half seven. Why?'

'He'll be pissed.'

'Well, he won't be too pissed to answer the phone, will he?'

'I wouldn't be too sure of it.'

'Oh, God preserve me from the Bishop family.'

'All right, I can but try. You got any ten pees?'

Pike rummaged in his pocket for change and came up with a couple of coins.

After a bit of scouting around they found a pub in one of the new buildings, designed to look like some old Victorian place and stuffed with expensive Christmas decorations. There was a pay phone at the bar and Noel dialled the number.

Pike stood looking out the window, half listening to Noel alternately pleading and shouting down the phone.

Chelsea Harbour looked like an empty stage set and from somewhere he heard a Christmas carol, drifting from a speaker, far off in the building somewhere. Pike felt suddenly very lonely. For some reason the thought of going back alone to his empty flat filled him with despair.

Alone. As he had been ever since Marti left him.

He could see the pointy top of the Belvedere, sticking out above the building opposite. He counted the floors up to Patterson. He couldn't see anyone moving up there, though the curtains were still open. Probably never closed them.

Was this really all that was left of them? The Alma crew? Noel and Chas, Pike, and those two up there?

He wondered what it would have been like if the scousers hadn't wandered into the pub all those years ago. After all, it was pure chance. They could have picked any pub in the area. They could have walked past the door, gone back to Finsbury Park, back to Liverpool. But they didn't. They chose the Alma. And that was that.

Glen Williams and Tony Creen. Pike knows their names, now. Though he didn't at the time. That night they were the fat bastard and the other one. Older than the crew, in their thirties. They were two lost little lamb-i-kins who had wandered into the lions' den.

He can see their faces so clearly now. It's funny, he can't really picture Mick and Colin clearly, Chrissie ... guys he'd known for six or seven years, but the scousers, two guys he knew for only one evening.

'Done.' Noel came over, slapping his hands together and blowing on them.

'And?'

'Chas was there.'

'When?'

'Last night. He stopped off to pick some things up.'

'Where was he going?'

'Dad can't remember.'

'For fuck's sake.'

'Look, it took me three ten pees to get that much out of him. He was rambling, talking bollocks. His mind's gone. It was like talking to a Martian.'

'Is he likely to remember any more when he sobers up?'

'He never sobers up, the old fart . . .' Pike glared at him, but Noel went on before he could say anything. 'He's better in the mornings. We'll ring him in the morning, eh?'

'Nah, sod it. We'll go up there. It'll save time.'

'To Swindon?'

'Yeah. It'll only take a couple of hours, won't it?'

'Yeah, but . . .'

'Come on, then. Let's go. D'you remember how we get to the car?'

'Hold on a minute. I can't just rush off for the night.'

'Why the fuck not?'

'I've got responsibilities.'

'Oh yeah? Like what?'

'Well, I . . . I've left Kirsty at home.'

'We're not taking your bloody girlfriend along, Noel.'

'She's not me girlfriend. She's me daughter.'

'Oh, fuck.'

TEN

Pike sat in the car and waited for Noel to come out of his flat. He'd said he'd only be a minute, and so far he'd been ten. Pike was starting to get cold. He'd kept the engine running for a while, but had turned it off when it had become evident that Noel wasn't going to be as quick as he'd said. He wondered if he should go in and see what the bald bastard was up to, but in the end he decided he couldn't be bothered to move.

He stretched and rubbed the back of his neck. The cold was making him stiff. Noel had left a packet of fags on the dashboard and Pike lit one. What the hell, it'd keep him warm. A car sounded its horn and he shivered. He looked out through the dirty windscreen. It had started to drizzle and drops of falling water glittered in the light of a street lamp. Down the empty street two old drunks tottered into a pub.

He never went into pubs any more. It cut him off from a whole part of London. London was made of pubs, there were pubs everywhere. On every street there stood one of these glowing, smog-filled dens.

Drink. That's what you did in this country. You drank. Sometimes you got drunk, but mostly you just drank, maintained a level, a balance of alcohol in the system. Once his whole life had been spent in pubs, every lunchtime, every night-time, lager and fags, fags and lager.

And the centre of it all, the heart of his world, his headquarters, his 'office', was the Alma. That was the place to be. Where every evening started and most ended up. After all, the landlord was one of their own. A lad. They'd got drunk together, gone to the football together, and wasn't it everyone's dream to have a mate run a pub? He remembered Chrissie's first night. It had been a riot. It had seemed like every lad in north London was there. Chrissie at the centre of it all, holding it together, half dead with drink.

And he remembered that last night, before the long hangover. The night of the scousers. Glen Williams and Tony Creen.

They hadn't been the brightest of blokes. They were already pissed up and full of themselves when they came through the door. But they were nothing, really. After clocking them the crew hadn't given them another thought. They were just two harmless tossers who'd wandered into their territory, and as long as they behaved themselves, didn't get too uppity, well then ... Well then ...

Lager and fags. The air solid. Brass fittings and optics gleaming. Carpet dark and sticky. The pub filling. Early-evening crowd. Noisy. Happy.

The crew are warming up, getting a few bevvies under their belts. Then all at once – there's no sign given, nothing is said – they understand that it's time to move on. Laughing and shouting they bundle out into the street. There's Patterson's Merc and Mick's van. Colin's bike. Colin's drawn the short straw, he gets the van with Mick. Noel and Chas get to ride in the Merc.

And Pike? Pike always does as he pleases. He sits in the back of Patterson's Merc, like it's a taxi. Patterson can play at being El Supremo, but Pike sits there in the back and looks out the window, saying nothing.

It's half eight. Still light, warm. They drive with their windows down, the stereo on full, pumping out dance music. They're pirates of the road, feared and fearless. They go where they please. Ah, yes, there's nothing to beat the exhilaration of driving at top speed while your body's alive with alcohol, and the drugs which Doctor Mick has administered are starting to kick in.

First of all they stop off for funds. Tonight they're working Romford. Last week it was Southend, before that, Watford, before that . . . ? Who cares? Who remembers? That's ancient history.

They park round the corner from a pub where they're not known and go in separately. They buy drinks and Pike stands alone, letting it come – the juice. The power. Looking round at the people in the pub. The fools. The wankers. The losers. Civilians. And the others, Patterson and the others, he can feel them waiting, too. Waiting for Pike to come on line. Waiting for the fury. He's shaking a little, his muscles tense. He feels cold. All that shit inside him.

Then it's time and he starts it, shoving Noel, picking a fight. Chas steps in, Patterson joins the argument. They barge about the place, knocking over tables, but Pike's still holding it in, waiting for the moment when . . .

There it is. One of the locals steps in, clips Pike with his fore-arm. Pow!

Pike goes off. The guy goes down. Total power. Maximum disruption. Full whack.

They trash the place and once the whole pub is distracted, once the landlord is lured away from his station, then little Mick vaults the bar and, guarded by Colin, empties the till.

Colin gives the signal and while Noel, Chas, Pike and Patterson allow themselves to be noisily lobbed out one door, Mick and Colin scarper out the other with the cash. Pike has one last go, smashes the pub door into someone's stupid face then it's back to the transport and on to another pub for a repeat performance.

Never fails.

And it's only one method, Plan B out of a whole alphabet of violent, small-scale, money-making schemes.

Tonight, two pubs yield them nearly five hundred quid, eighty quid each, enough for the evening.

Half nine they check out the talent at a disco pub on the Seven Sisters Road and find it lacking. Then Colin starts a fight for a laugh, slaps some geezer in pooffy New Romantic gear and they're obliged to leave.

So it's another high-speed chase to the kebab shop. Extra chilli sauce. Insult the Turks, belch loudly, get some beers for the journey, and back to the Alma just before eleven, ready for a serious session of after-hours drinking.

It's packed now. The pub is popular amongst the locals because Chrissie never shuts. Six months later he'll finally lose his licence, but tonight it's all systems go. There are other lads there, mates, half-mates and fuckwits. There are the usual old codgers, men who fifty years ago must have been hooligans like the new crop, but they've drunk their lives away, and are now content to play at being characters, in their hats, and their tatty suits, with their toothless grins, their tricks with cigarettes and their loud, cheeky wives. There are a few youngsters here, too, under-age drinkers trying too hard to be men, eager to please, sick in the bogs, if they can get that far. There's even a handful of students who squat the nearby estate and are always good for taking the piss out of.

And of course there's the girls, the alternative crew, the Alma Force, from fourteen to forty, hair done up, make-up on, jewellery, short skirts, high heels, foul mouths. Debbie, Kath, Louise, Shirley, Linda . . . and, of course, Marti.

Marti in a very, very small white dress, helping Chrissie out behind the bar.

This is it. Perfect. Heaven on earth. Their own small kingdom. They barge through the door like returning war heroes. The usual taunts are exchanged with the ladies. The usual insults and sexual threats are offered by each side. Then the stories begin. Reminiscences of tonight's campaigns, full of laughter and exaggeration.

But what's this?

At the bar, sitting on two stools. Sitting? They're still here. The scousers, Williams and Creen, even more pissed than before. Showing out, waving cash around, trying to act flash and buy everyone drinks.

'Come on, pal ... Come on, have a drink ...'

'What's with the scousers?' Mick asks Chrissie, and he tells them. He's been listening in. He's good at it. He comes across as a hopeless drunk, his brain gone, so people tell him things, expecting him to forget. But Chrissie remembers everything.

Some of it they find out from Chrissie. Some of it they find out later.

Turns out Glen Williams and Tony Creen were brought down from the Pool to help turn over a post office in Leyton. That was last week. Pike's heard about it, it was in the papers. They were evidently there for their muscle, not their brains. They'd been given their cut and by now they were supposed to be safely back home up North. But being morons they've stayed around to enjoy the bright lights of the big city and spend some of their hard-earned cash. Today they've been seeing Williams's sister, lives nearby. They've been showing off to her, showing her how they're big time, now. And on their way to the mini-cab office to get a ride back to their hotel in Finsbury Park they've passed the Alma. Well, how about a little drink, eh? A little drinkie. One for the road ...

And now it's closing time and they're still here, seduced by the cheery, beery London pub atmosphere. Seduced and fooled, made careless by drink.

Eleven o'clock, Chrissie locks the pub and pulls all the curtains.

Well, now, the scousers decide they've landed on their feet. This can't be bad. Money in their pockets and a pub that never closes, full of genial cockneys.

Cockneys.

They called everyone south of the Pool a cockney.

'Have a drink ... Come on, have a drink, pal ...'

They can stay. No problem. As long as they behave themselves. And if not ... well then.

There's some hard drinking done. Some serious drinking. The lads are settled in for the night, now. At half twelve there's an explosion of hilarity, Chrissie, bombed half-way to hell, comes out from behind the bar, writes 'Spurs' on the carpet with lighter fuel, and sets light to it. He dances round it like it's some mad religious ritual. When it's in danger of spreading he stamps it, leaving 'Spurs' permanently branded into the red, floral pattern.

A couple of the old women start singing a filthy song. One of the under-age drinkers starts a fight with one of the other under-age drinkers and they're both lobbed out to be sick on the pavement. Mick's speeding out of his skull, telling everyone about Marxism, and how Capitalism is a doomed philosophy. Colin's beating up the fag machine trying to get some money out of it, Chrissie offering encouragement.

It's steaming. Another Friday night at the Alma. People's faces shining, bloated, scarlet, stupid grins plastered all over them.

Now Chas gets Pike's attention. 'Look at those bastards.'

'Which particular bastards?'

'The fat, scouse bastard and the other one.'

Pike looks round. They're sat there on their stools, putting their hands all over Shirley and Louise.

'Those are London girls,' says Chas. 'Those are our girls.'

'They're nothing, Chas. Don't worry about them.'

'Look at them. Dribbling over them with their slack, scouser mouths, their hissing, slippery accents. Look at the bastards, buying them drinks.'

'They're just scousers, Chas. We don't have to even think about them.'

'It's not on, Pike. It's not on. It can't be allowed.'

'Tonight, Chas, anything is allowed.'

Chas gives up on Pike, wanders away to get one of the other lads interested. But nobody can give a fuck.

The drinking continues.

Little by little the pub empties, the regulars dribble away. Now it's the girls' turn to leave.

Even Shirley and Louise.

Well, have you ever seen two such heart-broken scousers? They'd thought they were in with a chance. Thought things were going swimmingly. No doubt they'd already figured out how they could get them back to Williams's sister's place and shag them on the sofa. But they'd misread the whole situation, they'd thought the girls had been crazy with lust, when in fact they'd just been taking the piss out of them all evening.

'Oh, come on girls. Come on . . .'

'Night, night.'

'Bye.'

'Dah, ya fuckin' slags.'

'Fuckin' cockney slags!'

Well, that's nice talk, isn't it?

It's all right for the lads to call their women slags and sluts, slappers, bitches and cunts, but not two uppity scousers. No way.

Williams and Creen are in the mean part of drunk now. Over the hill and hacking down the other side. Bitter and resentful. The lads have to put up with the usual whingeing, self-righteous, scouse self-pity. And now the northerners turn their attentions to the goddess behind the bar. To Marti in her white dress.

Marti don't care. She's an old hand at bar work, she knows how to handle lascivious drunks. She doesn't bat an eyelid, but Chas has had enough. He goes over and has a word with them, asks them politely to fuck off out of it.

'We've got every right to drink here,' whines the little one, Creen.

'Come on, lads, we're closed,' says Chrissie.

'Oh, yeah? Then how come youse lot are still here, then?'

'It's a private party.'

'Bollocks, it is. Give us another drink.'

They're hard men, these scousers. Armed robbers. Nobody tells them what to do.

Chas shoves Creen off his stool. Creen sloppily hits Chas, knocking him flat. Chas jumps up and faithful Noel steps in.

'Not in here,' says Chrissie. 'All right? Not in here.'

And the Bishops back off. Chrissie's the boss in the Alma. He has to be shown respect.

Now there's no one left. No one except the crew, the scousers and Marti, who's helping Chrissie to clean up. The scousers won't give up, they pester her, even go so far as to offer her money for it. Though this offer is accompanied by much giggling. They haven't been troubled any more by the lads, and they've made the mistake of thinking this is because they've established their authority over these soft, southern cockneys. They're top dogs here, as far as they're concerned, two tough-talking, hard-drinking men of the north.

At last Patterson has a word with Marti and the lads leave.

They wait round the corner, in a dimly lit alley leading between two shops towards the estate. Six of them, standing silent in the warm night, smoking. Pike, Patterson, Noel, Chas, Colin and Mick.

They don't have to wait long.

Five minutes later, Marti walks into the alley, Williams and Creen trotting at her side like hungry, happy dogs.

'Hello,' says Patterson, and they stop.

'All right fellers,' says Williams, trying to sound relaxed and casual, but they can see by his face that he knows he might have made a miscalculation. His eyes are big and round.

'Nice night for it,' says Chas.

'Yeah,' Williams laughs. Creen keeps a stone face. Trying to read the situation.

'Where you going?' says Colin flatly.

'Oh, you know . . .' Williams looks at Marti. She shrugs at him apologetically and steps away.

'Eh, fellers, no harm meant, eh?' Williams addresses his remark to Chas. 'We're all mates, eh?'

'Yeah,' says Chas. Williams laughs again.

Pike wants it started. It's going on too long. He wants to get into it. Get going. There's no frenzy yet, just the anticipation, like a junkie before the needle, like Marti smiling from the bed.

Now.

Without saying anything, he steps forward and brings his fist smacking into Williams's mouth. Williams bends over double, holding his face in his hands, blood dripping though his fingers. Creen bravely lets fly at Pike but Pike swats him back with his forearm and he tumbles sideways into the wall.

'What d'you do that for?' says Williams. 'I've lost a tooth.'

'There it is,' says Patterson helpfully and points to the ground where a yellow tooth lies on a paving stone.

'Thanks.' Williams leans down to pick it up and Patterson boots him in the face with all his strength. Soundlessly, Williams flips over onto his back and sprawls there and doesn't bother them again.

Pike's heart is pounding, now. The fire is lit. The whole night has been leading to this, this one pure moment of violence. This is what he lives for, the feeling of adrenalin washing his system, his brain focused, the tension falling away from his muscles ...

Creen sees that if he stays he's got no chance. Williams is down, he can't be helped now. It's six against one. The little scouser tries to run. Colin and Mick grab him and throw him back to the others. Chas brings his knee up and gets him in the bollocks.

'No,' Creen says, sounding disappointed, tired, and he staggers forwards, lower and lower, like a man walking downstairs. Pike finally drops him with a rabbit punch to the side of his neck.

'Come on,' says Patterson.

What happens next is cold, methodical and ugly.

What happens next is why Pike took sick and hid for ten years.

What happened next is why he still wakes in the night and can't get back to sleep, his mind filled with images of blood, spreading on the pavement, black like oil.

While Marti stood watching, the six of them kicked Tony Creen to death.

ELEVEN

'Does she ever talk?' Pike asked, turning off the Chiswick round-about towards the M4.

'No,' said Noel. 'Just plays her Game Boy.'

Kirsty was an ugly child, with wide-set boggly eyes, lank, greasy hair and unhealthy greyish skin. Noel said she was six, but she looked younger, stunted. Pike looked at her in the driving mirror, hunched over her electronic game, her face illuminated by a little clip-on light. She looked like something out of the Addams Family, but then, so did Noel.

'She don't half get through a lot of batteries,' said Noel.

'How d'you put up with that noise?' Pike asked, as a twee, beepy tune diddled out of the hand set.

'You get used to it. Don't notice it after a while.'

Since they'd picked her up in Shepherds Bush, Kirsty hadn't said a word. Not even hello.

Well, with a dad like Noel, what did you expect? Shirley Temple?

Traffic was light at this time of night and they were soon up the ramp and onto the flyover which carried this part of the motorway. As the Escort picked up speed it began to whine and rattle.

'Jesus,' said Noel, raising his voice to make himself heard above the racket. 'This is a shit car, you know, Pikey. What you driving a piece of crap like this for?'

'It suits me fine. There's no point in having a decent motor out my way, they just get nicked or smashed into.'

'But where's your pride?'

'It only makes this noise between forty and sixty. Once we get past sixty it'll settle down.'

'I'm embarrassed to be seen in it.'

Pike pulled into the fast lane to overtake a van and sure enough the noise died down. The car settled into a general hum.

'It goes fine,' said Pike. 'Good engine. Small for parking. I buy cars like this, run them into the ground, and get something else cheap. It's only got to last me till I go to Canada. There's no point in getting attached to a car, getting sentimental over a machine.' Pike glanced round at Noel who was staring out of the side window at a lorry carrying carpets. 'So you going to tell me, then? Or what?' he asked.

'What?' Noel looked round at Pike who nodded towards the back of the car.

'Your little bundle of joy.'

'It's a long story.'

'We've got plenty of time,' said Pike.

'I'll give you the abridged version.'

'Who's the mother?'

'No one you know. Alana. I met her in Vegas.'

'A Yank?'

'Middlesbrough.'

'What were you doing in Vegas?'

'Gambling. Let's face it, Pike, you've got to lose a shit-load of money in Vegas at least once before you die, haven't you? Otherwise you haven't lived. I had money, then. Chas and I had worked up a very neat little fake perfume scam. We were well bunced up, but for one reason or another we had to get out of the country and keep our heads down for a bit. But that's another story. Magic place, the States. Travelled all over. Course I wound up in Vegas. You should have seen me. Top hotel – they give it you for nothing if they think you're going to spend a lot on the gambling, and, boy, did I spend. Started off, right, I was on a roll, couldn't put a foot wrong. Charmed! My dosh was accumulating faster than crabs on an Essex girl. I had respect, my own place at the table – roulette, that's the game. I was Mr Bishop. They laid on a car for me, moved me to a better hotel, right above the casino. I had the works. I was big money. My pile just grew and grew, and that's how I met Alana. She was out there with the girls from her local bingo. Saved up for years. Proper girls on holiday, they were, off the lead and going for it. To her I was a big cheese, I was James Bond.' Noel chuckled. 'Bought meself a white suit, the bollocks. Had me hair done, manicure, saunas, sunbed, massage, you should have seen me, Pikey.'

'I can imagine.'

'Well, Alana, she was crazy for it; for me. That was the best sex I ever had that week. In that posh hotel, big round bath, bubbles, gold taps, champagne, steak, coke, and Alana … oh, she was beautiful. Small bird, but perfectly formed. Lovely. Lovely little tits. Lovely little face. Northern accent, but we didn't do much talking, so that didn't matter. And she was on holiday, showing out, really dolled herself up … It was like we were both in a film.'

'This story isn't going to have a happy ending, is it?' said Pike.

'No. But at the time, I'll tell you, my dick thought it had died and gone to heaven. You know what she said to me – the first night, back in my room, stripped to her undies, stockings and everything – you know what she said?'

'I hardly dare to think.'

Noel lowered his voice, leant towards Pike. ' "Noel," she said. "Noel, you can do anything you want to me … anything." Can you imagine?'

'No,' said Pike.

'What do you mean, "no"? She said I could do anything.'

'Like what?'

'Well, you know, anything.'

'Yeah. So you keep saying. What's anything?'

'Well ...' Noel glanced back at Kirsty, then put a tape in the machine, turning the volume up. It was Ennio Morricone.

'Use your imagination, for fuck's sake, Pike. She said "anything". I went hard as a tube of Smarties. I mean, isn't that the most horny thing anyone can ever say to you?'

'I still don't get it,' said Pike. 'I mean, what do you normally do?'

'You can't do everything to just any bird.'

'But what is there to do? Strikes me that unless you're some very specialized pervert, sex is sex. So, some bird says to me, "You can do anything you want." What am I supposed to think? That I can kill her, or what?'

'No.'

'You're not into pissing, or any other kind of bathroom antics?'

'No,' said Noel. 'What do you take me for?'

'So, once you've tried sucking, blowing, a bit of manual work, you on top, her on top, behind, upside down, tying her to the bedposts ... what is there?'

'Well ... anything.'

'So you keep saying. But what the fuck is anything?'

Noel thought about it. 'Now I come to think of it ... I don't know. I just remember thinking at the time, this is it, this is the horniest thing anyone's ever said to me.'

'And when it came down to it, what did you do?'

'Well, what you just said, I suppose ...'

'Which is what you normally do,' said Pike, patiently.

'Yeah, suppose ... Wait a minute, you missed out the tradesman's entrance!'

'You what?'

'Up the jakes,' said Noel.

'You're into that, are you?'

'Not particularly, no. I mean the idea of it is sort of saucy, you know, that someone might let you do it . . . that's exciting.'

'You did that with Alana?'

'No. She wouldn't let me. Said it was disgusting.'

Pike burst out laughing. He hadn't laughed properly for a long time. It felt good. Noel joined in.

'I didn't mind,' he said, rubbing his bald patch. 'Wasn't really bothered. But I tell you, that was the best week of my life.'

'And at the end of it?'

'At the end of it, I was skint and Alana was pregnant. Silly cow, wasn't on the pill.'

'You didn't think to ask?'

'She said I could do anything, didn't she?'

'You silly sod.'

'We tried to make a go of it, back in London. Stuck it for about a year. But Shepherds Bush just isn't the same as Las Vegas. The magic wasn't there. She let herself go, my white suit turned grey, we realized we didn't really like each other that much. So she buggered off back up North with Kirsty.'

'How come you've got her now, then?'

'Six months ago Alana turns up on the doorstep with Kirsty in tow. Says she's got a new bloke, and he wants to start his own family, doesn't want Kirsty around. So now I'm lumbered with her. Christ, it's hard work looking after a kid. Getting her to school, getting her home again, buying her shoes, taking her to the doctor's. I'll tell you, it's never-ending. The only thing that keeps her happy is that bloody Game Boy. Super Mario Brothers.'

Pike had no idea who the Super Mario Brothers were and he wasn't interested enough to find out. He felt old, though. Like he didn't have a clue what young people did any more. He was out of touch. Didn't belong here, didn't belong anywhere. Canada? What was Canada? A dream country, a fairy-tale land out of a book.

'Noel?' he said.

'What?'

'At least you've got her. At least you've got something real.' But Noel just laughed.

And so they drove to Swindon. With Noel playing Pike's film music and getting into it, even the Philip Glass. Watching the lights blur past, hypnotized by the rhythms, clicking with it.

'It's all right . . .' he said, nodding his head. 'It makes sense. You've just got to be in the right mood. Diddly-diddly-diddly-diddly . . . It's all right.'

Then he was off again, chattering on, filling Pike in on the details of his disorganized life. Pike letting him talk, happy to listen and not have to contribute in any way, trying to keep his mind off Chas, and the money, and the fuck-up he'd made of everything.

The driving seemed to take care of itself. Now and then he realized that for several minutes he hadn't been conscious of what he was doing at all. He couldn't remember driving, couldn't remember what had happened, as if the car had been driving itself. He was lost on a track of music narrated by Noel. An endless story of a scam, a hustle, a con, a beating, little wins, big losses, a drunken binge, a lost weekend of drugs and mayhem . . . And all the while, holiday brochure images of Canada flitted uninvited into his thoughts; the Rockies, pine forests, the Great Lakes, moose and elk in the snow, bears, Eskimos, Toronto by night, lobsters and old fishing boats, craggy coastlines . . . a Mountie.

'Like something out of a film.'

That's what Noel kept saying, playing the tapes. 'This, with the music, it's like something out of a film.'

'Is it?'

'I haven't been to the pictures in years,' said Noel.

'I go all the time,' said Pike.

'What about the football? You ever get to a match any more?'

'No.'

'Me either. It's ridiculous, I haven't been in about two years. When you think it used to be me whole existence. And now . . .'

'I watch it on the telly sometimes,' said Pike.

'That's not what football's about,' said Noel. 'Football's about having a laugh.'

'No, it's not,' said Pike. 'It's about being bloody miserable. Losing at home to, I don't know, Coventry. That's my memory of football apart from one game ...'

'1991, semi-final, Arsenal,' Noel butted in. 'At Wembley.'

'Yeah,' said Pike.

Noel laughed and sang, 'Where's your double gone? Where's your double gone?'

'That first goal,' said Pike.

'Gazza's free kick.'

'Yeah. I watched it on the box. Unbelievable. Even Barry Davis couldn't believe it. When that one went in, that was the one time I thought ...'

'I was there, Pikey,' said Noel. 'I was *bloody* there. At Wembley. *Nobody* could believe it. All the Spurs, we were just looking round at each other ... And when the second goal went in. Blimey. I'll never forget looking up the other end and seeing that sea of red. Motionless. It was like a dream. A good dream. Silent red and happy yiddos. It was like I'd spent my whole life preparing for that one moment.'

'Final was crap, though, wasn't it?' said Pike.

'Yeah,' said Noel despondently. 'But we won, I suppose.'

'Own goal, though. Felt sorry for Cloughie a bit.'

'Yeah. But that was it, for me. Haven't watched much since.' Noel stopped and smiled at Pike. 'Hey, this is all right, innit?'

'What?'

'Talking about the game. Like we used to.'

Now it was Pike's turn to smile. For a moment it had been fun. He realized that he never really talked to anyone any more, not even about trivial things – TV, films, football, sex. He hated Noel for getting under his skin, but in a way he was grateful to him for plugging him back in.

That was what football was all about. Not a sport, not twenty-two men running around on a pitch. It was about being with your mates. It was about being a part of something. It was about being plugged in. Belonging.

'This is it,' said Noel.

'Huh?'

'This is our turn off. This is Swindon.'

So they pulled off the motorway and the spell was broken. The journey became all stop-start, no longer a smooth, unbroken glide. They were back in the real world. Noel had to concentrate on giving directions and Pike had to concentrate on the driving.

Noel's dad lived on a faceless, modern council estate in a semi-detached brick house with half-hearted fake Tudor woodwork.

There was an eerie light. The street lamp out front was faulty, cutting on and off. Looking at the house was like you were looking at an old, flickering cine film.

The front garden was a mess. There were a couple of abandoned shopping trolleys lying among sacks of empty bottles and the burnt-out remains of an armchair. The lawn was uncut and over-grown with weeds. Dogs had dug up parts of it and it was bumpy and uneven.

Noel had become serious and guarded. 'We'll go round the back,' he said. 'There's no point in knocking, he'll probably be passed out.'

Pike followed him round the side of the house, Kirsty shambling at his side, still playing the game.

Noel stopped. 'One thing,' he said. 'Don't go in the back garden.'

'Why not?'

'Just don't, okay? Trust me.'

'Why can't I go in the back garden?'

Noel sighed. 'About a year ago his toilet got blocked and he hit on a novel way of unblocking it. He filled it full of petrol and dropped a match in the bowl. Blew the fucking thing up.'

'Jesus.'

'Yeah. So, now he shits into plastic bags and chucks them out the window. So don't go in the back garden.'

'Fine.'

'You can piss in the sink, but if you're desperate for a dump you can use Mrs Weller's bog next door. She looks after dad.'

'Noel, we shouldn't have brought a kid here.'

'I know, but you didn't give me much choice.' Noel pushed open the unlocked back door and they went inside.

Noel found the switch in the dark and a harsh fluorescent light flickered on.

The kitchen was disgusting. The sink was piled high with dirty dishes, mould growing from many of them. The surfaces, too, were cluttered with pots and pans, plates, half-empty tins, boxes and packets, foil take-away containers, fag ends, pizza boxes ... There were empty beer cans and bottles everywhere, a pile of four or five bin bags that looked like they'd been there for years. The floor was thick with a yellowish, sticky grease, patterned with black footprints. Pike's shoes stuck to it as they walked in.

And it stank. Of piss and beer and whisky and rotting food. An animal stink mixed with decay.

They hurried out of the kitchen, but the rest of the house was no better. It was hard to believe that one person could create this amount of filth and rubbish. Pike felt dirty, like something vile had got into his system. He wanted to wash his hands. To take a hot shower in a pure white, tiled bathroom.

They found Mr Bishop by the noise. He was sitting upright on the sofa in the sitting room, fully clothed and snoring loudly. He'd been sick and the front of his once white shirt was plastered with spew. There was a quantity of blood in the puke. He looked about a hundred years old, though he probably wasn't even sixty. He was wearing a black suit which was old and shiny, and a pair of cheap new trainers. His face was leathery, dark red, seamed and worm-eaten. His tongue, which protruded through yellow teeth, was green.

Noel frowned and looked ashamed. 'There's no point trying to wake him,' he said. 'Best to just leave him here. We'll quiz him in the morning, eh?'

'Jesus, Noel.'

Kirsty stood by the door, staring intently at her game, trying to shut out the world around her.

They heard a sound in the kitchen and a female voice rang out. 'Hello? Hello?'

'In here,' Noel called back and a young woman came in holding a long torch like a truncheon.

'Oh, hello Noel.'

'Hello Mrs Weller.'

'I was just checking.' She must have been about thirty; tall with short bobbed black hair. She was wearing faded jeans and a man's shirt.

'I heard the car and saw someone come in. I have to look out for him. They've robbed him before now. They know he's easy.'

'Thanks, Mrs Weller. But you shouldn't come in like that, it could be dangerous.'

'Oh, they're all cowards. They run at the first little sound. They're tossers, kids mostly.'

'Yeah, well thanks for looking out for him. He don't deserve it.'

She looked at the unconscious body and sighed. 'I try my best, but he's his own worst enemy, really. He's just a kid himself.'

'I don't know how you put up with him next door to you.'

'At least he's quiet.' She laughed.

'Oh, by the way,' said Noel. 'This is Pike . . . Dennis. Old friend.'

'Pleased to meet you,' she shook his hand and smiled politely.

'And this is Kirsty, my little girl.'

'Oh, so this is Kirsty . . .' She squatted down and said hello to the girl, who ignored her.

'Sorry,' said Noel. 'She's dead to the world when she's got that flaming machine on.'

'I know. My Darren's just the same.' She straightened up. 'You're not staying, are you?'

'Yeah, well, just the one night. We need to talk to dad about something. There's no point trying now.'

'I'll take Kirsty.'

'No, you don't have to …'

'I'd take all of you, but I don't have the room.'

'No, it's all right,' said Noel with a noticeable lack of conviction. 'We'll manage.'

'Noel. She's not staying here.'

'It's very kind of you Mrs Weller,' said Pike.

'Sarah.'

'Sarah.'

Noel leant over Kirsty. 'Do you want to stay the night with Sarah and Darren?'

Kirsty shrugged.

'She says thanks a lot,' said Noel.

Sarah took Kirsty by the elbow. 'Come on, then. We'll get you to bed.' She took her out by the kitchen and Pike and Noel were left alone with the snoring body.

'Welcome to the Bishops' country residence,' said Noel, bitterly. 'His Lordship is asleep.' He kicked his father's leg. 'You fucking old bastard.'

'Come on,' said Pike. 'Leave it. Let's go and get pissed, eh?'

'Yeah,' Noel smiled ruefully. 'Like father, like son.'

They went to the pub.

TWELVE

Pike got up at seven, tired, aching and hung over. He'd hardly slept all night. Noel had given him the spare bed and taken his father's room, which Pike didn't envy at all. His own bed was hardly ideal, an uncomfortable narrow affair with nylon sheets, but at least the room wasn't too dirty. It looked like it was mainly used for storage and was full of old boxes and suitcases, rather than abandoned food and empty bottles. The putrefying smell got everywhere, though, and Pike had lain there most of the night, itching all over, half awake, half drunk, feeling cold and lousy.

When he went downstairs in the morning he found the old man still asleep on the sofa, though he'd shifted himself from his seated position and was stretched out on his back.

Pike left him there and went outside. It wasn't fully light yet, a dreary, freezing Thursday morning in December. He ran round the estate for half an hour to get his body going. Pumping clean air into his lungs and trying to clear the stink which he felt sure was clinging to him.

He felt better after the run, more able to face the horrors of the Bishop house. On his way back he passed a row of shops. He bought himself a *Daily Mirror* and read it over a full cooked breakfast in a café at the end of the row. There was no way he was going to risk eating at Noel's dad's.

Feeling a twinge of pity for Noel he picked up a loaf of bread and a pint of milk before heading back.

Sarah Weller was paying the milkman at her front door when Pike arrived. She smiled at him and called out good morning.

Pike strolled up to her door. 'Was Kirsty okay?' he asked, and yawned.

'No trouble. You're up early.' Sarah was wearing pyjamas and an overcoat.

'Couldn't sleep.'

'Do you want a cup of tea, or anything?'

'I just had one at the café, thanks . . . But, go on, yeah. One more won't do me any harm.'

Sarah took him inside. 'The kids are still asleep. It's daft, really. Darren doesn't wake up at the crack of dawn any more, but I still do. Just got into the habit, I suppose.'

Sarah's little house was a haven of order and domesticity after Mr Bishop's. Pike sat at the table in the clean, bright kitchen while Sarah went about making some tea.

'Your husband not up yet?' Pike asked.

'God knows. I haven't seen him in two years.'

'Oh.' Pike looked at the back of Sarah's neck, where it was shaved up to the line of her short, thick, black hair and had a sudden urge to go to her and bite it.

'What do you want with the old guy, then?' she asked, making conversation.

'We're trying to find Chas.'

'He was down here the night before last.'

'Did you speak to him at all?'

'Not really, no. Just hello, and that.' The kettle boiled and she poured the water out into two cups.

'He didn't say where he might have been going on to?' Pike asked.

'No.' Sarah brought over the cups and sat down opposite him.

'This is very civilized,' Pike said.

'He was all right, you know, Mr Bishop, until his wife died. I moved in here about the same time as they did. I mean, he always drank, but I suppose she kept him in order, and when she went . . . Maybe he just thought, what's the point? You know? You married?'

'No,' said Pike.

'Divorced?'

'No.'

'Widower?'

'No.'

'Girlfriend?'

'Nope.'

'You're not very good at this, are you?' Sarah shook her head.

'What?'

'Conversation.'

'I don't know . . .'

'You've got to give me a bit of help, here.'

'I'm sorry. I've been kind of . . .' Pike stared at his tea. 'Out of action for a while. I'm not used to . . . Well, you know.'

'You been inside?' Sarah asked, matter-of-factly.

'No.' Pike smiled. 'But I might as well have been.'

'Mr Mysterious.'

'Not really. There's nothing to know.'

'You're not as old as you look, are you?'

'I wouldn't know.'

'What are you? About thirty-five?'

'Four.'

'Well, then. You're not as old as you look.'

'Are you always this personal with strangers?'

'I'm stuck here all day with a nine-year-old. I'll grab at any chance to talk to a grown-up, even a miserable sod like you.'

'You think I'm miserable?'

'Well you're not exactly the laughing policeman, are you?'

Pike shook his head and took a sip of tea. 'No.'

'Still,' said Sarah. 'Beats reading the side of the cereal box again . . . Just.'

'There you are, then.' Pike put down his mug. 'I'd better get back and see if Noel's up. Things to do, places to go, you know?'

'If you say so.'

'Thanks for the tea.'

'Any time.'

Pike looked at Sarah. She had very white skin and very blue eyes. 'It was very civilized,' he said. 'Very civilized.'

He went next door, letting himself in by the kitchen. There was a horrible, mucus-filled coughing sound coming from the front room.

Mr Bishop was up.

Pike met him in the hall. He was scratching his head and picking at the dried-on puke down the front of his shirt. He blinked up at Pike when he saw him. 'Who the fuck are you?'

'Friend of Noel's. We came down last night.'

'Last night?' Mr Bishop had a heavy East End accent.

'I'm with Noel.'

'Noel? Is Noel here?'

'He's asleep in your bed.'

'My bed . . .' Mr Bishop collapsed into another coughing fit. 'Cunt,' he said when it was over, but Pike couldn't tell if the old man was referring to Noel, to Pike, to himself, the cough, or just the world in general.

Pike followed him as he shuffled into the kitchen, shoved a pile of crap to one side of the sink and filled up his kettle.

'What's Noel doing here, then?'

'We came to talk to you about Chas.'

'Chas?'

'Yes, he was here, wasn't he? Last Tuesday night.'

'Tuesday night? Was it? I don't know.'

'Chas was here, and we need to know where he went.'

'Where he went? How the fuck should I know where he went?'

'Maybe he said something to you.'

'To me? Why should he say anything to me? He never fucking tells me anything.' Mr Bishop put the kettle on a gas ring and lit it.

'So you don't know where he might have gone then?'

'Might have gone anywhere.' He took a squashed packet of Embassy from his pocket. He tipped out a cigarette and, without offering one to Pike, lit it on the gas.

'Listen, Mr Bishop, this is important. Did Chas say anything at all about where he was going when he left here?'

'When he left here?' Mr Bishop snorted, chewed for a second, then spat into the sink. 'Tell you what,' he said. 'Why don't you fuck off and leave me alone?'

Pike wanted to take hold of the old man's crumpled face and smash it down onto the table top. Ten years ago he would have done. But he knew it wouldn't make any difference.

'I'll get Noel,' he said and left the room.

'Noel. You do that.' Mr Bishop shouted after him and followed it up with a volley of hacking coughs.

Noel was sound asleep, sprawled in his father's old double bed, wearing his underwear. Like this, his mouth open, his tongue out, his face slack, he looked like his father.

Surprisingly, the room wasn't too bad. It was reasonably tidy. The old man had made a pathetic attempt at keeping order in here. There was even a sort of little shrine to his late wife. Three photographs in fussy gilt frames were set out on a dresser with a few of her things, a silver-backed brush, a pair of pink-framed glasses, some dried flowers, pieces of broken jewellery.

Pike shook Noel, and carried on shaking him for over a minute until he finally came awake, looking dazed and disoriented.

'What? What is it?'

'Come on, Noel. Wakey, wakey.'

'Pike? What's the matter? What time is it?'

'Get up. I need you to talk to your dad. I'm getting nowhere with him.'

Noel looked at his watch. 'Christ's sake, Pike. It's half past eight in the fucking morning.'

Pike picked Noel up, lifted him out of the bed and dumped him on the floor. His long legs were pale and skinny and girlishly hairless.

'Downstairs. Now.'

'I'm freezing.'

Pike grabbed Noel's clothes and chucked them at him. 'Put these on.'

He stood there and waited while Noel clumsily dressed, swearing and muttering the whole time. Then the two of them went downstairs.

Mr Bishop was back in the front room, sat by the window looking out at the grey day, smoking and cradling his mug of tea.

'Hello, dad.'

'Dad . . .' He didn't look round. 'So you are here, then, Noel?'

'Yup. Listen, dad. Chas has gone missing.'

'Missing? Chas . . . Yeah . . .'

'You're the last person who saw him.'

'Saw him. Yeah. I was pissed, Noel. Pissed.'

'It doesn't matter.'

'Doesn't matter. No . . . Your old man was steaming. I don't remember. He picked some gear up.'

'What?' Pike asked.

'What? How should I know? Some of his boxes. Some of his stuff. You know Chas, always has stuff. Boxes of stuff, wherever he goes. All that junk. Never comes to see me. Just keeps his junk here.'

'Never mind about that, dad . . .'

'Never mind about that. Never comes to see his old man. Just like you, Noel. Never come to see me.'

'I'm here now, aren't I?'

'Aren't you? Only 'cos you want something. You don't care about your old man.'

'Tell me one reason why I should care? One fucking reason. You treated me like shit all my life, and now you're a hopeless old piss artist.'

'Piss artist.' Mr Bishop started to laugh and it inevitably turned into a cough. 'That's me. Piss artist.' He hurled his mug at the wall and it smashed, leaving a brown splash of tea. 'Picasso of piss.'

'Don't show off, dad.' Noel put a hand on the old man's shoulder.

'Don't fucking touch me!'

Noel let go.

'Junk. Rubbish. Crap. Shit. Full of it.' He got up and went to the window. 'He was here. Didn't stay. In and out. What do you think I am, a fucking storage facility, a fucking cupboard . . . ? Bath.'

'What?'

'What? What's what? He went to Bath.'

'Chas went to Bath?'

'To Bath. Said he was going to Bath. Made a joke of it. Said he wouldn't bath here. He'd bath in Bath.'

'You're sure of it,' Pike asked.

'Sure of it. Had to meet some fucking kraut. What's he want with poxy Bath?'

'Did he say whereabouts in Bath?'

'Bath. That's all he said. Made a joke of it . . .'

'Right,' said Pike. 'Let's get sorted. Noel, you ring Chas's junkie bird, Christine. Double check Chas hasn't been back there, been in touch. I'll go and get Kirsty from next door.'

'Then what?'

'Then we go to fucking Bath. What do you think?'

'You're all the same,' moaned Mr Bishop. 'You don't care about me. I'm just a piss artist. You don't care. Family's important to Londoners. The family. If your old mum was still here . . . You don't care.'

'Oh, fuck off,' said Pike and he went next door.

He felt oddly excited; he wasn't sure if it was the piece of information or the prospect of seeing Sarah again. An image of the back of her neck, where her hair was cut short, appeared to him and he tried to put it out of his mind.

This was no time to be thinking about that. It was just that seeing Marti back at Patterson's had jolted something loose inside him. He'd been indoors all this time, and now he was out, and it was icy out here. He knew that if he slipped he'd just keep on sliding.

THIRTEEN

'Where are you?' Christine's voice was flat and monotonous. No surprise there; everything about her was flat and monotonous. She acted permanently bored, like an adolescent.

'Where is that?'

You couldn't provoke any kind of extreme reaction in her, she accepted whatever happened with the same sullen irritation. Even when Terry hit her she hadn't seemed to notice. She had a big bruise on her cheek now, and she stroked it idly while she droned into the telephone. Basil wanted to take her by the shoulders and shake her, get some life into her, but she wasn't worth it.

'Where is that?' she repeated, then waited. 'Swindon? Give me the number so I can leave a message if Chas gets in touch.'

Basil fiddled with his ring, turning it one way and then the other. This was it. Contact had been made. They were back on the trail. Terry nudged the sulky girl and she made an irritated face at him. But she did as she was told.

She was writing the number down now. Terry looked at it and nodded. He didn't smile or anything, just nodded. Terry never smiled – he was a very serious man, probably the most serious man Basil had ever met – but Basil could tell that he was pleased. So Basil was pleased too. Terry had been angry when they'd lost Noel and the other bloke, the older-looking man, round Victoria. He'd been quiet and moody ever since and Basil had had to be extra careful with him, so he wouldn't fly off the handle. Things had been uncomfortably tense for a while, particularly waiting here in the girl's flat.

It had been a long night. Basil had slept on the sofa under a couple of coats. Terry had sat in a chair by the door the whole time, hadn't slept at all, in case the girl tried to get out, or something. She whinged and moaned and when Terry hit her Basil thought he might kill her. Basil had been scared and excited at the same time. But Terry hadn't killed her, he'd just hit her once, hard, and although at the time she hadn't acted like it hurt, she'd been perfectly co-operative ever since.

She was a druggie, a heroin addict. Basil hadn't been able to watch when she'd injected herself in the leg. He didn't like needles. He didn't like her, it was like she was sick the whole time, like she had flu, and it made Basil feel ill. He didn't like it here. He was glad that now they had a lead they could get away.

The girl hung up the phone and Terry took the piece of paper with the number off her.

'It's Chas's dad's,' the girl said. 'They're with Chas's dad … In Swindon.'

'This isn't the address, is it?' Terry asked her, folding the note neatly.

'No. Just the number.'

'Do you know the address?'

The girl shook her head.

'Will it be here somewhere? Will Chas have it written down somewhere?'

The girl shrugged. 'Dunno. They're not staying there, anyway. They're going to Bath.'

'Whereabouts in Bath?'

'Dunno. Didn't say.'

Terry passed the note to Basil and stared at Christine for a while, thinking. The girl lowered her eyes.

'Why don't I go through his stuff,' said Basil after a while. 'See if I can find any addresses written down; Swindon, Bath . . . anything like that.'

'Good,' said Terry. 'That is a good idea.'

Basil was happy to be of use, Terry's trusted and valued soldier. He went into the bedroom and sifted through Chas's things. It didn't take long. All Chas's documents and paperwork, all his personal stuff, was in one drawer, a few receipts, some business cards, a broken gold chain which Basil pocketed, a couple of biros, some car insurance crap, bank stuff, a book of matches, a pile of out-of-date credit cards in various names, a notebook with rows of figures and a doodle of a naked woman with big tits in it, a pile of envelopes, some bills . . . and there at the bottom a small pile of tatty pieces of paper with phone numbers and addresses on them. He sorted through them, then smiled as he found one with an address in Bath scrawled on it.

Still grinning, he stuffed the others in his pocket and returned to the front room with his prize.

Terry was standing still in the middle of the room staring down at the girl who was back in her armchair huddled over the electric fire.

'Look at this,' said Basil, holding out the piece of paper.

'What is it?' Terry said without looking.

'Bath address . . .'

Terry nodded. 'Good. You look after it.'

'What now?' Basil asked. 'Do we go to Bath?'

'How much of a start do you reckon they've got on us?'

Basil looked at his watch. 'Two or three hours. Trouble is, traffic's going to be bad getting out of town at this time of day. Could take us an hour, hour and a half, just to get onto the motorway.'

'Let's get shifted, then.'

'We could always get a train.'

'No,' said Terry. 'I never use public transport.'

'Right. Car it is, then.' Basil smiled and picked up his overnight bag. 'And no errors this time.'

'No.' Basil stopped smiling.

Terry looked at the girl and pulled his knitted hat down at the front. 'Stand up,' he said and she moodily got up out of the chair like it was the hardest thing she'd ever done.

'What?' she said, sounding bored, but looking a bit wary.

Terry cupped her bruised cheek tenderly. 'We're going now, my love.'

The girl grunted.

'And you wouldn't do anything daft, would you?'

'No.'

'You wouldn't try and get hold of Noel, or anything?'

'No.'

'No. You wouldn't. Because out of all the bad things in the world, I'm the worst, aren't I?'

'Mm.'

Terry nodded, then very quickly punched the girl twice in the face, right on the bruise. Short, solid jabs. It was over almost before Basil knew what he was doing. The girl went down, like a sack of potatoes, collapsed straight down onto her knees.

'There,' said Terry matter-of-factly. He didn't say anything else. He didn't have to. He'd made his point.

The girl didn't cry out or whimper, or make any sound of protest. She just crawled back into her chair and leant over the fire again.

Terry straightened his woollen hat. He'd already forgotten all about her. He hiked up his sweat pants and marched to the door on his short bowed legs. Basil followed, his heart racing a little.

'Bath, then?' he said as they clattered down the uncarpeted wooden stairs.

'Yes. Check out that address.'

'Might not be the same one, of course. Might not be where Noel's going.'

99

'Then we try Swindon,' said Terry.

'We don't have an address for Swindon, only the number.'

'It'll be in the phone book, won't it? Under Bishop. Match the number and bingo. It'll be in the phone book.'

*

'It'll be in the phone book,' said Pike.

'Under what?' Noel asked, paying the woman for the teas and the ice cream and coke. He still felt like shit. He'd drunk too much last night, and got up too early this morning.

'That's the tricky part,' said Pike and Noel watched as he went over to the pay phone on the wall.

They were stopped at a café, high on a ridge just outside Bath on the road into town from the motorway. It was overcast but the air was clear and you could see right out across a big green valley with farms and trees and little windy roads.

Noel gave Kirsty the ice cream and the can of Coke and she sat down at a table.

'I don't like ice cream,' she said.

'All kids like ice cream,' said Noel. He hadn't asked, just assumed that that was what she wanted.

'I don't like ice cream,' Kirsty said again.

Now he came to think of it Noel didn't like ice cream, either, never had. 'Well eat it anyway, honey.'

'I want to play Super Mario.'

'Well daddy's got to get some new batteries, hasn't he? You can't play your game for a while. Why don't you look at the nice view instead?'

'I don't like views.'

'Look, just sit there and look out the window and eat your bloody ice cream.'

'I don't like ice cream.'

'Then throw the fucking thing away. Just leave me alone for a minute, will you? I've got to help Uncle Dennis.'

'He's not my uncle. Uncle Chas is my uncle.'

Pike came over to the table with a local phone directory.

'I think I preferred her when she didn't talk,' said Noel. 'First chance we get we pick up some batteries.'

'There's no Mullers,' said Pike flipping through the phone book. 'Muller?'

'Herman Muller. Isn't that what Patterson said Herman the German was called?'

'Oh, yeah.'

'Said he'd pocketed Herman away in a nice little nest down here.'

'Yeah.' Noel nodded. 'If Patterson owns the place, it could be in his name.'

'Could be. But he's a devious sod.'

There were five Pattersons in the book, and they tried them all without any luck.

'Could be ex-directory,' Noel suggested.

'It's possible,' said Pike, wearily. 'But we can't give up yet.'

'I bet he's got property all over the place,' said Noel. 'Best way of looking after your cash. Instead of putting it in a bank, you put it in property. Harder to keep tabs on it that way.'

'And he wouldn't want it in his name, would he?' said Pike. 'Double protection. If his business goes under, if he goes bankrupt, it has to be in someone else's name to stay safe.'

'Marti,' said Noel.

'Exactly,' said Pike, and there, under M. Stoddart was an address and a number. Pike went back to the phone. Noel was about to go with him when Kirsty was spectacularly sick over the table.

'I told you I didn't like ice cream,' she wailed, her mouth stringy with mucus and saliva.

Noel took her into the toilet and cleaned her up as best he could. He swore and she cried in a pathetic self-pitying way which really got on Noel's tits.

When he came out Pike was by the table, looking out the big window at the view and finishing Kirsty's Coke.

'No luck?' Noel said.

'Don't know. Bloke answered the phone, definite trace of a foreign accent. Could have been German. When I asked if he was Herman Muller, he hung up.'

'What's the address?' Noel asked, mopping up the mess on the table with a handful of napkins.

'Royal Crescent.'

'Sounds posh.'

'Sounds like Patterson,' said Pike. 'Sounds just like Patterson.'

'Well, let's try it, then.'

'Yeah. Better than nothing.'

Once they got into Bath it didn't take them long to find the Royal Crescent. Everyone they asked knew where it was, there were even a couple of signs for it.

The Crescent was a wide semi-circular terrace, built of the same yellowish-brown stone as the rest of the city. Tall and elegant and really quite spectacular. It stood on a hillside above a small park in a commanding position. You almost expected to see a horse and carriage come trotting round the curving cobbled road.

'Don't say it,' said Pike as they got out of the car.

'Don't say what?' Noel asked.

'Don't say it's like something out of a film.'

'Well, it is.' Noel shook his head and surveyed the worn paving stones, the ancient black iron railings, the blue plaques on the walls, the evidence of a great deal of money through the windows. 'It's *Oliver Twist*, innit? *Dracula ... Upstairs Downstairs*. The whole place is like a film set. Living in London you forget places like this exist.'

'Come on,' said Pike, locking the car. 'Let's get on with what we came here for.'

The house was near one end of the crescent. They went to the front door and knocked the huge brass knocker. Noel peered in the window. He saw an empty room with fancy striped wallpaper but no furniture or carpet.

'Looks deserted,' he said.

Pike had a look for himself. 'Let's try the basement,' he said.

The three of them tramped down the wonky stone steps to a small courtyard and another door. Pike rang the bell.

They waited.

'There must be someone in,' said Pike, ringing again. 'Because they answered the phone.'

'Maybe he went out.'

Pike hammered on the door, then he stopped and yelled through the letter box. Still nothing. He moved to the window which was covered over with newspaper and banged on that. Nothing. It was fixed shut so he couldn't lift it.

'Here.' Noel quickly looked up to make sure nobody could see him and he gave the door a hefty kick with his heel. It didn't budge but a terrible pain shot up his leg and his whole spine jarred.

'Shit,' he said and he had to sit down on the steps, clutching the small of his back.

Pike was just about to try kicking it himself, when they heard the rattle of a chain and the sound of a bolt being slid.

Noel got up from the steps and walked over just as the door was opened by a slight young man with round, John Lennon glasses, very pale, acne-ravaged skin and greasy black hair cut short on the top and sides and long down the back. He was wearing a black T-shirt, boxer shorts and socks. He had a sort of piece of string with tiny beads on it round his neck. He blinked at them warily.

'What do you want?' he said with a mild foreign accent, looking from Pike to Noel and then Kirsty.

'Chas,' said Pike.

'You have the wrong address. Sorry.' The young man tried to close the door, but Pike put his hand on his chest and firmly pushed him back into the flat.

'Now, Herman,' he said. 'You know we have the right address.'

FOURTEEN

'You have to talk to us, Herman,' said Pike. 'Sooner or later. We're not going away. Now, has Chas been here?'

Noel could tell that Pike was still holding back, going easy on the guy, but it was difficult. He wouldn't talk to them; he wouldn't even look at them.

'Come on, Herman,' Noel said, trying to sound friendly. 'He's me brother, for fuck's sake.'

There was a long silence. In the end it was Kirsty who broke it. She'd been staring open-mouthed at all the computers in here and she finally went over to Herman and tugged his hand.

'Have you got any batteries?' she said, and held up her Game Boy.

'Hey, Game Boy.' Herman smiled. 'What are you playing?'

'Super Mario Land.'

'The first one?'

Kirsty shrugged.

'It's an old game,' said Herman. 'But it's a good one. I think I have some batteries.' He grinned at her and went to an old kitchen table laden with two huge colour monitors and three keyboards. The whole room was crammed with the stuff. Noel reckoned there must be at least ten different computers in here, on tables, desks, purpose-built black metal stands, even the floor. And it wasn't just computers, there were several telephones, a fax machine, a wall of music gear, tapedecks, CD players, amps, graphic equalizers, sequencers, a stack of stuff whose function Noel couldn't even guess at – sleek black boxes with knobs and VDUs. Everywhere you looked red and green lights danced and winked, and screens flashed information. Everything linked; wires came out the back of things they were never meant to and joined up with other machines, there were plug boards all over the place, studded with plugs. On a couple of surfaces there were half-dismantled pieces, their insides hanging out, wires sprouting, like they were being cannibalized for parts.

The room was warm and thickly carpeted; all natural light was kept out by the newspaper over the windows, and tiny half-hidden lamps threw soft patches of light here and there. Some kind of wishy-washy music was wafting out, abstract and soothing, and beneath the sound of the music there was an electronic hum, the buzzing of computers, the whirr of fans, now and then a little high-pitched cheep like a bird. In fact it reminded Noel of being in an animal house at the zoo, as all around the electronic machinery, perched on shelves and ledges, murmured and bleeped, blinked, stirred, and chattered.

Herman scrabbled around in a drawer before he brought out some batteries and he deftly fitted one into Kirsty's game.

'There you go,' he said, kneeling down by the little girl. 'You are Kirsty, yes?'

'Yes.'

'Chas told me all about you.' Kirsty's face lit up as the game came back on, and she fiddled and diddled with it.

'I can show you some secrets on there,' Herman said gently and Kirsty smiled.

'Where is Chas?' Pike asked, sitting down in a very high-tech office chair.

'I don't know where your Uncle Chas is,' Herman said to Kirsty.

'You have to tell us,' said Pike. 'We're not the only ones looking for him.'

Herman shrugged without looking up. 'Oh,' he said, as Kirsty made a face at her game. 'You must be careful and time your jump. I have some games here you might like, you know.'

'What games?'

'I will show you.' Herman led her over to a computer and tapped away on the keyboard for a few seconds, his fingers darting over the keys. Then he gave Kirsty a battered joy-stick.

'The right button is for fire, the left for jump. I have set you up with infinite lives.'

Kirsty sat down and studied the screen seriously. Noel watched as she guided some little fairy-type thing through a cutesy magic kingdom, zapping things with a magic wand.

'There is no point in my lying to your father,' Herman said, his eyes, too, fixed on the screen. 'One way or another he will come to the truth.'

'Talk to us,' said Pike, but Herman seemed not to hear. He sat on a chair, drawing his legs up into a yoga position. 'Do you think I should talk to your father, Kirsty?' he said after a long silence.

'I don't know,' said Kirsty. 'This is a good game.'

'He is Chas's brother,' said Herman. 'So, maybe ... Tell your father that I will talk to him, because I know that he will not involve me in what will happen now.'

'What will happen?' Noel asked. 'What do you mean?'

Herman shrugged again.

'Did Chas come here Tuesday night?' Pike asked.

'Yes.' Herman leaned close to Kirsty. 'I think you know he did, or you would not be here.'

'They're looking for Uncle Chas,' said Kirsty. 'He's run away.'

'Chas came to me with one of his schemes,' Herman said to her.

'Oh, no ...' Pike let out his breath slowly.

'Oh, yes, I am afraid. He was excited. He ... There is another scheme.'

'What other scheme?' Pike asked.

Herman put a hand on Kirsty's shoulder. 'Jump on the flower, darling . . . Yes, that's it.'

'What was his scheme?' Pike asked again.

'Chas would not tell me. He said that I must do only my part. You see, Kirsty, this . . .' He gestured round the room. 'This is what I do. Only this. What Chas did outside of this room was none of my concern. I only knew he had a scheme, but he needed investment. Without money he could do nothing, but with money he would make a fortune. Chas had no money. He came to me often, asked me to do something, find him some money, but it was always too dangerous. I have been in prison, I do not want to go back.'

'Prison?' said Kirsty.

'It is a bad place. A dungeon.'

'I know. Uncle Chas was in prison.'

'So what happened on Tuesday?' Pike asked patiently.

'Chas comes in the night. Happy, a little scared, I think. He says he has a way to get the start-up money . . . with my help.'

'He tells you he has the details of a building-society account with a lot of money in it,' said Pike.

'Yes . . . Mr Pike's account.'

'My account.'

'Yes. He says this account, if we get into it, the owner will not go to the police. This is the vital thing, because building societies are very difficult to hack into. In the end you will be uncovered. But if I know an account where nobody will say anything . . . All Chas needed was a few days, a week. Borrow the money for a week, make his fortune with his scheme, and then put the money back. But in that week, I must know that the man to whom the money belongs will do nothing.'

'He knew I'd come after him myself.'

'That was an acceptable risk. Kirsty, you should have seen how I did it. I already had the access device codes, the passwords to get on to the computer. I got them from a bulletin board. Then, when

I had the account numbers and the details, I could try my idea I have been having for a long time.'

Herman was excited now, talking fast and nodding his head. Like a different person. The lights from the screen reflecting in his glasses.

'You should have seen it, Kirsty. It was beautiful. First I put up a smokescreen, I hid Mr Pike's account. It was still there, but you couldn't see it. Chas made me put in my handle, the Red Baron, so that Mr Pike would know not to look any further. The message was designed to wipe itself out once it had been read. Then I moved the money. It is like *Star Trek*. You know, when they use the transporter ... Brrrrroooo ...' Herman made a sort of cooing noise. 'To be safe, if we need the time, the money was broken apart into a million pieces. Some of it went through Australia, some of it through Spain, some of it even went through Hawaii, all around the world ... And then I brought it back together again.'

'In Chas's pocket,' said Pike.

'In the end, yes. But it was a lot of money, so to avoid any suspicion, Chas picked up parts of it in different places, in different ways. Oh, it was beautiful. I had been wanting for a long time to try this technique out ...'

'I don't want to know,' said Pike. 'I only want to know where the money is now. Where Chas is.'

Herman pointed at the screen. 'Go to the right, darling. Just keep going fast and firing, they can't stop you.'

'Where's Chas?' Pike asked, more forcefully this time.

'Chas is dead.'

'What?' Noel jumped up from the table top he'd been perched on. 'What?'

'Chas is dead and I do not know where the money is.'

'Sod the money!' Noel shouted. 'Chas can't be dead. He can't be ...'

'When did this happen?' Pike asked calmly.

'Last night.'

'No, come on ...' Noel felt like laughing. He couldn't take this in. It was all too unreal.

'Mr Patterson came here.'

'Patterson?'

'He came with the woman, Marti. He was very angry that Chas was here. I am not supposed to see Chas. There was an argument. Upstairs. I was down here. I don't go upstairs. I heard them, the three of them, shouting. Then there are bumps. You know, pang, pang, on the floor. Then the shouting stops and Patterson tells me he is going. I ask where Chas is, he says Chas has already left, but I know this is a lie. Nobody can come in or come out of the house or I would know. So I watch as Patterson leaves with Marti, he carries a big bag, like a sack. It is a duvet cover I recognize. He puts it in his car. His black jeep with the black windows. His Cherokee. And they drive away. But I know that was Chas in the bag.'

'You don't know,' said Noel. 'You don't know for sure he's dead. You didn't see him dead.'

'He is dead. And now I have to be quiet. I should not talk. All I want to do is work here, that is all. I don't want to know about all that out there. I don't want to know about people and what they do, about their cars and roads and shops. I want you all to go away. I don't want to know about Chas and Mr Patterson, or you, all of you. I would like to be left alone.'

Herman took off his glasses and rubbed his eyes. Without his specs he looked even younger. Noel realized he couldn't be much over twenty.

'And the money?' Pike asked.

Fucking Pike. Why couldn't he just fuck off about his bloody money for one moment? He was becoming a bore.

'I don't know,' said Herman. 'Chas had it with him. He was ready to leave. He had collected it all. Now he is gone. The money? I looked. It isn't here. Patterson must have it.'

'Shit.' Pike got up and began to stalk around the room. 'I don't need this.'

'Hang on a minute,' said Noel. 'What about me? The bastard's killed my brother.'

'Fuck your brother, Noel. This is all his fault. The moron.'

'Well, fuck you, Pike! Have a little heart, eh.' Noel's throat felt tight. He knew he was on the verge of weeping. He turned away from the others.

'Look, I'm sorry, Noel,' said Pike. 'As sorry as I can be. But, let's face it, I was going to kill the cunt myself.'

'You wouldn't have.'

'I might have. I don't know.'

'Oh, fuck. What's going on?'

'Come on,' said Pike. 'Let's turn the place over. Check the money's not still here.'

'It's a waste of time, Pike.'

'You don't have to come with me,' Pike said flatly and walked out.

Noel felt very weary. Things had been ticking over very nicely. He had enough little sidelines on the go to be fairly comfortable. Being landed with Kirsty had thrown him into a spin for a while, but he'd got used to it, actually grew to quite enjoy it. He'd never tell anyone, but she gave him a bit of a purpose in life, a reason to get up in the mornings; even if she was small and ugly and never talked. And now ... Whatever you do, wherever you go, you end up treading in shit.

Once upon a time it hadn't seemed to matter. You were young, you arsed about, you drank, you had fights, you fucked when you got the opportunity ... And then one morning, that's what it had seemed like, one morning, waking up with a hangover, he'd felt like an old git, and it hit him, that's what he was. He wasn't a lad any more. It had all gone.

Fuck it.

He tramped upstairs after Pike, out of breath before he was even

111

halfway up. He could see Pike's muscles moving under his sweat-shirt. You couldn't always tell, with his baggy clothing and that, but Pike kept himself in shape. Right now, panting and sweating, Noel hated the man.

Noel had forgotten it was daytime, after the shuttered, artificial light of Herman's bunker, the sight of sunlight flooding in through big dirty windows was disorienting. He had to shield his eyes briefly.

The house was empty. Beautifully and expensively decorated, but perfectly empty. They searched every room, starting at the top, and it took them no time at all. Patterson had obviously never used the place, it was just a handy location to hide Herman. They found where Chas had been sleeping, probably once the dining room, a tall, elegant room with a dusty polished floor.

There was an old, stained mattress in one corner, a half-drunk bottle of white wine and an ashtray. Patterson had evidently taken Chas's clothes and anything else he might have left here.

And that was that.

'So now what are we going to do?' Noel asked, looking out the window at the overgrown back garden. 'We going after Patterson? We going to his place?'

'*We're* not going to do anything.'

'Huh?'

'We're not taking Kirsty along any more. This is getting stupid.'

'So what do you propose I do with her?'

'Go back to Swindon. Leave her with Mrs Weller.'

'No, Pike . . .'

'She shouldn't be with us,' Pike said wearily.

'Uh-uh, son. I'm not letting you out of my sight.'

'To tell you the truth, Noel,' Pike said, heading for the door. 'I don't want you along either.'

'Leave it out,' said Noel, hurrying after him. 'You're not getting rid of me. I'm seeing this through, all right?'

Pike turned on the stairs. 'And Kirsty?'

'We got no choice. She comes with us.'

'Noel . . .'

'Let's face it, Pike. We're not going to find Patterson, anyway, are we? The chances of him going back to Chelsea Harbour with Chas are fucking slim. So you might need my help figuring out the next step.'

Pike sighed and carried on down the stairs. 'I'm stuck with you, aren't I?'

'Yes. But first chance, we ditch Kirsty. Okay?' said Noel.

'First chance.'

They found Herman playing with Kirsty. The two of them had a joy-stick each and were laughing and shouting and peering at a screen about six inches in front of them. The room was filled with the noise of the game, music, explosions, bits of sampled speech. Herman smiled when they came in and left Kirsty to it.

'She's a good girl, Kirsty. She's funny. She has a good sense of humour.'

'Does she?' said Noel. 'I've never really talked to her.'

'Maybe you should do sometime.'

'Yeah, maybe I should.' Noel felt suddenly desperately sad for some reason. The tears which had been threatening to turn up finally broke and ran down his face. He felt very aware of the others watching him but he didn't care any more.

It wasn't as if he'd ever exactly liked Chas, but when it came down to it, he had loved him. Families, they were funny things. They made no sense.

Kirsty finished the game and Herman knelt down to give her back her Game Boy. 'You get to the end like I showed you, now? Then you can play some of these other games, yes?'

'Thank you.'

Herman handed her two or three other games and she clutched them in her tiny hand.

113

'Maybe you'll come see me again. I'll get some new games for you.'

'Thank you.'

Noel went over to his daughter, and he, too, knelt. 'Do you want me to look after them for you, chicken?'

Kirsty gave him the games, and he couldn't be sure, but she just might have smiled at him.

FIFTEEN

Basil decided he didn't like Bath. He hated it. Everything about it. The snooty people, poncing about in their expensive cars, the clean streets, the smart shops. Everything. The whole place was designed to make him feel dirty and stupid and insignificant.

Terry didn't seem to mind, he just strutted along like he always did, almost marching, except he didn't move his arms at all. He held them rigid, bent and slightly in front of his body, shoulders forward, head up, like he owned the town. But then Terry always acted like that. Basil felt good walking at his side. Basil felt proud. Everyone acted so bloody smug and arrogant, yet Basil knew that they were soft.

It had taken them ages to find somewhere to park and it turned out to be nowhere near where they were headed. They had to walk right through the centre of town and up a long hill. There were raised pavements here with railings and steps leading down to the road. And there were all these same old, boring, yellow houses, identical and monotonous.

The hill seemed to be going on for ever, and when they came to a pub Terry suggested they go in and get some more directions.

The pub was a small, tatty, dark affair. Bare, wooden floor, orange walls, a lot of smoke and a low ceiling. There was a jukebox playing an ancient Rolling Stones song, and a few locals were lurking in the gloom, laughing and chatting. Terry and Basil picked their way across the uneven floor to the bar where a bald, round-faced barman grinned at them.

'Hello, gents,' he said, with a yokel accent. 'What can I do you for?'

There were two more yokels leaning at the bar. About forty odd, with long hair and jeans, one of them wore a leather coat, the other had thick, black sideburns. They looked like druggie types, dope smokers. The sort of blokes you found working in junk shops, or selling second-hand records. Like the barman, they, too, grinned at the newcomers.

'We're just after some directions,' said Terry.

'Fire away,' said the barman.

'Do you know where the Royal Crescent is?'

'Hmm. The Royal Crescent. Now that's a tough one ...' The barman winked at the yokel with sideboards, who tittered.

'Do you know where it is, or not?' said Terry.

'The Royal Crescent? Well, now ... Let's see,' said Sideboards, scratching at his facial hair. 'I've heard of the royal mail ... the royal wedding ...'

'Royal seal of approval,' said the local in the leather coat and he barked like a seal. The three men laughed.

Terry didn't laugh. 'Do you know where it is, or not?'

'The royal seal?' said Sideboards. 'I think it's in the royal zoo, isn't it?'

The three men laughed even more.

Terry sniffed, then pulled his woollen hat down slightly towards his eyes. Very slowly he turned to face the man. 'I don't find you very funny,' he said quietly.

'Do you not?' said Sideboards, but he looked unsure of himself. He was obviously wondering how far he could push it. He looked to the barman and the other yokel for support. They were still giggling, they hadn't had Terry's one-eyed stare to contend with.

'Now do you, or do you not know where the Royal Crescent is?' Terry said patiently.

'Right hard man we got here,' said Leather Coat, and this seemed to give Sideboards a burst of courage. 'The royal croissant is on the royal breakfast table, next to the royal toast, I do believe.' This was too much for the three yokels and they let out great shouts of laughter.

'Fine,' said Terry and he grabbed hold of the man's bollocks.

Sideboards went white. Terry began to squeeze. Leather Coat tried to step in between them, but Terry grabbed him by the back of the neck with his free hand, and slammed his face down onto the bar.

'Jesus Christ!' said the barman.

Leather Coat staggered to a chair and sat down, holding his smashed nose in his hands.

Terry had forgotten all about him. Still squeezing, he leant very close to Sideboards. 'You do not say those things to me.'

Sideboards gasped and said 'no' in a very small voice.

'I'll call the police,' said the barman, but Terry ignored him.

'I am the man, see?' he said to Sideboards. 'I am the competition. I set the standards. Other men are judged against me. There's no two ways about it. There's no argument. I'm Popeye. I am what I am. Like day is light. No choice. No contradiction. I am a man, and man has control, you understand? Other men bore me. You're always trying to compete with me, but you can't, because I am the competition. I set the standards. When men shake my hand they try to squeeze. I say, "Don't size me. Don't compare yourself. I am better than you. I am the man. I am the competition." No competition. Now, where is it?'

'Straight up, first left, keep on going, you're there.'

'Thank you.' Terry let go. 'I just wanted directions. It was impolite of you to make a joke of it. A pub should be a place of hospitality and welcome. Do you understand what I am saying?'

'You're a fucking nutcase,' said the man with the broken nose. 'We were only having a laugh.'

Terry stepped over to him and stared down at him.

'I'm sorry,' the man said quietly.

'That's better,' said Terry. 'Come along,' he said to Smallbone. 'Let's go.'

They left the pub and Basil felt ten foot tall. Terry had proved it. He'd proved that this place belonged to them.

'That was magic, Terry,' he said. 'You showed them. Hah! You're king, Terry, you're the king.'

'People are stupid, Smallbone,' said Terry, and he hawked a great gob of phlegm into the gutter. 'People are backward, they don't see what is obvious, like the nose on their face. It's simple. I can see it, I can see what needs to be done, and I do it. They mess around. They complicate things. I don't like to hurt people, but if they misbehave they must be punished. They waste my time, and I won't abide that.'

'You've got it sussed, all right. You can do what you want. There's nobody better than you.'

'That's very true, Smallbone. That's very astute. You've hit the nail upon the head when you've said anything I want I do. That is the truth. I have control. I do what I want. What needs to be done. I have come full circle – I understand life, society, the human process. They must understand. Other men must understand, that I am the man.'

Terry stopped. They were in a side street of tall, noncy houses. Terry pointed to one of them. It had a big shiny door, the paint immaculate, brass knocker gleaming, an elaborate Christmas wreath fixed to it and fake snow sprayed around the panelling.

'See that house?' he said.

'Yeah ... ?'

'I could go in there. Right now, I could just walk in there and say, "What you have belongs to me." They couldn't argue. They couldn't stop me, I am not something that can be argued with. They would have to see the truth in what I say. But I don't need that, see? I don't need to prove it, and I don't need their things. So it's safe. If people behave, they are safe. I live a simple life. I am a simple man. I believe in God, in good and evil. I don't like bad language or strong drink. I am not a rapist. People should not need these things, only weak people succumb. So, people should know, instead of trying to better me they should accept what I am and feel safe with me. If I was prime minister, this country would be safe. People would sleep easy in their beds at night, unafraid of foreigners, of bad men, of evil doers and culprits.'

Basil laughed. 'You're right, Terry. You should be prime minister. Sort this country out. Get us out of the shit we're in. You should be in charge. Hah!'

'It's not a joke, Smallbone. I am serious.'

'I know you are, Terry. I am too. I could be home secretary, eh? Just think.'

'These are idle thoughts, Smallbone. Fantasies are not healthy. I was simply making a theoretical point. I was saying an abstract simile.'

'Right. Yes.'

'To fantasize is unhealthy. Only sick people dream.'

'Right. Yes. Sorry.'

Terry carried on walking. 'Now, we must attend to the matter in hand, not get sidetracked. Chas Bishop owes me money. Wages. Money I earned. I looked after him. It was a contract, and contract is law. Even a verbal contract.'

'Yes. That's right.'

'A man shouldn't break a contract. A man's word is all he has. Paper and writing means nothing. What he speaks, that is his meaning. If he defiles that he has nothing. I was good to Chas. He prospered because of me. I held him in my hand and he was safe. And now he treats me like I was unimportant, that it was all for nothing. I will look for him and I will find him. I have no doubt of

119

that, and I will take what is rightfully mine. Chas Bishop is a rich man, and I will have all his wealth.'

'He'll get what's coming to him, eh?'

'Yes.'

'And after? What will we do after, Terry? When this is all straightened out? What's next?'

'I haven't decided. One step at a time. One thing at a time. Focus.'

'But ... I mean. I'll still be ... You'll still want me. To drive for you, to help you, to be your right-hand man. You'll still want me around?'

'You are indispensable, Smallbone. I shall always have a use for you.'

Basil's hair stood up. He felt a spark of pleasure ignite and flare through his body. He smiled, turning away so Terry wouldn't see it.

Suddenly Bath looked all right. It was pretty.

Basil Smallbone was indispensable.

SIXTEEN

Pike sat down at the table in the motorway services and started to eat. The restaurant was crowded with people having their lunch, the high, glass-walled room was filled with noise. A man and woman standing in a corner playing guitars and singing Xmas classics were barely audible above the dense, deafening roar of voices. They were being completely ignored, but they grinned and strummed like idiots all the same.

The food was okay, though Pike could have done without the fake country fayre trappings of the place.

Noel approached the table, whinging at Kirsty, who was walking along playing her damned game. Noel's tray was packed with all manner of shite.

He sat down and began to noisily arrange the stuff on the table.

'That doesn't look very healthy,' said Pike, surveying the array of fried food, cakes, Coke, and biscuits.

'Like I care,' said Noel, ripping open a carton of milk.

'What about Kirsty?'

'Who do you think chose all this muck?'

'Yeah, but you're her dad, Noel. You have to set her an example. Offer her guidance.'

'Bollocks.' Noel tipped up the milk carton and emptied the contents straight down his throat. Then he crumpled it and tossed it onto the table top. 'That's better,' he said, his mouth rimmed with milk.

'How can you drink that stuff like that?' Pike asked. He'd never been fond of milk.

'It's good for you,' Noel said, tucking into his chips.

'Chinese never drink it.'

'So?'

'They don't eat any dairy products. They think westerners stink. Sort of rancid and cheesy.'

'For fuck's sake, Pike. I'm not going to go through life worrying about what I smell like to Chairman fucking Mao.'

'I'm only saying.'

'Yeah, well, unless you've got anything constructive, don't bother.'

'Listen, Noel, I'm sorry about what I said about Chas back there.'

'Mm ...' Noel didn't look up from his chips.

'I know you must be cut up. This whole thing's got to me, that's all.'

'Mutual.'

'I thought I'd done with it. The bad life. And now it's all come crapping down on me.'

'I know. And that's our fault, me and Chas. Well, Chas mostly I guess.'

'Yeah.' Pike put down his knife and fork and leant back in his chair. 'You remember when we used to go to the pictures?'

'Yeah,' said Noel.

'I used to love violent films. Killings, shootings, car smashes, blood everywhere.'

'*The Wild Bunch* used to be my favourite, didn't it?' said Noel. 'You were always on about it.'

'Yeah, must have seen it at least ten times. But afterwards. After Creen and Williams, when I stayed out of it, stayed in, I just used to watch videos all the time. As many as I could. At first I watched the same sort of thing. Violence. But the more I watched them, the more it sunk in what we'd done to the scousers. The more I watched them, the more I couldn't watch them. I started thinking,

122

when I saw someone blown away, what if that was a real person, with family, friends? What if those were real punches, real bullets, real blood.'

'They're just films, Pikey.'

'It started to get to me. Started making me sick. Went through a long patch I couldn't watch them any more. Had to watch comedies, space films, I don't know, cartoons.'

'So what's your favourite film now, then? *The Sound of Music*?'

'No. *The Wild Bunch*.'

'Hah!'

'It's a brilliant film.'

'You just said . . .'

'Yeah, well I got over it, didn't I? I mean, as you say, they're just films. It was me that changed, still can't watch some stuff without it gets to me.'

'Jesus, you have changed,' said Noel.

'I suppose I just thought about things too much. Realized what a stupid life it was. Realized it wasn't really that important if someone looked at you in a pub, if someone knocked against you and spilled your beer. Realized it didn't really matter if someone was cheeky to you. It's like that Terry Nugent twat fronting us out on the stairs like that. I can remember when I used to be like that, and it all seems so childish now.' Pike took off his glasses and polished them on a paper napkin. 'When I think I used to be like that,' he said, 'I cringe with embarrassment.'

'At least you used to be someone, Pike. You used to be a geezer. You had style, you had class. And when you went for it, when you turned it full on, there was no one to touch you. It was like ballet.'

'So I impressed a bunch of pissed-up, fucked-up hooligans, wired to their back teeth. Big fucking deal.'

'You're full of shit, Pike. That's your trouble. You need to flush it all out. You've been sitting stewing for ten years, like some kind of boil. You've got to get it out. You're one miserable bastard.'

'I thought I had it sorted.'

'Give me a break. You're one of the living dead. Tell you the truth, Pikey, I don't think this is about the money at all.'

'Huh?'

'That's just an excuse. You want this, Pike. Something in you wants it. I mean how much money was it really? Come on. Was it really that much?'

'Twenty-five grand.'

'Shit. As much as that?'

'Yep.'

'Well, my point still stands. You're Pike, always were, always will be, and the sooner you understand that, the better.'

'Noel?'

'Yes?'

'Twice now Patterson's ended up with my money.'

'And your bird.'

'What am I? Unlucky or stupid?'

'Maybe both.'

'Maybe you're right,' said Pike.

'I am right, Pike. You've fucked up your life. Do you never think that might have been you up there in the Belvedere, looking out over London? You were always smarter than the rest of us, I could tell that. You were a nutter, sure, but underneath . . . We all knew it was going to be you or Patterson. Now he's the one with the tasty flat, with Marti . . .'

'It's what I deserve.'

'Oh, fuck off.'

'What about Williams and Creen?'

'What about them?' Noel dropped his knife and fork and raised his hands in a gesture of despair. 'They weren't mourned. They were two small-time shits. Two scouse hard nuts who took a wrong turning.' He took a sip of Kirsty's Coke. 'Besides, Patterson was there with us, he don't seem to have spent the rest of his life crying into his beer.'

'And that's why he's there, Noel – in Chelsea Harbour – and I'm nowhere.'

'Forget it, Pike. It don't matter. Forget the scousers.'

'It does matter, Noel.'

'Yeah, I know.' Noel picked up his cutlery again and started back in on his food. 'I think about it, too. I have the odd nightmare. But fuck it, one day you've got to wake up. You've got to forget. You can't let that one moment fuck up the rest of your life.'

Noel was right.

One moment. That was all it took. One small moment to fuck up your whole life . . .

He pictured Creen going down, protesting, his shouts soon muffled.

Then he was rolling on the pavement beneath their feet.

'Come on fellers . . .' he pleaded.

And then they killed him.

Oh, that wasn't what they intended. It was a side-effect. They'd just meant to teach him a lesson. A lesson about territory and property and respect. But something went wrong. The kicking was certainly no worse than they'd dished out before. Perhaps it went on a little longer, perhaps they kicked a little harder, who knows? Perhaps Creen was weaker than others. He must have been frail, or something. Maybe he drank too much, maybe he had a feeble constitution. But whatever, he wound up dead.

It only took a few minutes. Admittedly he stopped resisting long before the end, but that was the thing about kickings, there was never an obvious point to stop. Once you'd started that was it, unless you had something better to do you just carried on indefinitely. The exciting bit was the build-up, the tension, the anticipation, the first few blows . . . That was the glory part. That was the fun part. To be with your mates in a berserk fury, hurting someone.

The final, relentless punishment was just something that had to be done. Crowding round him, jostling for a space. Kick, kick, kick ... Until there was no point to it any more, until they got bored.

One small moment, lasting for ever.

He's back there, back there again, as if it's still going on, as if they're still kicking the poor bastard, as if that's all there is, for ever without end, kick, kick, kick ...

Creen resists at first, puts up his arms to try and protect himself. But he's only got two arms and there are six of them. He can't move his hands around fast enough. It's pathetic. They swear at him for trying. Can't he just accept that this is the way it has to be?

His legs. His back. His arse. His stomach. His ribs. His neck. His head. His throat. His bollocks. His face. After a while it isn't like kicking a human being at all. You sort of forget what it's all about. It's just this thing. This thing lying there that has to be kicked. So they go on kicking, and somewhere along the line something snaps, his windpipe swells and blocks, his insides rupture, his brain explodes. Everything that can go wrong does.

They don't know he's dead at the time, of course.

Nor Williams.

Turns out Williams had a heart attack. Must have been about the time Patterson kicked him. But that was different. That was an accident.

The bodies won't be found till the morning, and even then it'll be several days before they're identified. Because the lads strip them of all their possessions – wallets, keys, licences. They clean them out. Quickly, efficiently, stuffing their pockets.

In high spirits, the evening a success, they go back to the Alma to celebrate. After a bit of knocking, Chrissie lets them in and they open a bottle of champagne. They're laughing, loud, excited, recalling every detail. Congratulating each other, showing off. Then they look through their haul. Nearly two grand in cash. Well, whoop de doo! More celebrating. They split up the proceeds.

Then Chas finds the key. A hotel key with a tag. Somewhere in Finsbury Park.

Conference time.

Listen, they had this much on them, maybe they've got more stashed back at their hotel. After all, haven't they been bragging all night about how flush they are? Haven't they been hinting that they're hard nuts, recently off a job? Well, let's face it, there's no harm in looking. And they won't go crawling back there for hours, state they're in.

Patterson takes charge, offers to go and check.

'We can't all go, now, can we? How would that look?'

'Yeah, you're right . . .'

'Yeah . . .'

'Should just be one of us. Meantime, you should all get home, in case someone's called the law. We'll reconvene tomorrow.'

'Yeah, good idea . . .'

'Yeah, Ian's right.'

'And if you find anything you'll tell us, won't you, Ian?' Pike speaks for the first time.

'Of course I will. I wouldn't shit you, Dennis.'

They look at each other and in the end Pike shrugs. He doesn't care. He just wants to get back and fuck the life out of Marti.

So they split up.

Pike takes Marti back to his place and they fuck all night. Pike so coked up he can't come. But he fucks with a fierce energy. He still has a lot to get out. To work off. Finally, near to exhaustion, with sunlight coming through the curtains and the birds twittering in the gutters he makes it. Comes inside her and collapses.

The perfect end to the perfect night.

That was the last time they slept together. It all went wrong after that. They found out next afternoon that the scousers were dead. Pike had never killed a man before. They had to keep low, not be seen together for a while . . . And Patterson?

'There was nothing there, lads. Just their suitcases. Whatever they had they must have spent. In the end they were all mouth. Better lay low for a while, though, eh?'

Well, they did lay low and that was when the fear started. He hated to admit it, but it was guilt, wasn't it? And a lad wasn't supposed to feel guilty. A yob, a thug, a hooligan, a berserker, they felt proud, not guilty.

And Patterson?

Patterson was gone. After a couple of months, Marti too. Said she was fed up with not shagging any more. But Pike couldn't fuck. Hadn't hardly fucked since. He couldn't get a hard-on. His blood had turned to piss.

As time went by they heard it on the grapevine that Williams and Creen had been paid nearly thirty grand. The law reckoned that it was the other guys who'd done the post office that topped them, to shut them up and get the cash back. It wasn't a very high-powered police operation, they were no doubt glad to be rid of a couple of twats, but arrests were made, some of the gang were picked up. In the end, though, they never pinned the murders on anyone . . .

And Patterson. Well, the lads could never prove it, but they knew. Must have been at least twenty-five grand he got from that hotel.

Twenty-five grand.

Two times twenty-five – fifty.

No. It wasn't about the money. It was about old times. The Alma days. Two dead scousers and one rich Jock.

It was about coming home.

SEVENTEEN

The noise of Terry's slap still rang in Basil's ears. It had sounded loud as a gun shot in the small, cluttered room. Now Herman sat holding his head in his hands. The force of the blow had shaken his whole body, and he'd staggered back, stunned, before letting himself down into the chair.

Basil was enjoying this.

'Right,' said Terry patiently. 'Now we've got that sorted. I'll ask you again. Where's Chas?'

'I have told you.' The young man's polite German voice had a little quaver in it that hadn't been there before. 'I do not know anybody n-named Chas.' It was almost a stutter.

'Then what was his brother doing here? What was Noel doing here?'

'I don't know.'

'You don't know?'

'It was nothing to do with Chas.'

'So, you do know Chas?'

Herman looked at the floor. 'You tell me one thing, you tell me another thing. You make me confused. I do not know.'

'You do not know what? You do not know where Chas is?'

'No.'

'I don't believe you.'

'You do not have to believe me,' said Herman. 'It does not matter to me.'

'It matters to me,' said Terry quietly.

'Very well . . . But what can I say?'

'I'll tell you what, my friend. Let's forget about Chas for a moment. You can give me Noel. I'll settle for him.'

'What do you mean?' Herman blinked at him.

'Tell me where Noel is. Tell me how I can get hold of Noel.'

'I cannot do that.'

'You said you were working for him,' said Terry, laughing. 'Now, surely you know how to get hold of him?'

'All right, yes. Perhaps. But I cannot tell you. It is business. There are rules.'

'Yes, my friend, there are rules.' Terry nodded. 'Let me tell you about the rules. Rule one, I am the ref. See? I am the ref, the captain, the manager, the coach, and I score all the goals. *Comprende*? Rule number two, you are nothing. You are less than nothing. You do not count. Therefore, *quid pro quo*, you do as I say. Rule number three, there are no rules, everything is allowed.'

Terry smacked Herman round the side of the head with one of his big, powerful hands, knocking the slight young man flying off the chair.

'Offside!' Terry said, and as Herman tried to pick himself up Terry hit him again. 'Handball.'

Herman decided to stay down this time, but Terry kicked him in the stomach with a shout of 'Goal!'

Herman curled into a foetal position on the carpet and stayed there.

'Okay,' said Terry, perching on the side of the chair, affable. 'Good game. Good game. I think we both understand the rules, now. So, perhaps you'd like to talk to me?'

'Yes,' Herman said, his voice barely audible.

'What's that? I beg your pardon? Speak up.' Terry cupped a hand to his ear.

'Yes,' Herman repeated, slightly louder.

'Fine. Get up. It's all right, I don't need to hit you again. Give him a hand, Smallbone.'

Basil helped the German to his feet, putting a hand under his upper arm. Herman felt very hot and damp and he smelled, a kind of animal smell. There was a livid red hand mark across one of his cheeks and his nose was running. He was shaking. He ran a hand through his hair and adjusted his glasses, amazingly, through it all, they'd stayed on.

'You have an address?' Terry asked. 'A phone number?'

'Yes.' Herman took a deep breath and sniffed. He was pulling himself together, becoming resigned.

Terry turned to Basil. 'You got a pen, Smallbone?'

Basil reached into the inside pocket of his jacket and took out a gold-look stainless steel biro.

'It's the one you got me,' he said, offering it to Terry.

'Huh?' Terry frowned and made no move to take the pen.

'When you first got out, remember?'

'I know what it is.'

Basil smiled, waiting for Terry to take it.

'What are you doing, Smallbone?'

Basil blushed.

'Why are you trying to give me your pen?' Terry was incredulous. 'I gave it to you. What do you think that was for? I don't want to waste my time writing things down. That's your job. Now find some paper.'

Basil felt like an idiot. He fumbled in his pockets for paper, aware that he'd gone bright red. He found the scraps of paper he'd taken from Chas's drawer and tested the biro on one of them.

Terry turned back to Herman who had sat back down at the table in front of a computer and was tapping at the keys.

'What are you doing?' Terry asked, suspiciously.

'You want Noel Bishop?'

'Yes.'

'Well, then ...'

The screen flipped between various images.

'What's that?' said Terry. 'What are you doing, there?'

'It's all on here ...' Herman tapped the buttons a couple of times and a list of names beginning with B appeared.

Terry snatched hold of Herman's arm and pulled his hand away from the keys. Then he grabbed the keyboard and lifted it off the table top.

Herman suddenly exploded into life, angry and frightened.

'Don't touch that!' he yelled, taking the keyboard back and cradling it like a baby. 'Don't ever touch that!'

'What are you doing?' Terry said furiously. 'Tell me what you're doing!'

Basil had never seen him like this before. Worked up. 'Terry ...' he said. But Terry ignored him.

'What's the matter?' said Herman, turning to the screen. 'I am trying to help. I am trying to give you Noel.'

'What are you doing? What are you doing fiddling about with that thing?' Again Terry snatched the keyboard away from Herman.

Herman lost his temper. He hit the screen with the back of his hand and almost shouted. 'Are you blind? Are you stupid? Can't you read?'

Herman looked up at Terry just in time to see Terry's head come hammering down into his mouth. He was knocked backwards off the chair and crashed to the floor.

Basil wasn't sure this was very helpful. It wasn't like Terry. Admittedly it was quite thrilling seeing Terry in action again, but he wasn't sure it was really helping.

Herman lay stunned on the carpet, blood from his nose and lips covered the bottom half of his face. He looked like someone playing 'dead ant'. Terry had hit him very hard indeed.

Terry himself had a round splat of red in the middle of his forehead, as if someone had thrown a tomato at him.

Herman groaned and opened his eyes. He sat up and gingerly touched his wounded mouth with his fingertips. He still had his glasses on. 'What did you do that for?' he asked, indignant. 'Are you crazy? What did you do that for? Stupid . . .' His speech was slurred, like someone whose mouth had been numbed at the dentist.

'Never call me stupid,' said Terry and he picked the monitor up off the table and brought it down onto Herman's head.

Herman flopped backwards and lay still.

Basil definitely wasn't sure about this. This wasn't very wise at all. Herman had been on the verge of giving them what they wanted, and now something had set Terry off and Herman was whacked out and the computer was bust. Basil was frightened, all the time he'd known Terry he'd been like a robot; single-minded, rational and unemotional. Now he seemed unhinged. Like a machine gone out of control. Like that computer out of 2001, mad and logical at the same time. Basil knew he ought to try and stop him, but he had mixed feelings. In this state there was no telling what Terry might do. He might even turn on Basil, and besides, Basil was fascinated. He wanted to see what Terry would do next.

Herman was quivering slightly, his eyes rolled back in his head, his eyelids fluttering. Terry knelt down next to him and grabbed him by the neck. Lifting his head up off the carpet, he whacked it back a couple of times. Then he stopped and looked around the room, his breath hissing through his nose.

'What is it?' Basil asked, hurrying over. 'What do you want, Terry?'

'I need something sharp. I want to fix him up.'

'Terry. Are you sure . . . ?'

'Get me something sharp, Smallbone. Make yourself useful. There's work to be done here.'

Basil looked around in despair and it suddenly struck him that there was nothing sharp in the room. It was all round edges, soft, like a child's room, there was nothing that could hurt you.

'Terry, there's nothing . . . Leave it . . .'

'Give me your pen,' Terry said.

'What?'

'Your pen. Give me you pen.'

Basil passed Terry the biro.

Just then Herman's eyes settled back into place and he stopped shaking. He looked a little more human. He said something in German which Basil couldn't understand.

Basil leant over him. 'Are you all right?' he asked. Herman looked at him and smiled vaguely, like he didn't know what was going on.

Terry pushed Basil away and forced Herman's head down into the carpet, turning it to one side. Then, his tongue between his teeth, concentrating hard, Terry stuck the tip of the pen into Herman's ear.

'Never call me stupid,' he said, and with a grunt he pushed the pen in. Herman moaned and his eyes went very wide.

'Terry . . .' Basil said. But Terry ignored him. He was in a world of his own now.

'Terry . . .'

Terry stood up. He looked very businesslike, methodical, as if he'd done this a million times before. Basil could picture him at work, a craftsman going about his job, a carpenter or an electrician or something. Practised, casual, yet highly skilled and efficient.

Herman tried to move, his head tilted, the pen pointing straight up out of his ear.

'Hold him still, could you?' Terry asked.

Basil reluctantly got down and took hold of Herman. Again he could smell that musky, animal smell, and feel the heat coming off him.

Terry put one foot on the pen and pressed down, forcing it further into Herman's head. Herman's mouth opened and he bared his teeth, his whole face screwed up in a silent scream. Terry strained for a moment and twisted his foot, then he began to stamp. Each

134

time the pen sunk in a little further, until it was about halfway. There was no blood or anything, and, after that first terrible rictus, Herman had stopped reacting in any way. He looked almost peaceful now, his lips slightly parted as if he was asleep. Basil thought he was probably dead.

'There,' Terry said.

'What do we do now?' Basil asked.

'Did you get the information? Did you get Noel's address?'

'No,' said Basil, feeling for a pulse in Herman's neck and not finding one. 'You broke the computer before I could get it down.'

'Never mind. We'll just have to go to Swindon and find the dad.' Just like that, as if it hadn't been important after all. As if none of it had really mattered.

Afterwards in the car, driving out of Bath, Terry was his old self, serious and unflappable. He sat looking out the window at passing scenery, making the odd comment – a house he liked the look of, a funny-looking dog, two hippies driving a van. He said nothing about what had happened with Herman.

Eventually Basil had to ask. 'Terry?' he said.

'Mmm.'

'How many people do you think you've killed, in all?'

'What do you mean?'

'I mean, you know ... how many?'

'Only the one.'

'What? Only one before now?'

'No. That was it. As far as I know I've never killed anyone before.'

'Oh.'

'Look at that. Look at that sunset. It's lovely, isn't it? Like a Christmas card, or something.'

Basil looked.

'Yes,' he said.

EIGHTEEN

Of course Patterson wasn't there.

At first that was all the receptionist at the Belvedere would tell them. 'He's not in, lads.'

'So, where is he?'

'I couldn't tell you that, lads. Even if I knew.'

They realized they weren't going to get anything out of the old geezer so they went back outside. After a bit of poking around they found the ramp to the residents' parking beneath the tower. They found a young car park attendant down there who knew Patterson's black jeep Cherokee, and he told them that Patterson had driven off yesterday and hadn't come back.

So they went back to the Escort and sulked for a while.

'I should have leant on Herman a bit more,' Pike said eventually, wiping condensation off the windscreen.

'You were like a tart with him,' said Noel. 'The old Pike would have smacked him as a matter of course.'

'Will you shut up about the old Pike, the old days . . .'

'But you were soft on him. And now we're nowhere. I mean, d'you reckon he told us everything?' said Noel. 'D'you reckon he was telling the truth?'

'Nope,' said Pike.

'D'you reckon he might know where some of Patterson's other property is?'

'Yep.'

'D'you reckon we ought to go back there?' said Noel.

'What do you think?'

'Bath, here we come.'

'Not yet,' said Pike. 'I need to pick some stuff up first. I've been thinking. If we do get hold of Patterson, we're going to need some kind of leverage.'

'You got a gun stashed away somewhere?'

'Better.' Pike started the engine. It was good to have a plan again. He felt energized.

'What is it?' Noel asked. 'What have you got? What's better than a gun?'

'Two wallets, a driving licence, an address book, an unpaid phone bill and a letter.'

'I get it,' said Noel. 'This is some new form of fiendish Japanese martial art.'

'Nope.' Pike drove out of Chelsea Harbour and turned towards town.

'Come on, Pikey, what are you on about?'

'It's who they belong to, Noel. That's what makes them dangerous.'

'And?'

'Williams and Creen.'

'You what?'

'I kept them,' said Pike. 'After we split everything up, I kept them. Don't ask me why. All these years I kept them safe.'

'Jesus.'

'Now, say Herman still won't co-operate. We simply tell him we've got this stuff, aren't afraid to plant it somewhere. Herman lets Patterson know ...'

'You kept them?'

'Yeah.'

'Pike? Are you prepared to go all the way on this? Open all that up again?'

'I don't know. But as long as Patterson don't know either we've got the upper hand. We'll flush the bugger out.'

'Weren't you worried, though, keeping it all? What if someone found it.'

'It's safe,' said Pike. 'Up at me mum and dad's.'

'I've never met your mum and dad.'

'Nope. And you're never going to. We get there, you stay in the car. I'll be in and out in five minutes.'

'Oh, come on.'

'I don't want you having anything to do with my parents, Noel.'

'Charming. I introduced you to my dad.'

Pike couldn't think of anything to say to that.

'Where they live, then?' Noel asked, sorting through the tapes.

'Hornchurch.'

'Essex? You an Essex boy, then, are you? I thought you were a north London lad.'

'Grew up in Peterborough.'

'Peterborough?'

'Moved to Essex when I was ten. Me dad used to work for the post office.'

'I always used to think you were a man of mystery, a loner, the great white shark of Tottenham. But your old man's a postman, somehow makes you more human.'

'Come on, Noel, everyone's got parents.'

'Yeah, but I thought your old man was probably a gangster, a crime boss, or a murderer, or something, banged up for life, on the run ... Not a bleeding postman.'

'He wasn't a postman. He worked behind the counter, got promoted, that's why we moved to Essex, got his own little sub post office.'

'Hey, is that why you gave the scousers such a kicking? Was it your old man's post office they done over?'

'No.'

'So it was just revenge for all postmen.'

'I never even thought about it until now.'

'What *have* you been thinking about all these years? Apart from your pension fund.'

'Canada.'

'Yeah,' said Noel, slotting the Philip Glass tape into the machine. 'I've been meaning to ask, Pikey, why Canada?'

'It's the third largest country in the world, and it's got a population the size of London.'

'There you are, see, nobody wants to live there.'

'That's how you look at it, is it?' said Pike.

'Why d'you think England's so crowded?' said Noel. 'I'll tell you why. Because it's popular. Best country in the world.'

'You sound like a proper hooligan, Noel. You sound like us on the way to Germany in '82. Ambassadors for Great Britain. Drunk on the plane, trying to shag the hostesses and fight the passengers. In-ger-land!'

'We were the most feared hooligans in the world though, weren't we?' said Noel. 'Eh? Weren't we? The most respected, the best organized, the most ruthless. An army, we were. And the rest of the world? Forget it. Soft. Soft shite. We showed them. We showed the fucking world. We were the best. And now you want to give it all up. You want to slink off to Canada with your tail between your legs.'

'But that's just it, Noel. It's people like you I'm trying to get away from. People like you in your Union Jack y-fronts. I can't stand all that shite any more. All that centuries-old garbage. I can't stand this old, old, fucked-up insignificant little country. And turn that fucking music down.'

'You can't listen to the Glass-man quiet. Full whack, diddly-diddly-diddly-diddly . . .'

Pike turned it down. 'Not now, Noel, I've got a headache.'

'Thing is, though, Pike. You can't get away. You can bugger off to Canada, but you'll still be yourself. You'll still have done what you done. You can't hide from your memories.'

'I can, though. I can hide from you and Chas and Patterson and all this. I can grow old in peace.'

'Stop! Stop the car!'

'Shit!' Pike hit the brake pedal and swerved over to the side of the road, his front wheel skidding into the pavement. He lurched forwards and the friction seatbelt cut into him.

A car behind blared its horn and swung round them, the driver yelling abuse.

In the back, Kirsty picked herself up off the floor and went back to her game.

'What?' said Pike, his heart racing. 'What is it?'

'Off licence.'

'Off licence?'

'Yeah. See . . .' Noel nodded out the window and undid his belt. 'I need a beer.' He opened the door. 'Won't be a minute. You want anything?'

'A bloody off licence?'

Noel got out. 'You want anything, or not?'

'No . . . Yes. Get us something not too strong, Fosters or something.'

'Rightio.'

Pike watched Noel as he strolled across the road and went into the brightly lit shop. Not a care in the world. He looked in his rear-view mirror. Kirsty was playing on as if nothing had happened. Maybe this was how Noel drove. He wondered what it must be like to have children. To create another human being out of nothing. He knew what it was like to reverse the process, to create nothing out of another human being, but this . . . ? It was all too weird to contemplate.

He'd come close once.

One night, he'd just made love to Marti when she announces that she's pregnant.

Pike doesn't know what to think. Asks her what she's going to do and she just shrugs, says she'll get rid of it. It doesn't bother her. She's had two abortions before. The first when she was fourteen.

'But don't you worry about yourself?' Pike asks, propping himself up on an elbow and looking at her skinny ribs and small breasts. 'About what it does to your body?'

'I don't care what happens to me,' says Marti, in a matter-of-fact way. 'I don't care what happens to my body. You can do what you like with it. I'll be dead soon.'

'How can you say that?'

'It's in my stars.'

'What, it said in the *Daily Mirror* horoscope "You are going to die today," did it?'

'I don't want to bring any more children into this world, Dennis,' she says, stretching and arching her back so that her breasts disappear altogether. 'It's all shit. I don't want any kid to go through what I went through. That first abortion, that was me dad's kid. Would have been me own sister. I don't want that. I'll be dead soon and that'll be the end of it. Good riddance.'

'You shouldn't talk like that.'

'We're not compatible, anyway, Dennis.'

'What d'you mean?'

'Our signs. The baby would be a disaster.'

'That's all bollocks, Marti.'

'Don't ever say that. It's what I believe in. At least respect that.'

'Yeah, yeah. I'm sorry.'

'We're not the same, you and me, Dennis. Your stone, for instance, it's a moonstone.'

'Come on, Marti . . .'

'No, listen. Don't you ever think that people have properties? Energies within them? They're like other things. Like a lion, or like fire, or water.'

'Yeah. If you say so.'

'It does mean something. It does . . .'

Pike kisses her. 'If you believe in it Marti, it's true, I suppose.'

Marti looks at the ceiling, smiling, like a little kid. Happy. 'I've been reading about the elements, about rocks and crystals. We're all part of the earth. Like you, Dennis, you're a rock.'

'What? Like concrete?'

'No . . . No. More like lava.'

'Lava?'

'Yeah. You ever seen lava? I saw some on the telly the other day. It was weird, looked like rock on the outside, all hard and black, but inside it was moving, flowing, on fire.'

'All right,' says Pike. 'So, I'm lava. What does that make you? What are you?'

'I'm dust.'

The car suddenly rocked as Noel clambered back in, holding a bulging carrier bag. He settled in the seat and strapped himself in. Pike put the Escort into gear and pulled away from the kerb.

Noel fished a four-pack of Four X out of the bag and pulled one of the cans free of its plastic necklace.

'You want one now?' he asked.

'I'll wait till we get there.'

'Suit yourself.' Noel popped the ring-pull and took a long swig. 'Perfection,' he said. 'Chilled to perfection.' He took another swig.

'You're a man of simple pleasures, aren't you, Noel?'

'Let me tell you about drinking beer, Pikey,' said Noel, taking another great pull. 'Let me tell you the philosophy of the four-pack.'

'I can hardly wait.'

'Now, behave. This is an important lesson.'

'Go on, then.'

'See this four-pack?'

'Yeah, I see it.'

'Well, this four-pack is the most beautiful thing in the world.'

'That's debatable.'

'No, it's not. Look,' said Noel, holding the cans up. 'Four prime-quality beers, straight from the fridge; ice-cold, condensation forming on the sides. Tall cans. Not little ones. Tall cans. Just the right amount in each one for a damned good drink.

'So you get your four-pack out and you settle down to watch the football, or a video, or something. You've got four cans, and you think, "This is it. I've got all this beer." And you think . . . well, you don't think, do you? You get stuck in. The first can, down in one, almost. Whoosh! It's gone. Why not? After all, there's plenty more where that came from. Look at all those cans you've still got left! Magic. You have a good belch and you're onto your second one. Now you take the second one a bit slower, don't you? You're not so thirsty, you can properly appreciate it. Not a care in the world. You're less than half way through your beers, no worries. Then your second one's gone, and you've got two left, and you look at them and you think, "When I started it seemed like I had all the beer in the world, but now look, there's only two left." It don't seem like so much all of a sudden. So you start on your third beer. And, fuck it, there's still one left, isn't there? But next thing you know your third can's empty and you don't even remember drinking it . . . And now there's only one left . . . What happened to all that beer? When you started out it looked like it was going to last all night. Looked like you might not even get through it all, might put one back in the fridge, have one left for tomorrow. But now it seems like you've only just started drinking and there's only one left. This is your last one. That's it. No more. So you take it real slow. Try to wait longer between swigs. Put it down to one side, try to think about something else, but every time you pick it up you can't believe how much you've drunk. How little there is left. It seems to be slipping down, dribbling away without you being able to stop it. Finally there's just one swig left. You can't really enjoy it, can you? Knowing that it's your last drink, after that there's nothing else, the fridge is empty. You're left with four plastic hoops and that's that. But you

143

drink it. You try and convince yourself you've had enough. But it's never enough. You always want more. Well, after your fourth beer there isn't any more . . .'

'So what's your point, Noel?'

'My point is, that's life, isn't it?'

'What is?'

'A four-pack. Life is a four-pack of beer.'

'Brilliant.'

'What I'm saying, Pike, is that you're on your third beer already. Christ, you're about on your fourth. It's gone, Pikey. You're not enjoying it any more. You should be on your second beer, still. You should be drinking without thinking, enjoying it without looking at the cans that are left. You're a three-beer man, Dennis. But not me, I'm a one-beer man still. All right, maybe two. Yeah, two. Even just thinking about this makes me a two-beer man, I suppose. But I'm in no hurry to get onto me third beer. I'm enjoying where I am. But you, you're sitting there grimly working your way through the four-pack, as if the sole aim was to finish it all as swiftly and efficiently as possible. You're not savouring a single drop. Get a fucking life, Pike. Get pissed. Kick out. Spend some money. Go full diddly like Signor Glass. They don't give you another shot. There isn't any more beer in the fridge.'

'Noel?' said Pike.

'Yes?'

'Will you do me a favour?'

'What?'

'Next time, will you buy a six-pack?'

NINETEEN

Noel couldn't believe Pike's parents' place. He could *not* believe it. It was a little bungalow in a side street in Hornchurch. The bricks had all been painted sky blue and the pointing white. Bright red wagon wheels had been fixed to the wall, and there was a tiny, fussy, ornamental garden out front. But the most unbelievable thing was the gnomes. About fifty of them, sitting on toadstools, smoking pipes, fishing in the pond, waving at the front gate . . .

'Gnomes,' said Noel. 'Nobody really has gnomes. Not in real life.'

'You stay out here,' Pike said, jabbing him with a finger.

'I mean, really, gnomes . . .'

'I won't be long.'

At that moment Kirsty woke up and started to cry.

'What is it, babes?' Noel asked.

'I want to go toilet.'

'Oh, please,' said Pike.

Grinning, Noel helped Kirsty out of the car. 'Lead the way, Pikey, old boy,' he said.

Pike went up to the red front door and pressed the bell. Noel heard elaborate chimes inside the house. He recognized the tune, he'd heard it on Melody Radio a couple of times, but he couldn't put a name to it. Possibly something about a black forest gateau.

Presently the door was opened by a small man in shirt sleeves,

145

high-waisted suit trousers and slippers. Behind him was a woman peering out at them through very thick pink-framed glasses.

The man had a mass of wavy, white hair, sticking-out ears, a red face and a huge nose. He was half as tall as Pike. His wife was tiny as well, or at least she was short, because she was very wide, as wide as she was tall – sort of square shaped.

'Dennis!' said the old couple, almost as one.

'Hello, mum. Hello, dad.' He made no move to kiss them or hug them in any way.

'Come in, son,' said the dad. 'And who are your friends?'

'Noel and Kirsty.'

'Hello there, Kirsty,' said the old fellow and Kirsty burst into tears again.

'Oh, dear,' dad said. 'Who's a sad little lady, then?'

'She needs the bathroom, actually,' said Noel.

'Of course she does.' Mr Pike pointed Noel to a door, and Noel led Kirsty away. As he closed the door he could hear the old couple fussing over Pike.

'It's been so long . . . You never call . . . You're looking fat . . . Are you well . . . ? Is something the matter . . . ?'

In the toilet there was a picture of Jesus on the wall, a rather gaudy affair in which the saviour had a very English complexion, all red hair and rosy cheeks. Beneath the picture was one of those little hand-embroidered messages . . . 'Christ is the head of this house. The unseen host at every meal. The silent listener to every conversation.' Noel felt suddenly self-conscious. His skin prickled.

'Come on, Kirsty, hurry up.'

When she was done he took her out to find the others. They were all gathered in the sitting room. The room was very twee but also rather untidy.

There were books everywhere and a clutter of mismatched orna-ments and pieces of furniture. Underneath a big picture window was a huge table with about fifty cactuses on it.

'Are you interested in cacti?' Mr Pike asked when he spotted Noel looking at them.

'Er ... No. Can't say that I am, really.'

'Oh, they're fascinating. Fascinating. Did you know for instance ... ?'

'Not now, dad,' said Pike. 'I'm afraid we're in a bit of a hurry. I just need to get some things from my room and we're going to shoot off.'

'You'll stay for tea?' his mother asked.

'It's half past eight, mum.'

'I think I've got some biscuits, somewhere.' The old woman struggled up out of her armchair.

'We can't stay, mum.'

'Come on, Dennis,' said Noel. 'We could force down a spot of tea. That'd be lovely, Mrs P.'

Pike scowled at him, but his mother waddled off to the kitchen, beaming.

'Mum ...' Pike called vainly after her. 'Mum ...'

There was a big old bulky TV below a framed and mounted teatowel depicting the Last Supper. It was turned on but the sound was down.

'Is this the match?' Noel asked.

'Yes,' said Mr Pike, coming over to stand next to Noel and admire the set.

'Forgot it was on,' said Noel. 'Any score?'

'Not to my knowledge. Would you like the sound up?'

'No, dad,' said Pike. 'It's all right.'

'If it's not too much bother, Mr P.,' said Noel. 'See how the boys are getting on.'

There was no remote control, Mr Pike had to go to the set to adjust the volume. The familiar, reassuring sound of John Motson and the white noise of cheering fans filled the room.

'See that,' said Mr Pike proudly, straightening up. 'You won't get a picture like that on a modern set. That's a solid piece of equipment, that. Valves. That's a perfect picture. Lifelike.'

Noel peered at the screen. If that was life, then most people obviously lived in a sort of thin fog. The brightness was up way too high and the colour was virtually turned off. There was also a slight ghost caused by a badly placed aerial.

'I'll check how mother's getting on with the tea.' Mr Pike left.

'Let's see if we can't fix this, then, eh?' said Noel, rubbing his hands together and kneeling on the orange, rose-patterned carpet before the massive set.

'Leave it, Noel,' said Pike irritably.

'I know what I'm doing. Televisions are my thing.'

'It's how he likes it. Don't interfere.'

'Come on, he'll be grateful . . .'

Before Pike could stop him, Noel had control of the knobs, and he soon had a sharp, colourful picture, with satisfying black shadows. He couldn't get rid of the ghost, but it was a marked improvement. Instantly, the football looked more exciting, more glamorous. He settled onto the sofa and tried to pick up the thread of the match.

He'd just worked out that it must be one all when Mr Pike came back in, carrying a teapot and a cake tin. He took one look at the screen and tutted.

'Oh dear,' he said. 'What's happened here? Have you been playing with it, Dennis?'

'No, dad.'

'Can't watch that. It'll do your eyes in.' Mr Pike soon had the picture fucked again and he sat down next to Noel on the sofa.

'Any action yet?'

'One all.'

'Ah.'

'I'm going up to my room,' said Pike.

'Okay, son.'

'Dennis used to be a very keen soccer supporter,' said Mr Pike once Dennis was gone. 'Used to be quite a useful little player, as well, when he was a lad. Don't know if he still keeps it up. He never tells us anything. Have you known Dennis long?'

'About fifteen years, I suppose.'

'We never see his friends. Never see him, if truth be told. Just pops by when he needs something. But there's always a bed for him here. Can I interest you in some homemade crumbly cake?'

'Thank you, very nice.'

Mr Pike opened the tin and manoeuvred out half a cake. He cut a slice for Noel but there were no plates. He was about to put it on Noel's outstretched palm when Mrs Pike came in with a tray of tea things and took over.

'There we are,' she said, handing Noel a plate. 'The best I could do at short notice.'

She leant over Kirsty.

'Would you like some cake? Some biscuits? A sandwich?'

Kirsty shrugged.

'Are you hungry, bunny?' Noel asked. Kirsty stuck out her lower lip, squinted at the tea things, then helped herself to a cheese sandwich.

'How old are you then, Kirsty?' Mrs Pike asked. Kirsty ignored her.

'She's going through a difficult stage, I'm afraid, Mrs P.'

'She's shy, isn't she? Dennis was very shy at that age.'

'No. Old Dennis? Shy?'

'Terribly shy. Always had his head buried in a book, never smiled, filled with doom and gloom he always seemed to be. Like he had the world's problems on his shoulders. Not like Harry.'

'Harry?'

'Den's big brother.'

'I never knew Dennis had a brother.'

'Oh, yes.' Mrs Pike fetched a photograph from the mantelpiece above the gas fire.

'Harry's the one in the middle with the plaque,' she said, handing it to Noel. It showed a large, fleshy-faced man with a moustache, wearing a cheap suit. He was standing with several other big fleshy-faced men with moustaches and bad suits.

There was something about the picture, something about the men ...

'Harry's a policeman,' said Mr Pike. 'Detective Inspector.'

'You're joking?'

'He's done very well for himself,' said Mrs Pike. 'Not like Dennis. Dennis just doesn't seem able to settle down, flitting about from one thing to another. He was such a bright little boy, but very sickly, always getting picked on ...'

'He reminds me very much of a cactus,' said Mr Pike. 'Prickly on the outside ...' But before he could elaborate, Dennis came back in carrying a shoe box and a carrier bag stuffed with clothes. He saw the tea things laid out and Noel tucking in and frowned. 'Oh, mother. I told you we weren't staying.'

'It's nothing fancy, Den.'

'I was just showing Noel Harry's citation photograph,' said Mrs Pike.

Dennis looked at Noel, but neither of them said anything.

'How is Harry?' Dennis asked, though he didn't sound particularly interested.

'Still hasn't got a girlfriend. Honestly, with you two, I don't know if I'm ever going to have any grandchildren.' Mrs Pike handed Dennis a cup and saucer. 'There you are, Den, you still take two sugars?'

Pike sighed. 'I suppose so.' He sat down in an armchair.

For the next quarter of an hour Dennis's parents tried to catch up on what he'd been up to, but as he hadn't been up to anything for the last ten years, the conversation was rather strained. Noel reckoned he hadn't told them about Canada, and he revelled in Pike's discomfort.

Finally the conversation completely ground to a halt, they sat there clinking cups and chewing, occasionally smiling at each other, while the football carried on as a focus of attention. In the end it was Kirsty who put an end to the proceedings. 'Can I go now,' she said. 'I'm bored.'

They all went out into the little hallway and Pike leant down so his mother could kiss him.

'Ah,' said Mr Pike, raising a finger. 'Hang on a minute.' And he scurried off.

'Will you be in touch, Den?' Mrs P. asked.

'I don't know, mum.'

'You could at least ring once in a while.'

'Yeah, I will.'

'Harry rings.'

'Well ... listen, mum. You couldn't lend us any money, could you?'

'Oh, Den. You never change.'

'There's a problem with my building society. I can't get any cash out. Just twenty quid, or something. I'll pay you back.'

'I shouldn't really.' Mrs P. shook her head and waddled off towards the kitchen. On the way, she passed Mr P. who had a small plant pot with him. 'There you go,' he said to Noel. 'As you're so interested in cacti ...'

It was a small spiny cactus. Like a green golf ball with spikes.

'Oh, thank you very much, Mr P., that's very kind of you.'

'It's a *Mammillaria bombycina*.'

Mrs P. came back and slipped something into Pike's hand without his father seeing.

Pike gave her a little smile. Then said briskly, 'Right, come on, Noel,' and tramped off down the front path to the car.

'He's all right, Mrs P.,' Noel said to the old woman. 'He's just got a lot on his mind at the moment.'

'He always did. Seven O-levels, you know?'

'I didn't know.'

'Could have got A-levels, but he gave it all up. Very moody he was, and Harry doing so well.'

'Treat it as you would any other plant,' said Mr Pike. 'Water in summer, give it a rest in winter, nice sunny spot ...'

'Don't you worry, I'll look after it. And don't you worry, Mrs P., I'll look after your Dennis.'

'Thank you, Noel. We used to think Dennis didn't have any friends. It's nice to finally meet one. There's so much we don't know about him.'

'Same here, it's been a real eye-opener meeting you.'

'Noel!' Pike yelled from the car, and Noel offered the old pair a guilty face. 'Better get me skates on, eh?'

'Noel! Move it!'

'Yes, it's been very interesting meeting you,' Noel shook their hands vigorously. 'I've learnt a lot about old Dennis. Here, I bet you even used to have a pet name for him, didn't you?'

'Noel!'

Pike was fuming. He should never have brought Noel here. What was he saying to them about him? He leant on the horn, and, at last, with a cheery wave, Noel came trotting down the front path.

He put Kirsty in the back and Pike started the car.

'Detective Inspector Harry Pike, eh?' Noel got in.

'Shut it, Noel.'

'Seven O-levels, eh?'

'I said shut up.'

'Sorry, Eeyore.'

Pike considered hitting Noel, but he laughed instead. He hadn't been called Eeyore in over twenty years.

TWENTY

Herman the German was dead.

Someone had stabbed him to death with a biro – in the ear. The poor sod obviously hadn't died straight away, he must have still been alive when his killers left, because now he was sitting at one of his computers for all the world like a busy man. It's just he wasn't moving, and there was the fancy gold biro sticking out of his ear.

'Get Kirsty out of here,' Pike told Noel, and Noel obliged. She had been staring at Herman with much interest. Pike supposed it wasn't that often you saw someone with a pen stuck in his ear.

Noel came back in. 'She's sitting in the sauna.'

'The sauna?'

'It's all right, it's not on. I told her it was a Wendy house.'

The two of them looked at Herman. Sitting there almost serenely.

'What do you reckon, then?' Noel asked. 'Patterson came back?'

'I don't know. It's not like him to leave things like this, it's sloppy.'

'It's his place. Nobody else would ever come here.'

'Yeah, but . . . I mean, what a way to top someone.'

'I know. Maybe he wanted it to look like a burglar.'

'A burglar would not stuff a pen in someone's ear.'

'It's weird, innit?'

'Weird.'

'What's he doing sat there, anyway?'

'Maybe he was catching up on some work.'

They both peered at the screen. There was a panel of funny symbols with meaningless words and phrases beneath them. TREELINE. KENNEDY. PAISTE INT.

'Shit,' said Noel. 'Look at that.'

There was a picture of a chess piece, and underneath it the word 'KIRSTY'.

'Well, what do you know?' said Pike. 'He's left her a message.'

'You mean he struggled up here just to leave Kirsty a message?'

'Maybe he didn't want anyone else to see it. Who else would know to look under "Kirsty" except us?'

'Could be. Could be he just set up some kind of game for her, or something.'

'So you're dying, and what do you do? Organize some games for a six-year-old.'

'He did seem to like her.'

'Yes, but there's got to be more to it than that.'

'Well, all right then, let's find out.'

They dragged Herman away from the table and left him in the corner. Then Noel found another chair and sat down in front of the computer, his fingers hovering over the keys.

'Right,' he said, clapping his hands and taking a deep breath. 'Right …' He clapped his hands together again. 'Okay,' he said. 'Now what?'

Pike stared at the keyboard, hoping, somehow, that he would suddenly understand how to operate a computer.

Noel extended one finger and tentatively moved it towards a button. Pike grabbed it and pulled it away.

'Let's not rush into this,' he said. 'We don't want to blow it up, or anything.'

'Maybe there's a manual,' Noel said.

'Did Herman strike you as the kind of bloke who'd need a manual?'

'No, but there's no harm in looking. We can at least look.'

Kirsty sat in the funny wooden room that she knew wasn't a Wendy house and concentrated on Super Mario World. It was nice in here. It smelled nice. It was warm and cosy. She'd never been in a room like this before.

Little Mario hopped and skipped about the screen. She'd never got this far before, she was fighting the Koopa King who was buzzing around in a little space-ship thing. But Herman had told her what to do. Since she'd talked to him she was much better. She liked him. He was a nice man, not like Mr Pike. Mr Pike was gruff and bossy. He always looked at you like you'd done something naughty. And Mr Pike was an old man, like a grandad. Herman was a nice young man. Herman could play games with you.

Suddenly she smiled. She'd done it. The Koopa King was gone. Mario had rescued Princess Toadstool. The game was singing a tune to her, things were flashing, numbers and things. She watched it for a while, some pictures went by, then there was a boring bit, just a lot of names, then it was finished. She turned it off and put it in her pocket.

Herman had promised her some more games. But Herman had been asleep. He didn't look very well. He hadn't said hello to her. Maybe he was dead. She waited, daddy had told her to wait here, so she waited, with her hands in her lap, looking around the room.

There was a metal basket in one corner with coal in it. That was probably a fire. There were no windows, only one in the door, and there were two wooden benches one low and one high. Maybe one was for children and one for grown-ups. Although she was on the lower one and her feet still didn't reach the floor. She stretched out her toes and she could just touch.

After a long while daddy came in. He had some floppy books

with him. He smiled at her and crouched down on the floor. He took hold of her hands. He didn't hold her very often.

'Honey,' he said. She didn't like it when he called her Honey. Her name was Kirsty. 'Honey. What's a mouse?'

She wondered if it was a trick. Everybody knew what a mouse was.

'A mouse on a computer,' he said. 'A computer mouse.'

'Don't you even know that?'

'No. But I bet you do.'

'Of course I do.'

'Would you come and show me?'

She slipped down off the bench and, holding daddy's hand, she went back into Herman's room.

Herman was still sitting in the chair but he had been moved away from the table, and he had a cloth over his head. He looked silly.

'What's Herman doing?' she asked.

'He's … He's sleeping.'

'Is he dead?' He was definitely dead.

'Yes.'

'Hmm. That's a mouse.'

Kirsty pointed to the little box with buttons on it that was attached to the computer by a long wire.

Pike felt desperately foolish, having to rely on this six-year-old girl.

'Okay, Kirsty,' he said. 'Herman's left a message for you. But we don't know how to read it.'

Kirsty looked at the monitor, then took hold of the mouse and wiggled it around on the table top. The pointer on screen moved to the picture of the chess piece. Kirsty clicked a button on the mouse a couple of times and the screen changed. There were two words in a box.

GAMES
CHAS

'Can you see what it says in Chas?' Pike asked, not sure if he was using the correct terminology.

'Can I play the games,' said Kirsty petulantly. 'He promised me some games.'

'In a minute.' Pike tried not to sound irritable.

'Later, honey,' said Noel. 'Let's just see what it says under Chas first, then you can have a play. It might be an important message.'

'All right.' Kirsty moved the pointer and clicked again, another box appeared, with just one word in it this time.

CARDIGAN

'Okay,' said Pike. 'Again.'

'That's it,' said Kirsty. 'There isn't any more.'

'That's it?' said Noel. 'Cardigan?'

'Yes. Can I play the games, now?'

'Yeah, go on honey.'

Kirsty set about clicking again, and in a while a colourful picture filled the screen and she was off, manoeuvring what looked like a yellow blancmange around a bizarre maze, while a series of bleeps and farts rang out.

Pike and Noel left her to it. They went to the other side of the room and sat on a very comfortable, state of the art, black, leather sofa.

'Cardigan?' said Noel, disgusted. 'What kind of a fucking message is Cardigan? He goes to all this trouble, you'd think he'd make it a bit clearer for us.'

'Maybe he was just, like, rambling. The nonsense of a dying man.'

'I don't believe this.'

'Did Chas have any particular cardigans of any significance?' asked Pike.

'Of course he fucking didn't. I mean what the fuck is a significant cardigan?'

157

'All right.' Pike thought for a bit, but didn't come up with anything.

'Maybe it's like one of them crossword clues,' said Noel. 'You know, like, er, cardigan, jumper ... horse ...'

'Shergar,' said Pike sarcastically. 'They've found Shergar.'

'It was only a suggestion,' said Noel. 'What about cardigan/Patterson. Like a rhyme, perhaps.'

'Still doesn't mean anything.'

'Doesn't rhyme, either,' said Noel, stretching. 'Well, it's too late now. My brain's not functioning. We'll have to sleep on it. We can stay the night at dad's again.'

Kirsty gave a disappointed shout, and banged her fists on the table. The game evidently wasn't going her way.

'Noel,' said Pike. 'Can you accept that we've got to leave her behind somewhere. She should never have seen this.'

'I know. You think I don't feel bad about it?'

'There's two people dead ...'

'I said all right. We can leave her with Mrs Weller till this is over.'

'Good, but it's gone half eleven, you'd better ring her, check it's okay.'

'Sure.' Noel stood up. 'Here, d'you suppose these are ordinary phones, or special computer phones?'

'I haven't a clue, but there's one way to find out.' Pike mimed a dialling action.

'Yeah, yeah ...'

While Noel scouted about for a phone, Pike went over to Kirsty. 'How's it going?' he asked. Kirsty shrugged.

'It's very difficult. If Herman wasn't dead, he'd show me how to do it.'

'I'm sorry about Herman. He was your friend, wasn't he?'

'Yes.'

'We better get going now, eh? It's well past your bedtime.'

'Can't I finish this?'

'Some other time.'

'Can we take it with us?'

'No.'

'I could play the game at home. Herman won't mind, he's dead.'

'We can't just take it.'

'But it's got my games on it, and the message about Uncle Chas.'

'Cardigan?'

'Yes.'

'You wouldn't know what it means, would you? Cardigan?'

'It's a place.' Kirsty bit her lower lip and wiggled the mouse furiously.

'A place?'

'Yes. We did it at school. It's in Wales. That's a country.'

'Of course.'

Kirsty grunted and kicked her feet. 'I lost,' she said. 'You were talking too much.'

'Sorry. But ... we'll take it with us, eh? A present for you. I'm sure Herman would have wanted you to have it.'

'You just said I couldn't take it.'

'I changed my mind.'

'Thank you.' Kirsty clicked some buttons and shut the computer down.

'No. Thank you. Without your help, we'd have been stuck.'

'Like a game?'

'More like real life, darling.'

Noel came over. 'It's sorted,' he said. 'Mrs Weller will take Kirsty.'

'Great.' Pike began to unplug the computer, supervised by Kirsty.

'And look what I found next to the phone.' Noel dangled some car keys in Pike's face.

'What's that?'

'Keys to Chas's motor. It must be parked round here, somewhere. Shouldn't be too hard to find. You can follow me back to dad's.'

'Okay.'

They found a box to put the computer in and packed it up.

As they were going out they took one last look at poor old Herman, sitting there with the cloth over his head and the pen sticking out the side.

'Funny bloke,' said Noel.

'Tough bastard in the end, though, wasn't he?' said Pike. 'Getting all that done, the state he was in.'

'Guess so. But why did he do it? I mean, I know he liked computers and that, but why go to all that trouble? To climb back up into the chair, to turn on the machine, program in all that stuff . . . Why didn't he just write it down, or something?'

'I don't know,' said Pike. 'Maybe he couldn't find a pen.'

TWENTY-ONE

Pike got out of the car and the cold bit into him, turning his breath into white clouds. It was a freezing night, very sharp and clear, the sky littered with stars. He grunted. He badly needed the toilet. He thought of Noel's dad, of the broken bowl and the garden full of shit.

'Noel,' he said. 'You go on in, I'll sort Kirsty out with Mrs Weller. I need a crap.'

'Okey-dokey. Don't be long, now. I don't want you sniffing around Mrs W.'

'Grow up, Noel,' Pike said, but he had to admit the thought was at the back of his mind.

'What about my computer?' Kirsty whined as Pike bundled her over to Mrs Weller's front door.

'It's in the boot, darling,' Pike said, 'I'll get it out in the morning.' He pressed the bell and waited.

'What if it was stolen?'

'It won't be stolen. This isn't London. It's too cold and I'm bursting.'

'But, you said ...'

Mrs Weller opened the door. She was wearing old jeans and a baggy cotton jumper. She smiled at Pike.

'Hi there,' said Pike. 'Sorry it's so late.'

'That's all right, come in quick before you freeze. Hello, Kirsty.'

'I've got a new computer, Herman gave it to me, but Mr Pike won't let me play with it.'

'Really? Maybe you can play with it tomorrow, eh? For now we'd better get you up to bed.'

'Herman's dead.'

'Really? Who's Herman? Your rabbit?'

'No, I told you. Herman's my friend, it's his computer.'

'Oh, okay.' Mrs Weller led her up the stairs, indulging Kirsty in what she obviously took to be childish nonsense.

Pike called after her. 'D'you mind if I use your toilet? Only, you know what Noel's dad's place is like . . .'

Noel checked that the car was locked then strolled over to the house. He didn't bother knocking, just went round the back again. There were lights on inside, but it didn't mean anything, dad could be awake, asleep, passed out, down the pub . . . At least the heating was on. The place felt reasonably warm. That was a bonus. Dad usually moaned he couldn't afford to have the place heated, he was always getting cut off.

He hurried through the filthy kitchen, trying not to breathe in, and went through to the sitting room.

He stopped.

'Oh, shit,' he said.

Terry Nugent was sitting there with a tall skinny bloke. The skinny bloke had a big red birth mark covering one side of his face. The two of them were on the sofa, on either side of dad, who looked miserable; colourless, deflated, half dead. His nose had been bleeding, there was dried blood caked all over his upper lip.

Terry got up when he saw Noel, stood there solid as a lump of concrete. He was wearing the same grey jogging pants and T-shirt he'd had on yesterday – a T-shirt in this weather? – and the blue knitted cap.

'Hello, Noel,' he said. 'Come in. Join the party.'

'Hello,' said Noel. 'What are you doing here, Terry?'

'You know what I'm doing here. I'm looking for your brother. Now, this stupid old fart says he doesn't know where he is.'

Noel looked at the old man, who raised his eyes and looked sadly back at him.

'You all right, dad?'

Dad looked down without saying anything.

'Course he's all right.'

'Dad . . . ?'

Terry took a step towards Noel. 'Don't worry about him.'

'Terry,' Noel felt very tired. 'Why are you doing this?'

'Something's going on, Noel, and you're going to tell me what.'

Noel instinctively backed off, but Terry kept coming, until Noel was up against the wall. Terry was at least an inch shorter than him, but it didn't make him any the less scary.

'Chas is dead,' said Noel, his voice small and strained.

'I don't believe you.' Terry's breath smelled. He had spots round his neck.

'It's the truth. He had a fight.'

'Oh, come on, Noel. I am not a stupid man.'

There was a huge, livid bruise on Terry's forehead, with an infected-looking puncture in the centre of it, like a burst boil. Noel's eyes were directly level with it. Noel wondered what poor sod had been the recipient of this particular piece of violence. 'Do you want me to tell you about it, or not?' he said.

'Go on, then, let's hear it.'

So Noel began to talk, self-consciously at first, but after a while it was like it wasn't him talking at all, he was just listening to this voice, telling a story, a story about Chas, how he'd wanted to rob an old acquaintance called Patterson, how he'd gone to Pike, then changed his tactics and robbed Pike instead. It was a story about twenty-five thousand pounds, about Herman the German and even about Terry Nugent himself, and it finished with Chas being killed.

When it was over, Terry was quiet, thinking about things, and Noel became aware that dad had slumped in his seat. The old man was crying. At least he believed him.

Chas had always been his favourite.

'No. I don't accept that.' Terry said at last.

'What do you mean? You don't accept that?' said Noel. 'Why not?'

'You're hiding him,' Terry said bluntly. 'You're protecting him.'

'I'm telling you the truth. What more can I do?'

'You can stop lying.'

'Oh, for fuck's sake, Terry . . .'

Terry hit him. A slap. His short thick arm came up, his hand open-palmed, and he belted Noel round the side of the head, so quick Noel never saw it coming, half on the cheek, half on the ear. His ear immediately felt very hot, and it rang with a piercing, high-pitched whine.

Noel felt sick.

He had only one thought.

How long was Pike going to be in the bog?

'It's very kind of you to let me have a bath,' Pike said.

'It's no problem.' Sarah Weller handed him a couple of thick green towels.

'I'm not keeping you up?'

'Don't worry about it.'

'I feel like I've been stuck in that damn car for weeks. Up and down the bloody M4.' Pike rubbed his neck.

Sarah smiled at him. 'There's plenty of hot water, so you can have it as deep as you like. I like it so full it's slopping over the top. Course it's ruined me kitchen ceiling.'

'Kirsty all right?'

'Asleep. Went out like a light.'

'And your boy? . . . Darren?'

164

'Nothing wakes him. Touch wood.'

'I'd like to meet him one day.'

Sarah smiled. 'Go on. Go and have your bath.'

Pike went into the bathroom. The bath was running and the room was filled with mist. It was a nice bathroom, clean and filled with women's things, women's and little boys'. There were jars and tubes and sprays, sponges and flannels, a clockwork frogman, a bubble bath in the shape of Bart Simpson, shampoo, conditioner, bath oil . . . Pike thought of his own bathroom. One towel, a scrubbing brush, shampoo and his shaving stuff. He'd never been very good at luxury. The last ten years he'd lived the life of a monk. He wondered when he could stop punishing himself.

He undressed and placed his clothes neatly on the toilet seat, then he tested the temperature, just how he liked it, almost too hot to bear. He turned off the taps and carefully got in, slowly edging his body beneath the steaming water. His icy feet burned and tingled, but he knew that soon it would feel like bliss.

Sarah had put in some kind of bath foam, or salt, or something, there was a pleasant woody smell with just a touch of sweetness.

Jesus, it felt good. Really, in the long run, the small pleasures were the ones worth living for. He lay there listening to the water dripping and sploshing. He closed his eyes. He was drowsy and slipped into a half-awake state, letting odd thoughts slip in and out of the front of his mind, trying not to let any bad ones sneak in, any about Chas or Patterson, or the pen in Herman's ear. He thought how old his parents had looked, their old age seemed to be accelerating, for years they'd appeared to stay the same age, but now, if he didn't see them for a few months it was like some terrible ageing spell had been cast over them. He thought of Harry and childhood days. Harry picking on him, beating him up at every opportunity. Until at the age of fifteen Pike had suddenly grown, and one day when Harry came home from school he sorted him out.

He wondered if the old couple would ever work out that Harry was gay, the ultimate bent copper. Maybe they'd always known, just wouldn't accept it.

He thought about leaving school, after his O-levels, how his parents had so desperately wanted him to carry on, do A-levels, go to college ... But he'd been sick of it, sick of being attacked as a swot, as a nice kid, sick of being a schoolboy ... That was when he'd started going to the football, and, two years later, by the time he met the Bishop brothers, he was unrecognizable, a big, hard teenager who wasn't ever going to let anybody see what was inside ever again ...

Pike jumped as the door opened, he instinctively sat up in the water and covered his privates with his hands.

Sarah came in, raised an eyebrow.

'Not shy are you?'

Pike didn't know what to say.

'Don't mind me,' she said. 'I give Darren a bath every night, I've seen it all before.'

'I'm not Darren,' said Pike.

'Yeah, I know.' Sarah laughed. 'It's just, when you've got kids, you forget. Here, I've made you a drink.' She handed him a large tumbler of neat whisky. 'Whisky all right?'

'Lovely.'

'I like to have a drink in the bath.' She put the glass on the end of the tub. 'Everything okay?'

'Yes. Ta.'

'I'll leave you in peace, then.' She went out.

Pike realized he was blushing, but hoped she'd just thought it was a hot flush caused by the bath.

Damn it.

What did it mean? This woman coming in like that?

He'd been too long out of circulation, he couldn't read things any more. All he knew these days was videos. His life was spent watching films. So if this was a film what would that scene have meant? Only one thing, because films went in a straight line. There wasn't room for a scene that didn't mean anything. You knew where you were with films. Man meets woman, they fall in love, they go to bed, there's problems, they fall out, they overcome their problems.

Happy ever after.

Well, sometimes life was like the films, sometimes it wasn't. If this was Hollywood the bath would have been huge and they'd have both got in, and the bubbles would have covered them. Not like these ones, these ones were almost gone. In real life the bubbles never covered you.

He took a hit of the whisky and felt it burn down inside him. He smiled. They both liked whisky. They both liked drinking in the bath ...

Noel was sat next to his dad on the sofa, his arm around him. Terry and the other bloke, Basil, were sat opposite. Basil. Noel almost felt sorry for him. He was long and thin and ungainly; big hands, a bony forehead and sunken cheeks. He was wearing smart grey trousers and one of those patterned nylon jumpers.

Dad was in a bad way, shivering, though the room was warm. He started to whine and whimper.

'Give him a drink, can't you?' Noel asked.

'Man should avoid strong drink.'

Jesus, Noel wanted to hit him. Just once. One punch, that was all he asked, then he could die happy.

'How long are you going to keep this up, Terry? It's getting boring.'

'There's no hurry,' said Terry. 'We can wait. I'm not tired. I don't need much sleep. Two hours a night, three at the most. People don't need as much sleep as they think. It's just laziness. You must understand you see ...'

Noel didn't listen any more, he was dog tired, but too scared to sleep.

When was Pike going to come back?

Terry had hit him three times now, and he was getting pissed off with it. The whole of the side of his head was burning. His eye felt slightly swollen and his cheek was horribly tender. His ear was still ringing.

There was no point in saying anything to Terry. He'd tried lying, said Chas wasn't dead, said he knew where he was, could take him there in the morning, but Terry had hit him just the same.

Terry was still rabbiting on. 'People are generally weak. The British people used to be a hard people, a strong people. We ruled the world. But our genes have been diluted by intellectuals, by immigrants, by students. We're a warrior race, fighting men, not artists and people who read books. We're a race of butchers and builders, soldiers, sailors, working men. But we've become soft, we've been corrupted by too much money, by the easy life, by television, immigration, by drink and junk food and social workers. People don't keep their bodies in order any more. The body must be hard. There's an apocalypse coming and we must be prepared for it. Look . . .'

Terry got up and went over to the door. 'See.' He punched his hand through the thin wood. 'I could do this to you.'

I bet you could, Noel thought.

Terry came back from the door and leant over Noel, pointing now at the ghastly lump on his forehead.

'See this,' he said. 'This could be you, as well.'

Noel stared at the lump, looked right into the hole in its middle. 'There's something in there,' he said.

'What?' Terry frowned.

'There's something in there. In your bruise.'

'Eh?' Terry straightened up. 'What is it?'

There was a filthy mirror set into a chrome and plastic sixties wall unit. Chas and Noel had given it to mum and dad one Christmas. Terry went over and squinted into it. 'You're right. What is it?' He touched it delicately. 'Smallbone, get over here.'

Basil scurried over. 'What is it, Terry?' He peered into the hole. 'It looks like . . . It's greyish white, like a piece of chipped plate.'

'It's his tooth,' said Terry.

'What?'

'It's the kraut's tooth.'

'Oh.' Basil looked distressed.

'Get it out.'

'Terry?'

'Get it out of there.'

'What with? I mean, you should see a doctor, really.'

'What doctor? I don't need a doctor. It's nothing. Just get it out of there.'

'I don't want to hurt you, Terry.'

Terry snorted derisively and picked up a box of matches from the stained and scratched coffee table. He took out a match and gave it to Basil.

'Use this.'

'I'm not sure.'

'Do it.'

Terry sat down and Basil carefully set about excavating the bruise. Terry made a great show of not flinching or wincing at all, but his good eye twitched a couple of times and he very definitely had his jaws clenched. Basil slowly grew more bold and poked around in the hole with more vigour, giving a running commentary on his progress. 'It's embedded . . . It's well stuck, no, hang on, yes, no, blast . . . I had it. Wait . . . Here it comes . . .'

Finally, with a great gouge, the tooth flicked out and rattled onto the table top. Basil picked it up and inspected it. 'Yup. Tooth all right. Or at least part of a tooth. When you nutted him.' Basil laughed. 'Bloody hell, you must have hit him hard, eh, Terry? Bloody hell.'

Terry didn't laugh. He took the tooth off Basil, glanced at it, turned up his nose and lobbed it away.

Oh dear, thought Noel. Oh dear, oh dear ... It was them. They were the ones who had stuck Herman with the pen. These two could seriously fuck up their chances of finding Patterson and getting things sorted.

Let's face it. These two could seriously fuck Noel up, and his dad, who right now was hugging himself, bent almost double on the sofa, repeating what sounded suspiciously like the Lord's Prayer over and over. When had dad become religious?

A mixture of pus and blood was slowly trickling from Terry's wound. He wiped it away with the back of his hand, leaving a smear across his forehead.

'Right,' he said. 'Now that little side show's over, let's get back to business. Noel, are you ready to start talking sense?'

'What do you want me to tell you, Terry? He's dead. That's all there is to it. I've told you all I can.'

'I want to know ... I want to know ... Everything. Clarity.'

'All right. Chas has been secretly working on the British space programme. He's in outer space. On his way to becoming the first North Londoner on Mars.'

As Terry hit him, Noel wished he'd kept his big mouth shut.

He remembered the scene in *Lethal Weapon* where Danny Glover is captured by the villains. The chief villain, the blond one, says something like, 'What are you expecting, a hero to come and rescue you? Well, there are no more heroes.' At which point Mel Gibson crashes through the door with a dead Chinaman on his back and proceeds to dish out a good kicking all round.

Unfortunately Noel was forced to concede that in real life the villain was right, there were no more heroes.

Pike had let him down. Pike was supposed to ride in like the cavalry and rescue him, but Pike wasn't going to do that, was he? Because Pike wasn't a proper hard man at all. He wasn't even a real lad. He was a nice boy from Peterborough with seven O-levels. He was some middle-class wimp who'd managed to bluff his way onto the Shelf at White Hart Lane. He'd made them all believe he was Pike the hard man, the loner, the man with no past. The king of violence, but it was just a sham. Make believe. A game. When it came down to it, Pike was a bottler. His roots came through.

No. Pike had disappointed him.

And Pike wouldn't save him now.

He was alone with his sad, fucked-up dad and these two arseholes.

Fuck it. What a stupid way to go.

TWENTY-TWO

The lights on the Christmas tree winked on and off. The only other illumination in the sitting room came from the flames in a fake coal fire; one of those gas ones, pretty realistic. If Sarah hadn't told him he'd have thought it was real.

There were cards on the mantelpiece, paper decorations around the walls, a big foil star hung from the ceiling. Pike felt like he was in one of those Spielberg-type films, where people had impossible, old-fashioned Christmases. He was sitting wrapped in a big towelling dressing gown. Sarah had half got ready for bed and was wearing the man's coat she'd had on this morning. He wasn't sure what she had on underneath, possibly nothing.

Between them they'd polished off nearly half a bottle of whisky, and Pike felt mellow. Yes, 'mellow' was probably the best word to describe the state he was in. Mellow and old-fashioned.

Sarah was in the middle of telling him all about herself – the husband who'd gone back to an old girlfriend, what it was like being a single mother, trying to get a better job. At the moment she was the manager of a small local supermarket, but she wanted to get trained, do something with her life. It was all reassuringly real, domestic, ordinary. Pike wondered if, when he went to Canada, he might find a woman like this. Easy-going, somebody to spend your life with.

It was always the same, when you weren't looking for something it was always there, and if you went out and looked you could never find it.

Then he told himself not to be a fool. What was he doing imagining a life with this woman? A woman he'd only just met ... But it was tantalizing, the shadows where her long legs disappeared into the coat, the way she ran her hand through her shiny black hair.

'What do you call that hair style?' he asked.

'Don't you like it?'

'I just wondered what style it was.'

'A bob, I suppose, with bangs ... Some people call it a Louise Brooks.'

'Who's she?'

'An actress, I think. In the twenties.'

'It makes you look Chinese.'

'Oh, thanks.'

'No, I like it. You've got nice hair.'

Sarah shrugged.

'It's funny,' Pike said. 'Women are very bad at accepting compliments, they always think you're taking the piss, but if you really are taking the piss they take it as a compliment. I don't know, they seem to find it much easier to be insulted.'

'Charming.'

'No, I mean, if a bloke takes the piss, women like that. They can cope with it. It's like if I said you were fat, or ugly, or something, you'd assume I was joking, assume I really thought you were thin and pretty. You'd laugh. But if I said you were beautiful you'd think I was some wanker coming on to you and I didn't really mean it, I was just after something.'

'So, you think I'm fat and ugly, do you?'

'No, I think you're beautiful.'

Sarah laughed. 'Now I don't know what you think.'

'There you are, see? Men, on the other hand, just like to be complimented. They lap it up.'

173

'You look old.'

'You told me that before. It's just my hair.'

'Is it?'

'Maybe I should wear a hat,' said Pike.

'I'm not sure about men in hats.'

'I know what you mean. Everyone these days wears baseball caps. They all just want to be Americans.'

'Promise me one thing, Pike.'

'What?'

'You'll never wear a baseball cap on backwards.'

'It's one of my ten rules for life.'

'What are the others?'

'Never wear red shoes. Never go shopping when you're drunk . . . I don't know, never wear braces and a belt at the same time . . .

'It's all a bit negative, isn't it?' said Sarah.

'How do you mean?'

'It's all things not to do. There's no positive rules in there.'

'Like what?'

'How about seize the moment.'

'I'm not that type.'

'No, I didn't think you were.'

Pike looked at the carpet.

'You're not a very happy man, are you, Mr Pike?' Sarah said after a while.

'Never thought about it.'

'You're all closed in, private property, keep out. Trespassers will be prosecuted.'

'I've got problems, same as everyone else, but I'm basically contented.'

'You pompous old fart.'

'I'm not old, I'm thirty-four.'

Sarah stood up and came over to him. She definitely had nothing on under the coat.

174

'Take your glasses off.'

Pike did as he was told.

'My, but you're a pretty little thing, Mr Pike.'

'Am I?'

'You've got an old head,' said Sarah. 'But you've got a young body. I saw that much in the bathroom.'

*

'Now then,' said Terry. 'Where's this daughter of yours?'

'At home.'

'Your father told us you were travelling around with her.'

'We were. She's at home now. We left her in London.'

'Smallbone, here, is particularly fond of little girls.'

'Terry.' Basil sounded indignant.

Terry was wandering around the room, picking things up and looking at them before chucking them away. 'You got any pictures of her here?'

'I don't know,' said Noel wearily.

'This her?' Terry was inspecting a photograph he'd found on the chrome wall unit.

'I don't know.'

Terry showed him the photo. It showed Noel and Kirsty and Kirsty's mother. It had been taken on Kirsty's fourth birthday. She'd been even uglier when she was younger. She looked like some kind of mad goblin.

'Yes, that's her.'

Terry gave the picture to Smallbone. 'What do you think?'

Basil hardly glanced at it. He was evidently embarrassed.

'Well?'

Basil muttered something inaudible.

'What?'

'I said she's not my type, Terry.'

'Not your type. She's a girl, isn't she?'

'Leave it, Terry . . . Please.'

Terry shrugged and dropped the picture on the table. The glass cracked.

Noel wondered if he'd be able to hold out till morning.

'Please, Terry,' he said. 'What can I say? What can I do?'

'I'm owed money, Noel.'

'I don't have money.'

'If I'm going to believe your story,' said Terry. 'Then this man Patterson's got my money.'

'Your money?'

'Chas must have got it for me,' said Terry. 'What else?'

'But that money didn't belong to Chas. He swiped it off Pike.'

'That's not my problem.'

'What are you saying, Terry?'

'You've got two options, Noel. One, you tell me where Chas is. Two, you tell me where the money is. I'll settle for either.'

'Chas is dead. Patterson has the money.'

'Where's Patterson?'

'I don't know.'

'Where's Patterson?'

Jesus, they were right back to square one. It was going to start all over again.

'Look, Terry. Chas is out of it. Can't you leave it now?'

'I want that money.'

'Pike wouldn't like that.'

'I don't care about Pike. Now where's Patterson?'

'Oh, fuck off.'

'There's no need for bad language. If you cannot express yourself without resulting in profanity, you show an impoverished vocabulary. Now, me, I speak the Queen's English. I speak the language of Chauncer and Shakespeare.'

'Who?'

'Chauncer.'

176

'Fine. If I spoke the language of Chauncer as well, maybe I could get you to understand what I'm saying.'

'I understand perfectly well what you're saying. And I understand that you're not telling me everything. I believe you know where the money is.'

'I don't.'

'Then where's Chas?'

'Chas is in heaven, for God's sake, Chas has gone to meet his maker, he is an ex-Chas, he is pushing up fucking daisies.'

'Don't blaspheme,' said Terry, and he smashed a plate of half-eaten fish and chips over Noel's head.

*

Sarah's bed was soft and it smelled of her, a hint of perfume and something more earthy. The sheets felt cold against his naked skin.

He watched as Sarah undid the belt of her coat and let it slip off her shoulders. Her skin glowed almost translucent in the half-light. She had round white breasts with very pink nipples. She smiled unselfconsciously and slipped in beside him.

'Brrr,' she said. 'It's freezing. Warm me up.' She held onto him and wriggled about. 'God, you're freezing, too,' she said.

'Sorry.'

'A cold fish.' She laughed. 'Mr Pike.'

He kissed her, savouring the unfamiliar taste of another person. Her hands moved down his body and he broke away from her.

'Sarah,' he said. His voice sounding strained, like a bloody teenager. 'Would you mind . . . ? No. I mean – can I just hold you? I just want someone to hold on to.'

'Do you?'

'Yes. Something soft, warm.'

'Something?'

'Someone.'

'Well, sod you, Mr Pike.' Sarah propped herself up on her elbows and looked at him seriously. 'I haven't had a shag in over two years. So don't give me any crap about kissing and cuddling. Now get on the case, or you can sling your hook.'

'Sarah ...'

She smiled. 'Do your duty and be a man, Mr Pike.'

Noel must have fallen asleep, because now he was being woken up. Basil Smallbone was shaking him, making his head bang against the back of the sofa.

'Come along,' said Terry. 'Up.'

Noel struggled to his feet and looked at his watch, it was half past two in the morning. Jesus, Terry was right, these guys never slept.

'What the fuck do you want now?' Noel asked.

'I've been thinking,' said Terry.

Great.

'We're not getting anywhere. You're still holding out on us.'

'Can't this wait till the morning?'

'The truth never sleeps.'

'Oh, for fuck's sake ...'

'Come on. Upstairs.'

'What's upstairs?'

'Up!'

Noel got up. His neck felt stiff. Dad was asleep, snoring loudly, his mouth wide open.

Terry ripped the phone out of the wall, and Noel plodded after him up the stairs, scratching himself. Basil followed.

They all trooped into the bathroom and Terry locked the door.

'This place is unholy,' he said.

The bath was filthy, covered in a thin, greyish slime. There was water on the floor where it had leaked from the shattered toilet. There was a smell of damp and mould, but that wasn't as bad as the smell coming from the bucket under the sink. Dad had obviously been using it as a temporary toilet. It was full and reeking. It looked

178

like some vile biological reaction had occurred to the contents, they were green and there was something growing on the surface.

The stink really was inhuman.

'Get that out for a start,' Terry told Basil. Basil took one look at it and told Noel to shift it.

Noel picked it up at arm's length and dumped it outside the door, turning his head to keep the stench out of his nostrils.

When he came back in Terry was perched on the side of he tub.

'I shall keep asking you the same question,' he said. 'Until I am satisfied. Where is the money?'

'I don't know.'

'Fine.' Terry turned on the hot tap. 'Undress.'

TWENTY-THREE

Sarah was asleep. Pike could see her soft and rosy in the dim light of the bedside lamp. Her hair was stuck to her forehead with sweat, her mouth open, one arm flung back, like a child. He wondered how quickly you could fall in love with someone. He had already made vague, four-in-the-morning type plans for spending the rest of his life with her, helping to bring up Darren who he hadn't even met, putting presents under the tree at Christmas. But he knew none of that would happen. He was going to Canada, and that was that . . . Just as soon as he got his funds back.

Fuck it. Everything came back to that. The bloody Bishop brothers screwing up his life. Here he was on the verge of feeling happy for the first time in ten years and . . . But, then again, if Chas hadn't nicked his money he'd never have met Sarah, and he'd never have . . .

He'd been worried at first, worried he wouldn't be able to get it up. He'd slept with a handful of girls since Marti had left him, but they'd all been disasters. If he wasn't so drunk that he didn't know what he was doing, he couldn't do anything. With Sarah he'd felt horribly clumsy at first, big and awkward and self-conscious. But she was so different, so relaxed, so into it, so little worried about what he thought, that he'd soon forgotten about all his problems.

He'd relaxed as well, and in the end, well, it was just like riding a bike. Except more fun.

He got up and went to the bathroom for a glass of water. The house had got very cold. His feet flinched, arching away from the tiles. He drank some water from a tooth glass and splashed some into his face.

He had to get away from Noel. From here on in, he wanted to go it alone. He could easily slip away now. He'd have to disable Noel's car, so he couldn't follow him for a while. The car he'd picked up in Bath, Chas's car. He could pour some sugar in the petrol tank, perhaps.

Yes. That was the thing. Keep moving. Do it alone. He didn't need anyone else. He certainly didn't need Noel, this was between him and Patterson.

As he went back to the bedroom to get his clothes he thought of Kirsty and looked in on her. She was fast asleep, her ugly little face scrunched up, snoring. He remembered the computer in the back of the car. He'd have to get it for her before he left. After all, she'd helped him out, back at Herman's.

Darren was in the other bed and Pike took a look at him. He was an ordinary-looking kid. An ordinary, suburban boy, just like Pike had once been. He hoped Darren would stay that way, not go down the road Pike had chosen.

Shit. What had he been thinking of? Planning a life with Sarah. She didn't need him. She didn't want any part of his world. It was just Christmas and everyone was feeling a bit sentimental, a bit lonely, there was an office-party atmosphere in the air. That's all Pike was, a snog in the stock room with someone you shouldn't be snogging, someone you'd never talk to again.

He added a new rule to his list. Never make plans in the middle of the night.

Trying not to look at Noel Bishop, Basil poured another kettle of boiling water into the bath.

Basil didn't like to look at Noel. He'd never been comfortable with naked adults, like at the swimming pool, or something. Grown men had horrible bodies. They were flabby and loose and the flesh sort of dangled everywhere. Basil didn't even like to look at himself in the nude. It was like looking at a corpse.

Noel's skin was very white, almost grey. He had a big, wobbling gut on him, and long, pale, very skinny, hairless legs. Like a girl's legs. He was shivering, with his hands held over his privates. He looked about ten years older.

It was freezing in here, despite the heat coming from the half-full bath, and, even with the bucket gone, the smell was almost unbearable. It reminded Basil of being back inside; slopping out. Standing there trying to clean your teeth while men emptied their shit into a basin right next to you. There was something about smells, something that got to you. The memories made him as nauseous as the stench.

'That should do it,' said Terry, inspecting the bath. He turned to Noel. 'You ready, then? It's bathtime.'

'I'm not getting in there.'

'Have you ever seen a crab being boiled? Pow. Instant. Now this water isn't boiling, of course, so it won't kill you. Leastways, I don't think it will. I've never tried this before ... but it's this place, you know? Filthy. I'm starting here, cleaning things up.'

'I'm not getting in there.'

'You'll only be ... What's the word? Not scorched, like scorched, scarred? No ...'

'Scalded?' Basil suggested.

'That's it, scalded. Let's look on it as an experiment.'

'I'm not going in there.'

'Then tell me where the money is.'

'It's not your money.'

'Bathtime.' Terry took hold of Noel by one arm and the back of his neck.

182

'Don't do this, Terry. I'm not a brave man. I'm not good with pain.'

'Where's the money?'

'Terry...'

Noel said 'Ow' and arched his back as Terry did something to him, Basil couldn't tell exactly what. Then Noel said 'Ow,' again as Terry doubled him over and held his face just above the surface of the water. Noel tried to twist his face away.

Basil no longer noticed the cold, he no longer noticed the stink. All his attention was focused on Noel. He'd never seen anyone this scared. It was awesome the way Terry held him, controlled him so totally.

'I don't have to do this, you know, Noel.' Terry pulled Noel back. 'There are other options.'

'I can't tell you any more.'

'Tell you what,' Terry said. 'We'll do it bit by bit. If I dump you all in in one go there's no telling what might happen. How about starting with a hand?'

'Please, Terry.'

Quickly, before Noel could say or do anything else, Terry dunked his left arm into the water and Noel screamed. Terry held it under for a couple of seconds then let Noel go. The hand and wrist came out scarlet. Noel clutched his arm to his body and fell into a squatting position, swearing. Tears of pain squeezed from his eyes.

'Jesus Christ, Terry. I've told you all I know.'

'Now the other hand,' said Terry and he hauled Noel up. Noel tried to squirm away, but Terry held him firmly, as if he was just a little kid. He held his other hand out over the water.

'All right, all right!' Noel yelled. 'All right. I'll tell you. Cardigan.'

'What's Cardigan?'

'It's a place in Wales. That's where the money is. That's where Patterson is.'

'Whereabouts in Cardigan?'

'I don't know. I only know Cardigan.'

'That's all you're telling me?'

'Yes.'

'That's all you know?'

'Yes.'

'I believe you. Thousands wouldn't.'

'Thank you.'

'But you should have told me before.'

'Sorry.'

'Now, as you haven't been entirely straight with me, I'll admit I haven't been entirely straight with you. You're going in Noel, all of you. Just say that my inquiring mind has got the better of the situation. I'm curious to know what will happen.'

'No, Terry. Please, Terry. Please don't do it . . .'

'Come on.'

Terry must have relaxed his grip because Noel managed to wriggle free. He scampered to the sink, but there was nowhere to go. Terry shook his head. He looked irritated. He took a step towards Noel.

Just then there was knock at the door, a pathetic, almost scrabbling sound.

'Noel? Noel?' It was Noel's dad. 'Let me in. What's going on?'

'Go away, dad,' said Noel. 'Please go away.'

Pike sat at the kitchen table and looked at the blank sheet of paper. He'd been going to write a note for Sarah, so it didn't look like he was sneaking off, but he didn't know what to put. Whatever he thought of sounded wrong. Like a thank-you note, or, worse, an apology. Finally he steeled himself and wrote simply, 'Goodbye'. But when he looked at it, it seemed awfully melodramatic. So, in the end he scrumpled up the paper and threw it away. He'd just go, and hope she understood.

Pike opened the door as quietly as he could and slipped outside into the dark night.

'Noel? What's up? What's going on?'

'Clear off, old man,' said Terry and he tried to get hold of Noel, who was twisting like a snake.

Basil looked round as the door handle rattled.

'Noel? Noel?'

'All right,' said Terry. 'Get him in here, he may as well watch.'

'No, Terry,' said Noel. 'Don't. Leave him alone.'

'Let him in.'

Basil unlocked the door and opened it.

He caught a brief glimpse of the old git standing there, holding the bucket, before he was hit full in the face with a cold, stinking sludge. He closed his eyes but it was too late. It got everywhere, in his nose, in his mouth, his hair, his ears. A clammy, slimy, evil mess of filth. Gagging, he fell to his knees.

It was all Noel needed, a second's distraction. Terry turned to see what was happening and Noel squirmed past him and sped for the open door.

He hopped over Basil, who was retching and puking on the floor, and raced past his dad.

Behind him he heard Terry, coming after him like a a greyhound after a rabbit, but Noel had fear on his side. He was down the stairs almost in one jump, he stumbled at the bottom and twisted his foot, but he was up instantly and moving again, through the sitting room, through the porch, and out of the front door.

The cold hit him like a physical blow, stinging his burnt hand.

There was mist in the air, everything was lit by the ghostly orange-pink glow of the street lamps.

Noel felt small and vulnerable out here, he was wilting from the cold.

What now?

He should have got the car keys. He should have got some-thing to cover himself. He was outside, naked, on a freezing December night.

Then he heard Terry.

'Get back here, Noel,' he said. 'Get back in here at once.'

Pike was just lifting the computer out of the Escort's boot when he heard the front door of Noel's dad's place bang open and he saw Noel come racing out, stark bollock naked. What was the silly sod up to now?

And then Terry Nugent came out and Pike realized.

Terry yelled at Noel. Noel stopped and turned, he looked defeated.

Terry grabbed hold of him.

'Hello there, Terry,' said Pike, and the two of them saw him for the first time.

Terry marched Noel over to the car.

'You keep out of this, four eyes.'

'Four eyes?' Pike gently lowered the computer back into the boot. 'That's rich coming from a bloke with only one.' He looked at Terry. He had some kind of virulent swelling on his forehead. 'Or is that another eye you're growing there?'

'Don't try it with me,' Terry said.

Pike glanced into the boot. The baseball bat he'd confiscated off the kids in the Dalston Cross car park was still there. But first Pike had to make Terry lose interest in Noel.

'You guys having some kind of a party?' he asked, and took hold of the handle.

'Don't try it with me,' Terry said again.

'Terry,' said Pike, 'you are a twat.'

Terry squinted, let go of Noel, and came at him.

Silly fucker.

In one swift movement Pike swung the bat out of the boot and smacked it into Terry's knee. Terry wasn't expecting this and the force of the blow knocked him off balance. Another whack to the other knee and Terry went down with an indignant yell.

Before he had a chance to get up Pike jabbed him behind the ear with the bat, end first, like a pool shot, and his face jerked down into the pavement.

'Shit,' said Pike. 'Look at that.'

'What?' said Noel.

'I've knocked him out.'

'Never.'

'Yeah, look. One blow. Shit. Would you look at that? I've never done that before. One blow and he's out like a light.'

'Thank you, God,' said Noel. 'Thank you.'

Just then Basil Smallbone staggered out of the house, wiping his face on a towel. He was calling for Terry.

'Over here,' said Pike, and Smallbone looked at them like a surprised bunny.

'This what you're looking for?'

'Terry, what happened?' Basil knelt by the still figure of Terry.

'He got hit,' said Pike. 'He's away with the fairies.'

'Terry . . .'

'I know,' said Pike. 'It's a bugger, isn't it?'

'Terry . . .'

'Who is this tit?' Pike asked.

'Basil Smallbone,' said Noel. 'He's with Terry.'

'Okay, Basil,' said Pike. 'Get Terry in your car and get the fuck out of here, all right? I don't ever want to see either of you again . . . Ever.'

'What have you done to Terry?'

'I think it's what you call a home run,' said Pike. 'Now, get him out of here.'

While Noel went in to put some clothes on Pike helped Basil put the solid dead weight of Terry's body into the Astra. Basil stank, he was blinking constantly, his eyes looked red and sore. Pike didn't want to know what was wrong with him.

Ten minutes later, Pike and Noel were ready to leave as well. Sarah had agreed to take Kirsty to stay with her mum on the other side of town for a few days, just in case Terry and Basil decided to come back. Noel's dad, the hero of the day, couldn't be persuaded to leave. He was full of cocky bravado.

'I showed them bastards, didn't I, son? Didn't I? Eh?'

'You showed 'em, dad.'

'If they ever dare come back I'll get 'em with another one of my special brews, eh? Ha, ha. He didn't know what hit him.'

'Dad, it was quite disgusting.'

'Ha, ha, ha.'

Noel was in severe pain, but he'd found an old stash of Chas's drugs in the house and was sorting through them for something he could use. His hand was packed in ice but the pain went straight from there into the front of his brain, like he had a red hot wire up his arm.

Just before they left Pike took Sarah aside.

'I'm sorry about all this,' he said.

'It's all right. A bit of excitement in my otherwise dull life. One way or another it's been quite a night.'

'I know. It was . . . It was good.'

'You have a way with words, don't you?'

'I can't say what I want to say, that I'd like to see you again, that I'd like to come back when this is all over, that you've woken me up. I can't say any of that.'

'Listen, Mr Pike. I don't want you coming back. Not like this. You're not a happy man. There's something in there.' She tapped his head. 'Something hidden that I want nothing to do with. You're a mess. I can't take on two kids at once.'

'Yeah.' Pike grinned as best he could. 'And thanks for everything.'

'Well, thank you, Mr Pike.' She formally shook his hand and gave him a mocking smile.

Pike turned and walked away.

Sarah called after him. 'But if you ever do get your shit together, you'll know where to find me.'

TWENTY-FOUR

'You did everything?' Noel asked, rummaging in the shoe box full of pills.

'Everything.'

'Like what?'

'Use your imagination.'

'So, while I'm in there being boiled alive by Terry Fuckwit, you're abusing the next-door neighbour.'

'I didn't abuse her. Everything we did was by mutual consent.'

'You bastard.' Noel popped a pill into his mouth.

'Go easy, Noel.'

'I'm in pain, here. Severe pain. Drastic problems require drastic action.'

Pike shook his head.

The roads were pretty well deserted at this time of night, and they were making good time. Pike had to admit it was more fun driving Chas's big green Mercedes 250 than his battered old Escort. It was probably as old as his car, but it was in a different league. Somebody had obviously looked after it – probably not Chas – it seemed to just slide along the road, its powerful engine ticking away. The sound system was better, too. Noel had found it locked in the boot. Chas had left an Al Green tape in the glove compartment and the soothing sounds filled the car.

Pike would have enjoyed it more if he hadn't been dog tired, however. He hadn't slept at all tonight and he wasn't used to it. He'd toyed with the idea of trying out something from Chas's pill box, but as Noel didn't seem to be sure what any of it was, he didn't want to risk it.

The high suspension towers of the Severn Bridge loomed up into the night sky ahead and Pike looked at the clock on the dashboard, it was just gone three. 'I'm going to pull into these services,' he said. 'I'm asleep at the wheel, here.'

'I'll take over if you like,' said Noel.

'You can't drive with that hand.'

Noel held his scalded hand up and twisted it, inspecting the damage. It was red raw and blistered.

'I don't know,' he said. 'Might take me mind off it.'

'We'll see.'

Pike parked the car in the largely empty Severn View Pavilion car park and they went inside to the welcoming lights of the building.

They got themselves some coffee and sat in the window looking out at the great bridge.

There were a few lorry drivers scattered about, a bunch of young people in leather jackets who looked like they might be in a pop group. Some solitary men in suits. A vanload of disabled teenagers, sitting in wheelchairs. The atmosphere was subdued, but there was an undercurrent of excitement, of adventure. They were all staying up past their bedtime. They owned the night.

'It's not fair,' said Noel, stirring his coffee, round and round and round. 'I've fancied Mrs Weller for years, and you just stroll in there, say hello, and the next thing you know you're test-driving her Slumberland. You always were a jammy bastard when it came to women. Years I've fancied her.'

'She's got that great haircut.' Pike yawned.

'What the fuck's her haircut got to do with anything?'

'It's the first thing I look at in a woman.'

'Her haircut?'

'I guess I'm a hairstyle fetishist. Anything that looks like it's been thought about, you know? I don't mean like a perm. I mean, like, plaits. Jesus, I love plaits. Any style where the hair's tied up.'

'Pigtails?'

'Pony tail, bun ... those black birds, round London with those weird styles, all knotted and tight. Sometimes I'll follow a girl because she's got her hair fancy at the back, in a ball, or a bow, or, yes, plaits. I even used to like that Fergie style, you know, pulled tight and overlapping, like one of them loaves. I know I'm not supposed to, but I used to love that style.'

'You fancy Fergie?'

'I fancy her hairstyle. She doesn't have it any more, anyway.'

'So she's safe from you, then?'

'Pony tail, pins, you know, that sort of Spanish look. Anything fancy like that. Anything interesting. Wet look, dyed, Mohican ... Sarah. Even caught myself fancying Sinead O'Connor once, because of her hair. Or lack of it. And you know the thing I like best of all?'

'What?'

'The nape of the neck. Exposed. Sends me wild.'

'Jesus.'

'Nine times out of ten, though, the girl on the tube doesn't live up to the hairstyle. Doesn't live up to the back of her neck. Sometimes I try not to look at their faces. Preserve the fantasy. But I do love the back of a girl's neck.'

'Me, I like arses,' said Noel.

'You surprise me.'

'Arses and long legs. Tits, of course. A nice face. Long hair, I think I like long hair best.'

'Long hair's good,' said Pike. 'Long hair, short hair ...'

'Yeah, I know, the nape of the fucking neck.'

Pike yawned again and rubbed his face. He was losing it. 'Maybe we should just find a hotel,' he said.

'A Scottish accent,' said Noel.

'Huh?'

'For some reason I go wild for a Scottish accent. Can't resist it.'

'Right.'

A young woman in shiny grey trousers, green shirt and matching green baseball cap cleared some crap off their table. All the staff were dressed like this.

Pike watched her walk away, his vision blurring. 'What about it, then?' he said. 'Shall we find somewhere to kip?'

'Nah, we've got to press on,' said Noel. 'Onwards and upwards. We've got to get to Cardigan.' Noel's eyes were wide and black, glistening. He was rocking back and forwards in his seat, still stirring his coffee.

'Noel. You can't drive.'

'I'm focused,' said Noel. 'Trust me. Besides we ain't got enough money for a room. We need your mum's twenty quid for petrol and I'm skint.'

Pike rested his head in his hands. He was too tired to fight. It seemed easier to just lay back and give up, let Noel carry him for a while.

'I'm all yours,' he said.

So it was Noel who paid the toll at the bridge and manoeuvred the big car over the black waters of the Severn Estuary into Wales.

Pike settled back in his seat and closed his eyes. The quiet hum of the engine was soothing. Al Green sang about love and devotion. He tried to think ahead, but he had no plan. Nothing beyond reaching Cardigan and finding Patterson. Tracking him down in his black jeep Cherokee with the tinted windows. With poor bloody Chas in the back of it wrapped in a duvet cover.

And Marti in the front with Patterson.

In this state, halfway between wake and sleep, he saw a composite picture of her ... Marti as she had been when they'd first met, nearly fifteen years ago. Then Marti as she had been when they were going out, those four years. Then Marti when he'd last seen her, at Patterson's; older but unchanged ... Still like a little girl fooling everyone she was a big girl.

But the strongest image was that first time, when he'd first seen her in the Ship on Mare Street. Maybe he'd always think of her as she had been then.

A Saturday afternoon. The pub crowded; a wedding. The happy couple have been married at the town hall just down the road. The place is noisy with laughter, packed with men in cheap suits and women with too much make-up. A few jolly old people wearing hats. There are big plates of sandwiches out on some of the tables and a tray of chicken drumsticks on the bar.

It's summer, no football. Pike and the Alma crew are already half-pissed when they roll up. Half-pissed and looking for a laugh. There is instant tension. The Alma boys can tell when they aren't wanted. They're outsiders. But that just makes them want to stay. To be difficult. It's a free country, isn't it?

Marti is with the wedding party, best man's girlfriend as it turns out, fiancée. She's been through a few fiancées by now. She's seventeen, but could pass for twenty-one. Later on Pike will find out that, fresh from the bath, naked, scrubbed of her make-up, she could pass for twelve. She's slim and small, sort of delicate-looking.

She's a bridesmaid, in a shiny pink-white dress, and still has her hair up, some over-elaborate style with fake flowers in it. That's probably what makes Pike notice her. That and the look on her face. Christ, she knows what she's doing. She owns every man in the place and she knows it.

Her fiancée, the best man, is a tall, bony geezer with a broken nose. A Hackney lad. The groom is a handsome dark-haired boy, a bit Greek-looking, wearing a fancy suit. Black with silver flecks.

Pike gets talking to Marti, insults at first, then, leaning at the bar, he starts to chat her up. He's cocky, he has the crew with him, he's out to impress ... Best man starts to shoot him glances, his mates say something to him, in the end he comes over. Starts a row with Marti. Not Pike, Marti. That's all Pike needs to know, the guy is basically chicken shit.

'Leave me alone,' says Marti, drunk. 'I can talk to who I like.'

'No, you fucking can't.'

'Yes, I fucking can.'

Best Man takes her arm, she pulls away.

'Why don't you leave her alone?' says Pike, and that seems to give the guy some guts. He grabs Pike by the collar and shoves him back against a pillar on the bar. Presses his head back, lifting him slightly. He's tall.

'What did you fucking say?'

Pike looks at the others, at Noel and Chas, at Mickey and Colin, sees their expectant faces, their excited grins. Then he sees Patterson. Different from the others. No expression, just staring at him. Knowing. Seeing right through him to the little swot. Knowing that Pike has to do this, has to keep on doing this for ever, or he'll be lost, unmasked.

And Pike turns it on. He goes for it. He's got no choice, complete loss of control. Unnecessary level of violence.

He grabs a soda siphon off the bar and whacks it into the side of Best Man's head. Best Man goes down, Pike boots him in the teeth before he can get up, then he picks up a stool, hurls it over the counter into the optics. Two wedding guests try and stop him, try and take hold of him, but Pike hardly notices them. He's in a world of his own now, and the rest of the crew are on the move, causing maximum damage.

What follows is a blur, the juice turned full on. Pike's consciousness, the reasoning part of his brain, is pulled back, shoved down and hidden away inside him somewhere.

In the middle of it all he notices Marti, standing there, impassive, unimpressed, just watching. Other girls are screaming, 'Stop it! Stop it, you bastards ...'

But not Marti. She's just watching. Watching the chaos she has created.

Pike goes to her and kisses her full on the mouth. She lets him, opens up, uses her teeth. He grabs her cunt and she squirms against his hand. When he pulls away he notices blood on her lips, somebody must have hit her in the face.

The best man's up now, he throws his arms round Pike. Pike runs backwards full pelt into the wall and the best man falls off. Pike kicks him again.

There's the groom, still immaculate in his suit, trying to keep out of it, sheltering the bride. But the world isn't like that, and he has to be told.

Pike pushes a glass into his face.

Then it's time to leave. Their work is done, there'll be cops here soon if the landlord's on the case. They all run out, laughing, out into the afternoon sun. And somehow Marti's with them. She gets carried along, down the street, into a car. There's a crazy ride north, back to their own turf ... and the day goes on, wild with drink and drugs. Exaggerated tales of today's outing. Boasts and lies and excess. Too much of everything. Like they're trying to eat the world, do it all now before they turn into one of the toothless old gits who sit round the edges of the pub in their trilbies, grinning and winking and drinking bitter as the afternoon sun streams through the windows and obliterates them.

Come six o'clock Pike's in bed with Marti, fucking the little thing, throwing her around the room. And the cut on her lip opens, so that, by the end of it, they're both smeared with her blood.

He knew it then, that she was crazy, but he didn't care. He found out why later, years later, when she felt able to talk about it. She'd had a lousy childhood, no childhood at all really. All she'd ever known was sex and violence. Violence and sex. She wasn't happy but what did he care? As long as he could fuck her. And he could. He could do anything he liked to her, as long as he was

Pike. As long as he was unbeaten. As long as he was the biggest shit around.

When she'd propositioned him at Patterson's, on the seventh floor of the Belvedere, he'd felt a momentary flood of desire. All those nights came back to him, all those afternoons, those mornings. In cars, hotels, flats, toilets, trains, beaches, fields, alleys. With her clothes on, her clothes off, in the underwear she bought. With each other, in front of the mirror, with the video camera on, with his friends, her girlfriends . . . Four years of debauchery, until that one night when it had all gone wrong, and Pike wasn't Pike any more.

Sarah had been different. He'd never known it like that before. It hadn't been hard and vicious, it hadn't been like a fight . . . It had been like a dream, where you think you're somebody else.

With their two faces swimming in his mind, merging, separating, he drifted off to sleep, and the car sped on deeper into Wales.

TWENTY-FIVE

Basil Smallbone couldn't get rid of the smell. He'd showered for half an hour, scrubbing himself raw. He'd clawed the insides of his nostrils with his fingernails, he'd cleaned his teeth over and over, he'd dumped his filthy clothes outside in a bin – thank God he'd brought some clean ones along in his overnight bag – but still the foul stink seemed to cling to him.

He was in a motel off the M4. The place was hell. He couldn't adjust the heating and it was stiflingly hot. It had livid orange walls and a brown carpet and Basil felt like death. He'd wanted to get Terry into a bed, didn't want to drive around with him unconscious in the car, but the place was being renovated and the only room they had available had only one double bed in it.

Terry had woken long enough to be got out of the car and into the bed, but since then he hadn't stirred. He'd been terribly disoriented and couldn't remember anything about what had happened; which was probably a very good thing. Basil felt utterly humiliated. He'd never forget running out of the house covered in shit and seeing Terry lying unconscious beneath Pike.

What had gone wrong? How had Pike beaten him? He must have been waiting, must have taken him from behind. Pike and Noel obviously had a plan worked out in advance. Terry could never have been bettered in a fair fight.

Well, Pike was going to pay for that. Basil would see to it.

He turned off the light, stripped to his vest and underpants, got into bed next to Terry and tried to sleep. It was no good. All he could think about was the smell, and now his eyes were starting to sting. He must have got soap in them, after all, he'd used enough of the stuff.

He got up and went back into the bathroom, splashed some cold water over his face and looked in the mirror. His eyes were very red, and when he pulled down the eyelids their undersides were yellowish. Bloody soap. That was all he needed.

There was a shout from the bedroom and Basil hurried back. Terry was sitting up in bed, looking round the room in some confusion.

'You all right, Terry?'

'What is this place?'

'It's a motel, remember? I thought it best we rest up for the night.'

'Why?'

'You hit your head, Terry.'

'Yes. Yes, that's right.' Terry put a hand to the lump above his left ear. 'What is this place?' he said again.

'A motel.'

'Yes.'

'You don't remember how we got here?'

'No. I don't ... I must be tired. What time is it?'

Basil looked at his watch. 'Half four.'

'At night?'

'Yes.'

'I don't get it. What is this place?'

'It's your head, Terry. You must be concussed, or something.'

'Listen, Smallbone. I'm having some problems here ...' Terry broke off suddenly and yelled – 'Ah!'

'What is it?'

'My knee. My knee. What's happened to my knee?'

'There was ... There was a fight, Terry.'

Terry's face cleared. He understood. 'Pike.'

'Yes,' said Basil, quietly.

'Crept up on me, ambushed me. Got me in the knee. Ow. Both knees. Ow. I can't bend my legs.'

'You remember the fight?'

'What fight?'

'It doesn't matter.'

'We were going somewhere, weren't we?' said Terry, frowning. 'In the car.'

'We have to get to Cardigan, Terry.'

'Cardigan?'

'In Wales.'

'Right . . . Where did you say, again?'

'Cardigan.'

'Yes. Chas. Chas, he's got the money, hasn't he?'

'I don't know, Terry. I don't know how much of what Noel told us was true.'

'Noel?'

'Chas's brother.'

'Right . . . Where did you say we were going, again?'

'Cardigan. Look, I'll write it down for you.'

'No. Don't write it down. What do you want to write it down for? I'll remember. You don't need to write it down. Ow, what's the matter with my knees? I can't straighten my legs.'

'You should sleep. Maybe you'll be better in the morning, eh? Maybe you'll remember things.'

'Yes, yes . . .' But Terry got out of bed.

He winced as he put his feet down, and stood in a sort of crouch. Then, grunting with the effort, he hobbled to the window and looked out.

There was a car park out there, a few cars, some lorries, couple of vans.

'What is this place?' Terry said. 'Why have you brought me here?'

'Please, Terry. Get back to bed.'

Terry opened the door, letting in a blast of cold air, and went outside. 'It's the middle of the night,' he said, looking up at the sky.

'Yes.' Basil came out. 'Get back to bed. You need to rest.'

'Stars,' said Terry.

'Yes.'

Terry smiled. 'They go on for ever. My father used to show me the stars. He had a telescope.'

Basil took him by the elbow and gently led him back inside. He helped him into bed and Terry sat there, blinking. He looked like a child and Basil felt a surge of pity for him.

'You'll be all right, Terry. In the morning. But you need to sleep now.'

'Yes.' Terry lay down and Basil tucked him in. He closed his eyes and Basil turned out the light.

'Don't turn the light off,' Terry murmured, and Basil put it back on.

'Thanks, mum.'

Basil sat and watched over him until his breathing slowed and he began to snore.

Basil rubbed his eyes. If anything they were getting worse rather than better.

Pike would pay for this, and that bastard, Noel. Hitting Terry when his back was turned. Basil would make sure they were punished. First Pike, then Noel, then Noel's dad, the evil old cunt. He'd drown him in a bucket of his own shit.

He went into the bathroom again and turned on the shower. This time he'd get really clean.

Pike was woken by the deafening sound of Philip Glass bursting out of the car's speakers.

'Christ, turn it down, Noel,' he said and looked out of the

window. They were just passing the huge industrial park at Port Talbot with the steel works rising up at the heart of it.

'Look at that,' said Noel. 'Will you take a look at that.'

Set away from the motorway in the middle of a wide, flat plain between the hills and the sea, the steel works were lit up by thousands of white lights, strung along the iron buildings like fairy lights. Tall, thin chimneys spouted great jets of flame up into the sky. And clouds of white smoke hung in the air.

'Come on,' said Noel. 'Come on, Glass-man ... We need the right music, here, give us them wiggly bits ... Come on, go for it ...'

Suddenly the music exploded into manic, deafening arpeggios, it was *The Grid*. The track that could send you round the twist.

'Yes!' said Noel. 'Perfection. Give it full diddly, Philip. Diddly-diddly-diddly-diddly ... go for it, full whack!'

Pike looked at the speedometer. They were going over a hundred.

'Jesus, Noel. Slow down, will you? We don't want to be stopped. Specially the state you're in. What have you taken, anyway?'

'I took them all, I figured something had to help the pain. Uppers, downers, sideways ... You know what I think's happened? They've all cancelled each other out, and I'm perfectly normal. Only it's a really intense sort of normality, *do you know what I mean*? Like the most normal you could ever imagine. So fucking normal I'm super normal. Like, more normal than anyone's ever been before. An incredible, intense kind of normalness. Yes, everything is perfectly normal. Like this seat cover, it's beige, right? Only it's a really, really, ordinary beige. Just, you know, beige. And that's it! Hah! Beige. B-e-fucking-beige. Nothing's changed. This music sounds just exactly like it always has done, only more so, more exactly the same than you ever thought possible. Exactly the same! Not different in any way at all. Completely ordinary ... I tell you, Pike, things are so ordinary, I don't think I can take it any more.'

'Fuck it, Noel, you're going to have to stop. You can't drive like this. Next services you stop, okay?'

They hammered through some road works, the car banging and bouncing on the uneven surface.

There was a new piece of motorway under construction here. Next to the existing one, up on pillars; starting nowhere and going nowhere.

'I can't stop, Pike.' Noel was staring straight ahead, his eyes wide and unblinking, his teeth clenched.

'You fucking stop or I'll stop you.'

'We just keep going till we come off the other side,' said Noel and he giggled.

'Slow down.'

The motorway ran out, turned into an ordinary road. There were ugly little semis along the side, a drive-through Burger Master, an Esso station.

'I'm not going fast,' said Noel. 'This is an ordinary speed. It just seems fast to you. I mean, say you were in a jet flying overhead, well, then we'd look like we were hardly moving, say you were on a satellite . . . Hey, look, Gwasanaethau Services. This is weird. *Déjà vu*. I could swear we've already been through Gwasanaethau.'

'It's Welsh,' said Pike. 'It means services.'

Noel laughed loudly, like a machine gun, 'Ha-ha-ha-ha-ha-ha-ha.'

'We'll stop, eh?' said Pike, trying to sound calm. 'Get some coffee, some water, can of Coke or something. Get your shit together.'

'No way, José.'

'Look, fuck it, Noel, we're nearly out of petrol. We need to fill up.'

'I don't need petrol. I'm running on rocket fuel.'

They passed a sign.

'Roundabout,' said Pike. 'Slow down.'

Noel ignored him.

They passed another sign and Noel read it out. 'Ar afwch nawr . . . Reduce speed now. Bollocks.' He put his foot down.

'Noel.'

The word SLOW was painted across the road in big white letters.

'Ha!' said Noel. 'That's a joke, innit? SLOW? I'm going FUCKING FAST!'

'Noel!'

There was a car on the roundabout.

Pike closed his eyes and pulled the hand brake up.

The Mercedes went into a screaming spin, end round end, down the middle of the road. The scenery blurred around them, like they were on a fairground ride, round and round ... Pike was sure they were going to die, that the car would flip over or someone would hit them, but at last they came to a halt, half way round the round-about, miraculously facing in the right direction. Philip Glass still belting out of the speakers.

'Fuck,' said Noel. 'Let's do it again.'

'Pull off the fucking road,' said Pike.

'Okay, okay, okay. Everything's under control.'

Noel started the engine and drove on slowly.

A little way on they came to the services exit and pulled off the main road.

These services had a wood finish and huge sloping roof, like some kind of Swiss barn. Noel parked and killed the engine.

The music stopped. It was suddenly very quiet.

They sat for a few minutes in the car staring out at the night, not saying anything. Drained. Finally Pike roused himself and he got out of the car.

'Come on,' he said, and he went inside.

Pike felt sick from the adrenalin rush. He passed the bleeping, flashing machines in the reception area and went through to the restaurant. The light was very bright in here and everything seemed frozen, like a flashbulb had just gone off. He went to a table and slumped in the seat, stared blankly at the small 'No Smoking' sign.

Noel came in and sat next to him, resting his hands on the table top. His fingers were dancing and drumming.

'What do you want, Noel?' Pike asked, his voice coming out cracked and hoarse.

'I want money and a flash motor,' said Noel. 'I want anal sex, I want oral sex, I want to give Naomi Campbell a pearl necklace, I want to take drugs and drink until I'm sick, I want a place in the fucking sun, I want my own private beach, with one of them jet-ski things. Fuckit, I want my own small country to rule, I want to be able to smoke fifty cigarettes a day, a hundred at weekends, I want to eat shit food, and take a crap undisturbed. Pike, I want to go full diddly like Philip Glass, like a fucking rocket, a Catherine wheel, I want a battery-powered dick to startle the ladies, I want threesomes, foursomes, I want to be on top, underneath, behind, backwards, sideways, upside down. You see, Pike, when I go to the bog there's blood in my shit, I cough up blood at night, my hair's fallen out, I'm overweight, unfit, I'm white, I'm thirty-five and I've got acne. I'm an ugly bastard, but I'm going to be a six-pack man, fuck four-packs, fuck low-alcohol lager, I'm going for high octane, I'm going to the end with this one. I don't want to wind up a drooling old fart, sitting wanking in some home, fantasizing about the nurses, fantasizing about what might have been, thinking "What if?" "If" never happens. "If" is for losers. See that? That out there. The world. The night. The stars. I want all of it. All of it, Pikey.'

'Yeah, Noel, but now. What do you want now?'

'Oh, right. Double egg, chips, beans and a cup of tea, please.'

TWENTY-SIX

'What's the matter, Smallbone?' Terry sounded peeved. 'Put your foot down.'

'I can't, Terry. It's my eyes.'

'What about your eyes?'

'They sting, Terry . . .' Basil couldn't stop blinking. It felt like his eyes were full of grit. When he'd woken this morning the whites were dark red and the lids were swollen and puffy. Now they wouldn't stop watering and they stung like buggery.

'I think I might need to see a doctor, Terry. I think they might be infected.'

'No doctors. We don't need doctors.'

'Well, a chemist, then. Get some eyedrops at least.'

'There's no time.'

'But I can't drive like this, Terry. I can't see . . .' Basil felt like weeping for real. Terry was still groggy and confused and Basil wasn't sure whether Pike hadn't done some permanent damage to him. His short-term memory didn't seem to be working at a hundred-per-cent efficiency. They'd had this conversation about Basil's eyes about five times, now. The only thing Terry seemed able to hold onto was their need to get somewhere, though he couldn't always remember where. And it was going to take for ever at this rate. Basil was driving at about thirty miles an hour.

'Terry, I've got to do something. It's getting worse by the second. I'm going to be totally blind soon if I don't do something.'

'We can't afford the time.'

'Well, why don't you drive, then?'

'No. You're the driver.'

'But I can't fucking see!'

'There's no need for bad language.'

'Please, Terry . . . Look, there's some services up ahead. It won't take me long.'

The services turned out to be little more than a garage with a shop, but it would have to do.

'I'll only be five minutes,' said Basil, undoing his seat-belt. 'I'll get some Optrex, or something.'

'What for?'

'For my eyes, Terry. My eyes.'

'What's wrong with your eyes?'

Basil got out of the car and slammed the door. He stumbled into the shop and groped his way around. In the end he had to ask the sales assistant to get the eye drops. He went back to the car, sat in the driver's seat and bathed his eyes in the little plastic cup. After a few seconds of agony it was bliss. The pain eased and he could see again. They drove on, but slowly the pain crept back, until it got so bad he had to stop and repeat the process on the hard shoulder.

They went on like this mile after painful mile. The motorway ran out and although the road was a decent dual carriageway, Basil was now going less than twenty.

Terry wasn't helping, he kept asking the same questions over and over; where were they going? Why were they going so slow? What was the matter with his knees? Basil was frazzled from lack of sleep and his bloody eyes, and eventually he could stand it no more.

'Terry,' he snapped. 'Please, shut up. I can't concentrate.'

'I'm sorry, Smallbone. I just can't seem to get a grip on things.'

'Maybe if you thought about something else, take your mind off what's going on.'

'What do you mean?'

'Tell me a story, or something. Fix on that.'

'All right. What story?'

'Tell me something that happened to you. I don't know, why don't you tell me how you lost your eye.'

'My eye?'

'Yes, you've never told me. What happened to it?'

'It was in Spain,' said Terry.

'Yes?'

'Yes. You ever been?'

'No,' said Basil.

'Don't bother, it's rubbish. It's just like England except it's really hot. All the shops, the pubs, the people, everything's English. But hot. It's ridiculous, you sweat all day and if you take your shirt off you burn. It's too hot to sleep at night. It's too hot to move during the day. I went for two weeks with my mum.'

'Really?'

'Yes, to Malaga. It's a dump. Some nice pubs, I suppose, but it's so hot. Mum wouldn't go out of the room. Just used to sit there all day watching telly, soap operas and that, in Spanish.'

'When was this?'

'When I was eighteen. I'd been working in a cold storage place, like a giant fridge, carting meat and fish fingers about the place. You had to dress up like you were going to the North Pole, gloves, fur-lined coat, boots, it was nutty, but it was a laugh, nice and cool. I got laid off. Used my money for a holiday. Thought I'd take my mum away. Dad had died that year and she was a bit blue, you know? She had her faith. We used to pray together. But I thought a nice holiday might help. Only it was so hot. It got to me. I mean, you know me, I am usually quite a casual person, nothing much gets to me. I'm pretty good-natured, but in this heat I started to get a bit irritable.

208

I used to drink beer to try and keep cool, and with a combination of things, I suppose I started to get a bit irritable.'

'Sorry, can you see that sign, Terry? I can't see what it says.' They came to a roundabout and Basil could barely keep his eyes open.

'Go straight on.'

'Straight on? You sure?'

'Go straight on.'

'I thought it said Cardigan off to the right.'

'If you know what it said, why are you asking me?'

'Give me some help here, Terry.'

They were crawling round and round the roundabout. Basil trying to get a fix on the signs.

'I am sorry, Basil. To tell you the truth I didn't see the sign.'

'How could you not see it?'

'I forgot. All right? I forgot for a moment where we were going. I forget things . . . Smallbone?'

'Yes?'

'Why are you driving so slowly?'

'I'm blind, Terry. The eye drops didn't help.'

'What eye drops?'

'Look, read that sign there as we go past. Does that or does that not say Cardigan?'

'Yes, yes. Cardigan must be that way.'

So, next time round Basil took the turn-off, and they soon found themselves climbing up a hill past a huge ugly grey castle into the town of Carmarthen. Basil pulled over and bathed his eyes again, and they stayed clear long enough for him to ascertain that they were on the right road.

But Basil was very frightened, now. He had to see a doctor.

Ha. That was a joke. How could he see a doctor when he couldn't open his eyes?

'Come on,' said Terry. 'Let's get going.'

'Please . . .' Basil got out of the car. It was raining. He turned his face up towards the sky and let the cool water fall onto his aching eyelids. He wiped them, causing the pain to shoot right into his skull.

He tried to ease his eyes open, they fluttered, then blinked. Through his tears he could see a vague, watery haze. He closed his eyes. He heard the passenger door slam and Terry's footsteps on the pavement.

'Smallbone,' he said. 'I need you. All right? I can't do this without you. You can't let me down.'

'I'm sorry, Terry, but if we could just get to a doctor's.'

'All right. You know I don't believe in doctors. But if that's the only way. When we get to Cardigan.'

'Thank you, Terry . . . But you really will have to drive.'

Terry said nothing. Basil could hear him breathing close by.

'Terry?'

'I can't drive, Smallbone,' he said, his voice sounding very small.

'Oh.'

So that was it. That was why Terry used him. That was why he needed Basil around; he couldn't drive. Basil felt almost sorry for him. He couldn't help but laugh.

'Well,' he said. 'You're going to have to learn.'

'No. No, I can't. I don't drive.'

'It's easy, Terry.'

'No. End of discussion. I'm not going to drive.'

'Look, we'll go slow. I'll talk you through it. Honest, it's easy. We've got no choice.'

Again there was a long pause from Terry, before he said quietly, 'Okay.'

'All right. I'll try and get us out of town. You watch what I'm doing and when we're on a quiet bit of road, you take over. All right?'

'All right.'

Terry helped Basil back into the car and Basil groped for his seat-belt. Even the simplest things suddenly got complicated when you couldn't see anything.

He felt the car rock as Terry settled into the other seat.

'Do you know anything about driving?' Basil asked.

'No ... Yes. I've seen you do it. I've watched people.'

'The only fiddly bit is the gears. Otherwise it's pretty straightforward.'

'Okay.'

'You've got to press the clutch when you change gear ...'

'The clutch? What's the clutch?'

'The left pedal. You have to press it down, to disengage the engine, then you change the gear. Like this ...'

'Okay.'

'Right, this is the gear stick. This is first, second, third, fourth ... You start with first, then go up as you get faster.'

'What are the other two pedals?'

Basil realized that this wasn't going to be easy. 'Just watch,' he said.

Somehow he got them safely out of town, and he stopped the car to let Terry take over.

Twenty minutes later Terry managed to get the car moving without stalling and they lurched down the road. The engine revved wildly, the gears crunching, but they were moving.

Basil was instantly overcome with terror. It was bad enough trying to teach someone to drive from scratch, but when you couldn't see anything. When you couldn't tell if they were about to do something incredibly stupid. He felt completely helpless.

'Keep the speed down, okay?'

'Don't worry ...'

Terry was deadly silent. Basil was aware of his immense tension and concentration. He could hear his heavy breathing. His little grunts as he did anything. Basil was lost in a world of sounds – the warp of the wipers, the hiss of the road, the hum of the heater ... A blaring horn.

211

'What was that?'

'Somebody hooted at me. I swerved a bit as they were going past.'

'Never mind. No harm done. You're doing fine. Now, you understand about junctions and roundabouts?'

'Yes, I think so.'

'Good.'

Basil's heart leapt as Terry stamped on the brake and he was flung forwards. The car stalled.

'Junction,' Terry said flatly.

'All right, well done. Start her up again. Then ... what do the signs say?'

'They don't.'

'What? There must be a sign.'

'They don't say where we're going.'

'Is it in Welsh maybe?'

'Maybe.'

'Okay, go straight across, I guess.'

Five minutes later they came to another junction, again Terry said there was no sign, again they went straight on.

'Maybe if you talked to me, Terry. It might take your mind off what you're doing, you might find it easier.'

'Okay ... All right.'

'You were telling me about Spain.'

'Spain?'

'How you lost your eye.'

'Yes ...'

'You said you were getting irritable.'

'Yes. It was really hot, you see, and I was drinking a lot. I'd go to pubs at night and drink beer. I had a couple of scraps. Men would pick fights with me and I'd have to sort them out. Nothing serious. Until one night I tried a different pub. There was Spanish people in there. All men. No women. That suited me, women shouldn't go to bars, they cause fights. When it's just men it's usually nice and quiet.

Anyway, a couple of Spaniards start talking to me, very smartly dressed, they were. One of them's in a suit, in a casual style, like an international playboy figure. The other one's wearing a leather jacket, expensive. I wondered how he could wear a leather jacket in that heat, but he seemed all right. Maybe as he was a Spaniard he didn't notice the heat so much. Anyway, we are having a drink, a couple of hours pass, and maybe with all that sweating I got drunk. I would not normally get drunk, but tonight I am drunk. So, then these lads come in, not English lads, Spanish lads. They're just the same as English lads, really, but a bit thinner. And they start giving everyone in there a hard time, pushing their weight around. Generally being a nuisance; lacking in respect. And when they start in on my two friends, I suppose I must have lost my temper. I gave them a smack – there was only three of them, and they were Spaniards, so it was not difficult. I flattened them and they got out of there quick. They understood, now, you see? So then it's drinks all round. I'm a big hero, till the law shows up. Spaniard police, with guns. My two friends tell me I had better make myself scarce, because the lads I sorted must have got the law. So they take me out the back way, the two Spaniards, and they've got a jeep out there, open-topped. They offer to take me out to their place for the night, until the police have forgotten all about looking for me. I was not going to argue. I could see the sense in what they said, it was a nice night and I had always fancied a ride in one of those open-topped jeeps. It's about a twenty-minute ride out to their place, and it's like a mansion. Up on a hill, really posh and modern. I thought to myself, this is a nice place. So we have some more drinks, very friendly, and next thing I know ... Hang on, junction.'

'Okay. Is it signposted to Cardigan?. A407?'

'Don't worry ...'

'Is it signposted?'

'I'll go left.'

'Terry ...'

'Don't worry.'

But Basil did worry. He was beginning to worry a great deal about Terry's lack of interest in road signs. He was beginning to wonder if they'd ever make it to Cardigan.

But they had to, didn't they? Because they had to see to Pike and Noel.

So, one way or another, they were going to get to Cardigan.

TWENTY-SEVEN

'Sometimes,' Noel was explaining. 'A Bloody Mary is the only option.'

'We'll wait till the pubs open,' Pike argued. 'Or go to a hotel bar, or something.'

'No, no, no. Very few people know how to prepare a decent Bloody Mary, and Wales is not known for its self-indulgence and imaginative approach towards drinking.'

'Well, can't you just get a can of Special Brew, or something?'

'No. The only thing that will restore me to humanity is a Bloody Mary.'

'Come on then, get the vodka and tomato juice and let's get going.'

'We shall need a little more than that.'

In fact they needed a lot more than that. The list included Worcester sauce, Tabasco, sherry – 'cream is best, just a dash' – nutmeg, black pepper, lemon juice and finally celery salt. This last item proved the most tricky, but by some miracle the supermarket did have some.

'It would benefit from some ice,' said Noel, picking up a pack of cheap glasses. 'But on a cold day like today that's not essential.'

'Jesus, Noel,' said Pike, grabbing the glasses and putting them back on the shelf. 'Leave them. We've only got about five quid left.'

'So what difference does it make? What else are we going to do with five quid?'

Pike couldn't think of anything to say to that. Noel put a hand on his arm.

'I've lost a brother,' he said. 'My hand's on fire. I haven't slept all night. I've taken a potentially fatal cocktail of drugs. Come on, Pike, allow a condemned man his dying wish.'

'Go on, then.' Pike put the glasses in Noel's basket and watched as he shuffled up to the till and paid for it all with the last of their money.

They were in Safeways in Cardigan, on the far west coast of Wales. They'd arrived on a cold, drizzling, foggy morning as the dark sky was beginning to be streaked with bands of silver light. Silver which soon turned grey.

Everywhere grey. The whole town was made up of grey, stone buildings. There was nothing pretty or frivolous and every other house was pebble-dashed – with the same grey gravel. Ugly cottage after ugly cottage. There was an isolated, desolate feel to the place, it seemed huddled against bad weather. Though Cardigan was a major town in this part of Wales, it had a small, mean air about it. Maybe it was just that they were tired, maybe it was the miserable morning, but Pike and Noel didn't instantly warm to the place.

It was half past eight now, and people were going to work, shop workers hunched in their winter coats, office workers with umbrellas, vans and lorries rumbling in the narrow streets.

The town was obviously geared towards summer holiday trade, there were toy shops, beach shops, newsagents selling postcards and trinkets, all depressing and dead in the middle of winter.

Noel prepared the drink in the back of the car, like some mad chemist; a pinch of nutmeg, a pinch of celery salt, two grinds of black pepper, generous splashes of lemon juice and sherry, and finally the Worcester sauce and the Tabasco.

'It should burn,' he said. 'Like liquid fire. Most people put in some girly drop of hot sauce and a measly drop of the Worcester. Not me, not me.'

Finally he was ready. He offered Pike a taste but he declined, it was too early in the day for him, then took his first taste. A look of sheer pleasure came over him. He closed his eyes, smacked his lips and grinned.

'Ah, the sun has risen. God is in his heaven and all's well with the world.'

So, with Noel in the back getting drunk, Pike drove around looking for accommodation. Most places were closed for the season, but they were eventually directed out of town to a place on the Aberystwyth road.

They were in luck, The Penparc Guest House had a sign saying they were open.

They parked out front in the empty car park and looked at the house. Mercifully, it wasn't pebble-dashed. It was a two-storey, white-painted building with a large single-storey extension added on at the side.

'How are we going to pay for this?' said Pike.

'Something'll come up. Don't you worry.'

Noel winked and got out of the car. Then he went over and rang the bell next to the frosted-glass front door.

Presently the door was opened by a small grey-haired woman with horn-rimmed glasses and a string of pearls over her twin set.

'Good morning,' she said, with a sing-song Welsh accent.

'Hello there,' said Noel. 'I know it's rather early in the day, but do you have some rooms free? You are open?'

'Yes? I'm open all year. You never know . . .'

'Excellent. And you have some rooms?'

'Oh, yes . . . Two rooms, you'll be wanting?'

'I think so.' Noel grinned at her.

She turned round in the little porch and they followed her inside.

'How long will you be staying, gentlemen?' She said as she led them into a small side office.

'We're not quite sure,' said Noel. 'Couple of nights. Could be longer.'

'You are up here on business, is it?'

'We're looking at properties,' said Pike. 'For an agency.'

'I see ... I'd better take your names, gents.'

'Yes,' said Noel. 'I'm Mr Glass, and this is Mr Pekinpah.'

'Pekinpah?'

'Yes,' Noel said. 'With an H.' He spelled it. 'Sam Pekinpah.'

The old lady laboriously printed their names in a register. 'Very good, Mr Glass,' she said at last and looked up.

'Please, call me Philip.'

'Okay, Philip. Now, I'm Mrs Jones ... Elsie.' They shook hands.

'Very pleased to meet you, Mrs J.'

Mrs Jones fished two keys off hooks and took them upstairs.

There was a flower theme to the decor. There were framed prints of flowers on the flowery wallpaper. There were flowery carpets, flowers in vases, even pictures of flowers on the light switches.

The rooms were small and flowery, with single beds, but they looked like heaven to Pike. As soon as the others were gone he pulled the curtains, undressed and went to bed. The bed was very soft, an old-fashioned affair with springs which sagged almost to the floor, but he didn't care. It was warm and quiet and he was soon sound asleep. Deep and dreamless.

He woke at two o'clock feeling vaguely human again. The bathroom was down the corridor and there was an electric shower in it. After showering he dressed in his dirty clothes and went to Noel's room. He knocked but there was no reply. He tried the door. Locked. He knocked again, then went downstairs.

There was a large dining room in the extension. There were more flower prints in here, as well as flower mats on the tables, only two of which, out of the fifteen or so, were laid. There was a clock on the wall and a barometer. Sliding glass doors gave out onto a well-kept back garden with a little ornamental pond in it.

'Pike!'

Pike turned to see Noel in the doorway waving at him. His scalded hand was inside some kind of plastic bag.

'What the fuck's that?' Pike asked.

'Mrs J. used to be a nurse.'

Mrs Jones appeared and smiled at Pike. 'Good afternoon, Mr Pekinpah,' she said. 'Philip told me all about spilling the kettle on his hand. It's not too serious, but this will keep it from getting any worse.'

Noel showed Pike his hand. Inside the bag, which was taped to his wrist and smeared with a thick transparent gel, the skin was pink and large flakes were peeling off it.

'I feel a hundred per cent better already,' said Noel.

He looked awful. Red-eyed and slightly wild. He obviously hadn't slept.

'Can I have a word, Philip?' said Pike.

'Sure, Sam.'

Pike opened the glass doors and they went out into the garden. The cold, damp air felt refreshing. The garden was well looked after, with neat beds and thick springy turf.

'You need to sleep, Noel. I don't want you going barmy.'

'Nonsense. Me and Mrs J. have been getting on like a house on fire. If that's not the wrong expression for this part of the world.'

'I'm sure you have, Mr Glass.'

'Yeah. Sorry about that. It was all I could think of at the time.' Noel kicked a stone into the murky pond. 'Besides, you can talk,' he said. 'Fancy telling her we were looking at property. The Welsh love that, don't they? English hobnobs coming down here and buying the place up. I bet she's a member of Plaid Cymru. She'll probably murder us in our beds.'

'Yeah, probably. But, please, we've got to remain inconspicuous.

If something does go off with Patterson, I don't want any shit from the local plods.'

'Yeah, yeah.'

'So, will you get some rest?'

'I can't sleep, Pike. Look at me. I'm on Planet X.'

'You're in Wales.'

'Well, keep reminding me, or I'll lose the plot. If I don't concentrate for a minute this all seems too weird.'

'Just take things nice and easy.'

'Nice and easy does it every time,' said Noel and he winked.

'Right. First we've got to find Patterson. I guess we can start with the phone books . . .'

'Already done it. There's no Patterson, no Marti Stoddart, even tried Muller. No joy. If he does have a place up here and he does have a phone, it's in somebody else's name.'

'Okay, listen. I'm going to drive around, see what I can pick up. You can come with me if you don't arse about, but I'd really rather you went to bed.'

'I'll come with you.'

'Come on, then.'

They went back inside and Pike closed the door. He got the car keys and his sheepskin jacket from his room and they went out front to the car park.

'We could do worse than try the petrol stations first,' he said, getting into the Mercedes. 'See if any of them have seen a black jeep Cherokee with tinted windows. There can't be many of them knocking about Cardigan. Then we'll try the pubs.'

'Good thinking, Batman.'

'Noel. You've got to promise me you'll behave.'

'Nil problemmo.'

'Just bear in mind that Patterson topped your brother. That's partly why we're here.'

'That's totally why I'm here. I keep forgetting about it, then it hits me again. Chas is dead. Shit, I know he was a twat, but he was my brother. We grew up together, we shared girlfriends ... Well, I had access to some of Chas's cast-offs. I mean ... He was my big brother, but I always looked after him. He was stupid – you know that – he was always getting into stupid scrapes and I'd always be the one who had to try and get him out of them. He'd have some scheme and I'd have to pick up the pieces when it all went wrong. But this time I wasn't there for him, was I? I feel guilty, Pike. I feel like it was my fault. If I could have only been there.'

'Then you'd probably be dead, and all, Noel. You're not a fighter.'

'That's why I've always had to use my head. Jesus, I'm no Einstein, but I was always the brains of the family. He was never any use without me, and I let him down ...' Noel began to cry.

'Oh, Jesus, Noel. Get your shit together, will you?'

'I'm sorry ...' Noel looked at his hand. 'I guess I'm still a little fragile after last night. I don't want to go into shock. That's why I don't want to go to bed. If I stop moving, if I close my eyes, I'm back there in dad's bathroom, with Terry Nugent about to boil me alive. I've never been more scared in my life, Pike. Terry Nugent is seriously round the twist.'

'We're shot of him, now.'

'Yeah ...'

'He's not going to find us down here, is he?'

'No ... No ... It's just ...'

'What?'

'I wish you'd killed him, Dennis. I really wish you'd killed the bastard.'

TWENTY-EIGHT

'We're lost, Terry. Can't you grasp that? We've taken a wrong turning. Why won't you read the signs? Why won't you help?'

'There are no signs.'

'There must be. Jesus, unless we've strayed into such a remote
region that the roads are too small for signs.'

'Yes,' said Terry bluntly. 'That must be it.'

'No. All roads have signs.'

'There are no signs.'

'I don't know,' said Basil. 'Maybe Wales is different. Maybe they
don't have signs in Wales.'

'Yes.'

'Then we'll have to read the map. Find out where we are and you
can look it up in the map.'

'I don't read maps. That's not what I do. That's your job.'

'But I'm blind. I can't open my fucking eyes.'

'Don't swear.'

'Terry, Terry, all right, Terry. Look, we'll have to ask directions.
If you see anyone you'll have to stop and ask the way.'

'Okay. We'll do that.'

The car jerked forwards and they were off again. Basil had no
idea how long they'd been driving around like this. It was like
some terrible dream which you could never wake from, an endless
journey into blackness. Into nothingness. A world without signs.

The only thing that kept him from going crazy was listening to Terry's story about how he'd lost his eye, although every time they were distracted Terry would lose the thread and have to go right back to the beginning.

Actually, now he came to think of it, Basil wasn't sure if the story wasn't driving him crazy, as well. If only Terry would get to the end, or at least give him some hint of how he'd lost the eye.

Terry was off again now, repeating the part about how he'd realized the two Spaniards were arse bandits, that it had been a gay bar and that was what all the trouble had been about. And now Basil was going to have to listen to his theories on homosexuals again.

'It's not that I don't like them, or anything. Not like I've got anything against them. I mean, it's been years since I used to go out with the lads queer-bashing. You know me, Basil, I am a tolerant man. I accept people for what they are. I accept you, after all, and you fornicate with little girls. That is not the point. I just do not want them coming near me, having anything to do with me. I do not want them touching me, or touching my food. There should be some island somewhere that we could send them all to, so they could be happy and we would not have to put up with them corrupting our environment. Either that or they should be sterilized.'

'Sterilized?'

'So they can't mate.'

'But they ... Oh, never mind.'

'Where was I?'

'The one in the suit just put his hand on your leg.'

'Right. So, I get the picture now. It all becomes clear to me. And I tell him I am not interested, but he doesn't pay any attention. He starts to try and feel me up again, so I smack him. The thing is, he seems to like it. Well, this is too much for me, I need to get out of there fast. But I'm in the middle of nowhere, and I don't know how to get back to Malaga. I am thinking I might have to kill the two of them.'

'Where was the other one all this time? The one in the leather jacket.'

'I'm coming to that.'

'Sorry.'

'So I smack him again and now he goes all soft, like a little girl. Starts apologizing, and I'm thinking, good, maybe now we can have a civilized drink. Because he's actually quite an interesting person, an educated man with interesting views on the world. But he keeps jumping up and down, popping in and out, getting snacks and drinks and stuff and, about twenty minutes later, he says he's got something to show me. So I follow him into this other room, and there's his friend, strapped to the wall, stark naked. I've heard about men like this before. S and M, they call it. Sado and Masochism. Men who like to be beaten up by other men. I have had enough by now, I kick the playboy in the privates, hard as I can, and he goes down wheezing. I look at the other one, the one tied up like a turkey, and see that this has given him the most colossal, you know, erection. So I've gone to kick him in the privates when I stop dead. I've seen something. I nearly fainted. I have seen many things in my time, but never this. He's got this huge great metal bar through the end of his, you know, his . . .'

'His nob?' said Basil.

'Yes. That. Like a dumb-bell, right through the head. I'd never seen anything like it. And you know what I thought . . . ?'

'You thought, Christ, that could have somebody's eye out.'

'Eh?'

'Nothing. Never mind. It was a joke.'

'Right . . . Where was I?'

'The bloke tied to the wall had a bar through his nob.'

'Yeah? Look, I'm going to have to go back a bit, or I won't get it straight.'

'Terry . . .'

'We're having drinks, right . . . In a bar . . .'

'Terry, please ...'

'Wait a minute. There's someone.'

The car jerked to a halt.

'What do I have to ask him, again?'

'Find out where we are and how we get to Cardigan.'

'Oh, right, yes.'

Basil heard Terry wind down his window. He tried to listen, but couldn't hear what the man was saying. At last Terry closed his window and started the car.

'Well?'

'We're a bit out of the way. It's a bit of a drive.'

'Just keep asking as we go ... And there has to be a signpost soon.'

Fifteen minutes later they were lost again. Terry had forgotten the man's directions and they hadn't seen anyone else. Terry still kept on insisting there were no signs, so whenever they came to a junction he guessed the way. They drove on in tense silence like this until Terry announced that they'd come to a dead end.

Terry struggled with reverse but eventually managed to get the car turned round, only bumping it twice.

'This is crazy,' said Basil. 'We don't know where we're going.'

'We'll be all right,' said Terry.

'I'm in agony, I'm going bananas, I'm going blind, and we're lost in some kind of stupid, crazy country with no signposts.'

'Should I go left or right?' The car juddered to a stop and the engine cut out.

'Jesus, Terry. I don't know. I don't know where we are, do I?'

'Don't blaspheme.'

'Oh, Christ! Let me try and have a look.' Basil wrenched his door open and got out of the car. He stood there breathing fresh air. He could hear the scream of seagulls, and very near, the sound of the ocean pounding on rocks. He smiled.

'Terry? Terry?'

'What?' Terry called back from inside the car.

'Is that the sea, Terry?'

'Yes.'

'Well, then. Cardigan's on the coast. We can just follow the sea. Are we north or south?'

'North, I think.'

'You think, or you know?' Basil had to shout above the wind.

'I think the man said we had to drive south.'

'Then we're okay.' Basil felt a surge of energy. This was better. Now everything would be all right. He thought he'd try opening his eyes again ... Yes, there was the sea, grey and rough under a grey sky. He turned. There was the car ... The road ... The pain was coming back, worse than ever. His vision was blurring, filming over. With a supreme effort he took one last look.

And there, right in front of the car, was a road sign.

Fuck.

'Terry?'

Terry got out of the car and came over to him.

'What? Are you all right?'

'There's a sign. What does it say?'

'There isn't a sign.'

'There. A sign. I saw it.'

'You can't see. You told me you couldn't open your eyes.'

'I saw it ... What does it say?'

'There's nothing there, you must have imagined it.'

'No!' Basil made his way to the car, his arms outstretched. He collided with it and felt his way to the front, then the side of the road, then the sign.

'Here. What's this? Eh? It's a road sign. What does it say?'

'It doesn't say anything.'

'Come on, Terry. It must say something.'

'No. No, it doesn't. It's not a sign. It's just a ...'

'What? What is it?'

'It is a sign, but it's nothing to do with us.'

226

'Well, what does it say, then?'

'Nothing.'

'What does it say? Jesus, Terry, can't you read? What does it say?' Basil stopped, shocked. Suddenly everything became clear. 'You can't read, can you, Terry?' he said softly.

Terry said nothing.

'That's why you need me. You can't read. That's why ...' Terry still said nothing. 'It doesn't matter, Terry. We'll find someone else to ask the way. You should have said, you should have told me. I don't mind. We'll find directions. I'll get a doctor. I'll be your eyes again.'

'You are blind,' said Terry huskily.

'It's just an infection, from the bucket. I need antibiotics, or something.'

'It doesn't matter any more,' said Terry.

'I know.'

It was ironic. It took losing his sight to make him see, to make him understand. All that Terry had done, his irrational rages, his whole attitude, everything ... It had been so obvious.

The poor sod couldn't read or write.

He felt Terry's hand on his shoulder and he shivered. 'Look, Terry. As you say, it doesn't matter. A lot of people can't read. I won't tell anyone. Hey, I could teach you, Terry. Soon as my eyes are better. I could teach you to read. I'm your mate, Terry, you can trust me.'

'I'm not a stupid person.'

'No. Of course you're not. It doesn't matter about reading. I would never tell anyone. Never.'

'Come back to the car.'

'Yes. We'll ask directions.'

Basil felt Terry turn him and push him along the road.

'Terry, this isn't the way to the car. Terry, the car's that way ...' Basil tried to force his eyes open again, but it was no good, the pain was too intense.

'Come on, now . . . Terry.'

Basil felt the wind in his hair. There was a salty taste to it.

'It's a secret,' said Terry. 'It must always be a secret.'

'It will be. Terry . . .'

'Enough, enough.'

'Please . . .'

Terry pushed him and he was in space.

His one thought, as the breath was pulled from his lungs, was that he'd never know the end of Terry's story, never know how he'd lost his eye.

He gritted his teeth. He was glad, now, that he couldn't see. It made the drop unreal.

The first jolt, as he hit the rocks on the side, sent him spinning, so that now he didn't know what was up or down, couldn't tell if he was falling any more.

Maybe he was flying.

He laughed. He was a bird. He was airborne. He was going up not down.

The second jolt, as he hit the bottom, killed him.

TWENTY-NINE

'They just asked if I'd seen a black jeep Cherokee,' said Julie Pickford.

'What time was this?' Handsome looked at himself in the full-length mirror by the bed. Looked at his long, pale, naked body, thin and muscled. The tattoo on his right arm, a tiger, up near the shoulder so it could be hidden by his T-shirt. His black hair tumbling down onto Julie's face.

'I don't know,' said Julie. 'About five – six. It was dark at any road.'

'What were they driving?'

'Green Mercedes 250.'

'You know your cars.'

'Comes of working in a garage. All I've got to do all day is look at cars.'

Handsome liked the look of his body as it moved over Julie, his buttocks rising and dipping. He was like a big cat, a panther. So different to Julie's softness, her roundness. She was a bit plump, truth be told, puppy fat, but she was a lively little thing.

'So what did you tell them?' Handsome began to move faster, ripples spread up Julie's body as he slapped into her.

'I said I had seen the jeep. Said it'd been in twice. Ow, careful. It was only afterwards I thought maybe I shouldn't have. That's why I told you.' Julie gasped, and her small fingers dug into his shoulders. 'Not so hard,' she said.

Handsome grinned. 'If you see them again, ring me on me mobile.'

'All right.'

He was close, now. He grunted between strokes.

'What did they look like?'

'Old. One had specs and grey hair. The other one was bald, ugly bugger.'

'Yes.' Handsome came, grunting loudly. Then he pulled out and flopped down next to Julie on the wrinkled sheets.

'You done well, Julie. You done well to tell me.'

'As I say, I didn't think anything of it at the time, but you know . . .'

Handsome kissed her on the tit. 'I'd better get going.'

Julie sat up in the bed and looked down at him. 'Can't you stay the night? My parents aren't back till tomorrow.'

'Nope. Things to do, you know.'

Handsome rolled off the bed and slipped on his briefs. He ran a hand through his hair, straightening out the tangles.

'Will I see you tomorrow?' Julie said, pulling up one of the sheets to cover herself.

'Maybe.'

'Handsome . . .'

'Listen, babe,' Handsome snapped. 'You remember what I told you. Don't twist my melons. Don't try to pin me down. I'm not like that, I'm a loner. I'm a free spirit. You try and turn me into your hubbie and I'm gone. Disappear into the night.'

'I'm sorry.'

'Right. I'll be round the garage, anyway.' He pulled up his leather strides and fastened the big silver belt buckle. He'd bought the belt in Dallas, genuine rattlesnake skin. The buckle genuine silver. It'd cost him four hundred dollars. He loved the weight of it. The way it clanked when you did it up.

'Got to keep an eye out for your visitors, haven't I?' He wriggled into his T-shirt and shrugged on his leather jacket.

230

'Are you sure you can't stay,' said Julie plaintively. 'I'll give you another blow job, if you like.'

Handsome laughed. 'That's a very kind offer, little girl, but I'm a busy man.' He slid a hand under the sheet and grabbed her.

'Keep it warm for me, eh?'

Julie giggled and he kissed her. She smelled of sex.

'See you, sweet stuff.' He winked at her, put on his shades, and left the room.

If he got his skates on he could catch Miranda at the pub before she left.

Ah, Miranda. The perfect woman. Couple of years older than Handsome, with bleached blonde hair. She had it all sorted. Lived in a cottage behind the pub. She was soft and warm and loving in a no-nonsense kind of a way. She made breakfast in the mornings, she mended your socks and she didn't get on your case the whole time.

He grinned again.

What a bastard he was. That's what he told people. 'Yeah, I'm a bastard, aren't I?' In the olden days he would have been a scoundrel, or a cad or a bounder, or something, all those types you read about in books, but, this being the late twentieth century, he was most definitely a bastard.

He was his own man, from the dark side, and he dressed the part. Always in black. Everything – from his biker boots to his genuine Harley Davidson leather jacket and his Guns 'n' Roses T-shirt. The man in black, with his long black hair and his black aviator sunglasses – always wore them, never took them off. Day and night, he always had his shades on. Except when he was making love with a woman. Then he'd take them off. They liked that.

He went out into the chilly night. With the shades on he couldn't see much and he had to lift them to find his way to the Land Rover. He got in and checked himself in the rear-view mirror. Looking good. Feeling good. Another two or three days and he'd be out of this shit-hole and away, a wealthy man.

He started the engine.

Yep. A wealthy dude.

Shit, he'd come a long way since he was main man at Nottingham university. The man with the contacts, the biggest dealer on campus.

Handsome.

He'd been called Handsome since he was a teenager, and he *was* quite handsome, in a sort of seedy Byronic kind of way. It was hard to keep his weight down as he neared thirty, but the drugs helped. It was just he'd have to keep the drinking under control, there was nothing worse than a fat arse in leather trousers. But he looked good. Hard and mean. The biker from hell – except he wasn't a biker. He'd had too many friends die on bikes to risk that. It was enough to look the part. It had the desired effect on people. Fear and respect. He liked to walk into a pub, swagger in, and know that people were looking at him, afraid of him. It was even better when he was with Noddy, roaring round the Welsh countryside in the Land Rover, with their shotguns hidden under the seat. It was just like they were in *Mad Max*.

Handsome and Noddy were security for this part of the operation. Later on they'd handle the selling but for now they just had to make sure everything was hunky-dory. So far, of course, nobody had bothered them. That's why the Doc had chosen this part of the country. So they spent their time practising knife-throwing up at the farmhouse. Knife-throwing and crossbow drill. They were getting pretty good with the crossbow. Their chief goal was to down a gull. Noddy had got close to one, sort of grazed its wing, but so far they hadn't scored a direct hit. They'd also had a couple of goes on the shotguns, but got told off. The Doc gave them a bollocking, told them not to be silly arses. He had a licence to shoot on the land but didn't want to attract any attention, risk anyone coming up to investigate.

So it was the crossbow and the knives.

He put a Nirvana tape on. It was a quiet bit, he waited for it to explode into noise and power and he joined in.

'Yeh, yeh, yeh, yeh, yeh . . .'

Shit. Life was good. Just so long as these characters snooping around didn't fuck things up, and he had a theory about them, anyway.

He got to the Bunch of Grapes just before ten. Couple of people looked round as he sauntered in. They were used to him in here.

Noddy was at the bar, he had a fresh pint in front of him, and Miranda was serving another customer, leaning over, showing off her big tits.

'All right?' Noddy asked with his rich west-country accent as Handsome slipped onto the stool next to him.

'Yeah.' Handsome smiled at the Soldier Boy. Noddy smiled back, he knew where he'd been.

Handsome called over to Miranda. 'Pint of Landlord, please darling.'

Noddy favoured army surplus, camouflage gear, netting, bandanas, big boots, lots of belts. Somewhere between Rambo and a South American jungle fighter. That's why Handsome called him the Soldier, or Soldier Boy. They all had nicknames, just like gangsters. They weren't like ordinary people, after all.

'Someone was in here,' said the Soldier. 'Tell him, Miranda.'

'Two blokes come in,' she said.

'Yeah, I know,' said Handsome. 'One bald, one with grey hair.'

'That's right. How d'you know?'

'They've been poking around everywhere. You tell 'em anything?'

'Nope.' Miranda handed him his pint. 'But I did get their address.' She grinned.

'Excellent.'

'I'm not just a pretty face. I told 'em I'd get in touch with them if I heard anything.'

'Where they at?'

'Penparc Guest House, it's out on the Aber' road.'

'Yeah, I know it. Listen, the bald one, did he have, like, long hair round the back and sides?'

'Yeah. It was a well horrible haircut.'

'Sort of pot belly? Long skinny legs?'

'Yeah, that's him. You know him, do you?'

'I think I might. It's Chas's brother. We was warned he might turn up looking for him. The one with him must be Dennis Pike.'

Miranda went down the other end of the bar to serve someone else.

'They might need to be frightened off,' said Handsome.

'Right on,' said Noddy. 'I could do with a bit of action. This security lark can get a bit dull at times.'

'We got to be careful, though,' said Handsome. 'Everything'll be ready in a couple of days, we don't want anything screwing it up now.'

Noddy scowled into his pint. 'I knew it'd be trouble, when bloody London showed up.'

'I always thought he was a poser,' said Handsome. 'Pretending to be a hard case ... but when he drives up with a fucking body in a bag.'

Noddy chuckled and shook his head. 'Fucking hell,' he said. 'Nutter. You know, we should have got shot of him there and then. We don't need the hassle.'

'What the fuck. Two days' time we'll be out of here. Flog the gear, happy new year, and I'm gone. Outta here.'

'You still aiming at Thailand?' Noddy asked.

'Yeah. Shack up on the beach with some under-age tart as my personal slave. What about you?'

'I thought I might hit the States, hang out in Miami, or Malibu, maybe even Hawaii, have a go of some of that surfing.'

Miranda came back over. Leant on the counter, her big tits squashed up in her top.

'You staying the night, then, Handsome?'

'Don't know. We got something to sort out first. Depends how long it takes. Leave the key under the mat.'

'All right, but if it's too late don't bother. I'm a bit knackered.'

'Maybe I could pop round in the morning, quick bunk-up before work, eh?'

'Listen to you, you smooth-talking bastard.'

'You wouldn't have me any other way. I'm your bit of rough.'

Miranda looked at him, the trace of a smile hanging around her mouth. 'You're just a big kid, Handsome,' she said and ruffled his hair.

THIRTY

'A splendid meal, Mrs J.' Noel slapped his belly.

'Well, I'm glad you liked it.' Mrs Jones collected up their plates. 'It's nice to have someone to cook for. Perhaps you'd like a drink in the lounge. I've got some brandy. Or whisky, if you'd prefer.'

'Now, that's what I call hospitality,' said Noel, getting up from the table.

'I've lit a fire in there. It's quite cosy.'

'Splendid.'

Noel and Pike left the dining room and crossed the hall into the lounge. They settled into two flowery armchairs on either side of the fireplace and sat listening to the crackle of burning logs and the steady tick-tock of an ornate clock on the mantelpiece.

Noel stretched out his legs. 'I could get used to this,' he said.

'With any luck we won't have to,' said Pike. 'Once we find Patterson, that's it, home.'

'If we find him.'

'We'll stake out that petrol station. He could come back.'

'It's a long shot,' said Noel, picking his teeth.

'It's the only shot we've got at the moment,' said Pike.

Mrs Jones came in with a tray holding a couple of bottles and three crystal glasses.

'What's it to be, then, gents?'

'I think a whisky for me,' said Noel.

'Yep,' said Pike. 'Whisky'd be nice.'

'Well, I think I'll join you, then.'

Mrs Jones poured out three massive glasses of whisky and handed them round.

'I tell you it's bloody impossible finding someone to have a decent drink with round here,' she said, settling into a third armchair. 'They're buggers, the Welsh, you know.'

'You sound like a native, though, Mrs J.'

'I am, Cardigan born and bred. Every year I tell myself I've got to get out. Everyone's so bloody gloomy and miserable all the time. They don't know how to enjoy themselves. Do you know Poole at all?'

'Can't say that I do,' said Noel.

'I have a sister who moved to Poole. She keeps asking me to come and join her.'

'And why don't you?'

'What would I do with myself in Poole? I've been running this place longer than I care to remember. I have some guests, you know, come back every year. I wouldn't like to let them down. I could sell the guest house but it wouldn't be the same. My heart is in it, you see?'

'You run it single-handed?'

'Since my Dickie passed on. God rest his soul. My two daughters do help me out in the summer, when it's busy, like. But it can get awful lonely in the winter. Don't know why I bother sometimes, really, keeping open, but I suppose it keeps the loneliness at bay, having the occasional guest. It fills a hole, you know? Shines a light in the empty darkness.'

'Well, you've certainly made us feel very welcome,' said Noel. 'Cheers.'

They all three took a long, meditative sip.

And so they chatted like this for an hour or so, until Mrs Jones fell asleep and started snoring loudly in her armchair.

'You know,' said Noel, re-filling his glass. 'There's some good people in the world. You forget that, sometimes, leading the sort of life I've done. You start to think everyone's greedy and self-serving. You think every last member of mankind is venal and damaged in some way. But there's another world, isn't there? A world we sometimes get a glimpse of, like when you're coming into Heathrow and you look down on all those funny little houses, like a kid's game. It's a world in which people are kind and neighbourly, they don't all want to hurt you or nick your wallet. They'll offer you a cup of tea, give your car a push if you break down ... but I can't settle in that world, I've tried, but one way or another bad luck's followed me around all my life.'

'That's not bad luck,' said Pike. 'That's Chas.'

'Yeah, probably.'

'We're not allowed into that world, Noel,' said Pike. 'We're banished. Ever since we topped Williams and Creen we've been exiled.'

'You're back to that again, are you? Always back to that. Why can't you leave it, put it out of your mind? All right, so you did a terrible thing, and it made you feel like a cunt, but people do worse things. The way I see it, it wasn't necessarily one of my boots that did for him.'

'It's not that, though, Noel. You don't understand.'

'Understand what?'

'When I realized what we'd done, what I'd done. When I realized I'd killed two human beings ...'

'I know, you felt terrible.'

'No, that's just it. I felt great. That's the problem. I felt pleased. I had a warm feeling deep inside. I enjoyed the fact that I'd killed them. I wanted it to be one of my boots.'

'Jesus.'

'And that's what made me feel bad. That's what took me out of circulation for ten years, gave me nightmares. I was scared of myself, of what I might do. You see? I might try and do it again. Because there's no bigger buzz. After killing someone everything else is just toothpaste.'

'Fucking hell, Pike.'

'It proved to me I was a man. I'd finally become what I'd always wanted to be – a hard man. No more pretending. No more bullshit. But it's like making a face and the wind changing. It's like making a wish for something and realizing you can never go back. I was stuck with it, with being, basically, a monster.'

'But you're an all right bloke, Pike ... I mean – I don't know what I mean.' Noel took a pull on his whisky and prodded a log on the fire with his boot. 'So, what are you going to do, for the rest of your life? Just hide?'

'I don't know. I've been thinking about it a lot these last couple of days, and I don't know any more. Maybe I've been kidding myself.'

'You worry too much. You think about things too much. That's what comes of living alone. You know what you should do, Pike? Have a go. I mean, Christ, what have you got to lose?'

Before Pike could think of an answer the doorbell rang, two musical chimes, and, as Mrs Jones showed no signs of rising from her slumber, Noel hauled himself up out of his chair.

'I'll see who it is,' he said. 'Shame to wake her.'

He padded across the thick hall carpet and into the little glass-walled porch. He found a light switch, flicked it on and opened the front door.

There was a man there, dressed all in black and wearing dark glasses.

'Hello, Noel,' he said. Noel struggled to place him, he wasn't expecting it to be someone he knew.

And then he remembered.

'Handsome? The fuck are you doing here?'

'That's just what I was going to ask you, Noel.'

'I'm looking for someone.'

'I know you are,' said Handsome.

Noel heard a sound behind him and he turned to see Pike standing in the hall watching them.

'Mr Pike, I presume,' said Handsome.

'What's going on?' Pike asked.

Handsome nodded over his shoulder for them to come outside. Noel turned to Pike and shrugged. Pike came out.

There was a Land Rover parked in the car park next to the Mercedes and Noel recognized the bloke leaning against it with his hands in his pockets. Noddy, wearing a long leather coat. He nodded to Noel, but didn't smile.

'Now, Noel,' said Handsome, lighting a fag. 'This isn't for you.' He flicked his match away into a flower bed. 'We don't want you here, all right?'

'I don't get it,' said Noel. 'What's it got to do with you?'

'Just listen, Noel. Don't try and act tough. Just listen.'

'Who are these people?' said Pike and Noel told him.

'Look,' said Handsome, blowing out smoke theatrically. 'We're handling a very delicate situation up here. The Soldier and I are security, and we don't want any outsiders muscling in and fucking things up, all right?'

Noddy came over and stood next to them, feet apart, hands still deep in his pockets. He was six feet tall, well built, and looked like he thought he was in a spaghetti western.

'We don't want trouble,' Handsome said. 'There's really nothing here that concerns you. So just go. All right?'

'Listen,' said Pike. 'It's cold out here. Do you two want to stop playing silly buggers, or what?'

'There's no need to get unreasonable,' said Handsome, and he made a signal to Noddy with his eyes. Noddy opened his coat to show them that he was holding a shotgun down his leg.

'I'll tell you what you can do,' said Handsome, smiling. 'Is that your car?'

'Yes,' said Noel.

'Right. You go and get your things, check out, or whatever you need to do, get in that car and drive back home to the Smoke. This isn't for you. We don't want you here. We want you to forget you were ever here. Otherwise we could make things very nasty for you.'

'It's late,' said Noel.

'All right. To show you that we're not unreasonable people. Go to bed, have a good night's kip and you can leave in the morning. There. That's fair, isn't it?'

'You in this with Patterson?' Pike asked.

'I don't know any Patterson. And from now on I don't know you two.'

'You're protecting Patterson?'

'I told you I don't know any Patterson. Now go to bed, and I never want to see either of you ever again.'

'Tell Patterson he's wasting his time,' said Pike. 'There's only one way this is going to end. There only ever was one ending.'

Handsome stepped forward and took hold of Pike's mouth with one hand, pinching his cheeks on either side.

'Listen, you senile old git, I've told you.' He waggled Pike's face from side to side. 'I don't know anyone called Patterson. *Comprende*, asshole?'

Handsome let go and gave Pike a little slap.

'Asshole? What's an asshole?' Pike asked.

'You're an asshole.'

'I know what an arsehole is, but what's an asshole?'

'Shut it, clown.'

Pike sighed and looked away muttering, 'Everyone wants to be an American.'

'Don't worry about it, old feller,' said Handsome and he gave Pike another patronizing little slap.

'Good night, campers,' said Noddy, and, laughing, the two of them got into the Land Rover and roared off into the night.

'Well, what do you make of that?' asked Noel, watching their rear lights disappear into the distance. The smell of exhaust fumes hanging in the night air.

'I think that our friend Herman the German may very well have not told us the truth, Noel.'

'That's a distinct possibility, Pike. Highly distinct. So, what do we do now?'

'We finish our drinks, get a good night's sleep and see what tomorrow brings.'

'Good idea.'

THIRTY-ONE

Terry Nugent was struggling to find the heater controls when the silver-grey Audi pulled out of the side road. Terry saw it too late, twisted the wheel to try and avoid a collision but hit the front side of the other car and careened off the road into a stone wall.

The engine raced for a moment, whined, then cut out. Steam curled from under the bonnet. Terry got out and looked at the damage. The whole of the front was stove in. He looked at the Audi, it was barely scratched. The driver opened his door and climbed out. He was a businessman type in a suit. He looked at his car, he looked at Terry's car and finally he looked at Terry.

'I'm saying nothing,' he said.

'You've spoiled my car,' said Terry. 'You've squashed it.'

'I'm saying nothing.'

'Look at my car.'

'You were going too fast, anyway,' said the businessman. 'I couldn't possibly have seen you.'

'I wasn't going fast. I was going slowly. It was your fault.'

'I'm saying nothing.' The businessman got a small leather folder from his pocket and opened it. He slipped out a pen.

'You'd better give me your name and address, details of insurance.' He looked at Terry, pen poised in mid-air.

Terry got back in the Vauxhall and tried the engine. It wheezed and something clanked, shaking the whole car.

'Hey!' said the businessman, leaning in the window. 'You've scratched my car, you know. You can't just drive off. I need full details.'

'It was your fault,' said Terry again.

'I'm saying nothing. Name?'

'You've broken my car,' said Terry and he got out.

They were in the middle of nowhere, surrounded by fields and trees. He hadn't passed a house for at least five minutes. The sky was heavy and grey and looked like it might start raining on them at any moment.

'Name?' the businessman repeated, an edge of impatience in his voice.

Terry went over to the Vauxhall and took all his stuff out.

'What do you think you're doing?'

Terry walked to the silver car and opened the door.

'I said what do you think you're doing?'

'I'm in a hurry,' Terry said and sat down. The controls were different to the ones in Basil's car, but not so different he couldn't work out what was what.

'Look. What the bloody hell do you think you're doing?' The businessman yanked the door open.

Terry got out of the car and head-butted the bloke, causing the pus-filled lump on his forehead to explode. The businessman sprawled off the road and into a ditch. Terry felt a wave of faintness wash through his head, everything seemed to buzz. He shook himself, squeezed his eyelids shut and took a deep breath. In a few moments it cleared and he was back to normal. He looked at the businessman, who was sitting in the ditch staring up at Terry, very white except for the yellow and red egg-burst just above his eyes. He looked shocked and frightened.

Terry wiped his forehead, sniffed, and pulled his cap down. He gazed at the man, he gazed at the cars. His mind was a blank.

Dammit. He'd had things under control. Butting the man had set him right back.

Never mind.

He could sort this out.

He was on his way somewhere. Yes. Think. Somewhere in Wales.

What would Basil have done in this situation?

He'd have looked at some writing. That was where all the clues were. All the answers. In writing.

He'd taken everything off Basil at the beach. Climbed down the cliff and emptied his pockets. So much paper. So many bits of writing.

He pictured Basil coming out of Chas's bedroom in London, paper in his hands. That's how they'd found the address in Bath. Maybe the new address was written in there somewhere. Basil hadn't thought to look before.

Yes. This was good thinking. This was clear thinking.

He pulled the pile of paper from his pocket.

The man was still sitting in the ditch, shivering slightly. Like an animal that had been hit by a car.

Terry sat down next to him on a rock and gave him all the stuff. 'Read this to me,' he said.

'What?' The man looked at him with wide, shiny eyes.

'Read me these writings. On the paper. Read it to me.'

'I don't understand.' The man sounded sad.

'Look. It's very simple,' said Terry. 'I want you to read me all these bits of papers.'

'Read it?'

'Yes. Is that such an unusual request? I mean, can't you read?'

'No ... I mean, yes.'

'Right.'

'I'm sorry. I'm sorry.' The man blinked twice and began to read, his voice shaky. 'Eggs, milk, Jaffa cakes ...'

'No,' said Terry. 'Just addresses. Names and addresses.'

'Right. Sorry.' He shuffled through the paper. 'Andy, 32 College Road ...'

'No.'

'Herman, 6 Royal Crescent . . .'

'Yes,' Terry smiled. 'I remember him.'

And so the man read on, sifting through the scraps, until suddenly Terry stopped him. 'Read that one again.'

'Hill Farm, Cardigan.'

'That's it. That's the place.'

'And there's a map,' said the man, showing Terry the paper.

'A map? Tell it to me. From here. Tell me how I get there.'

The man studied the scrawled diagram for a while. 'Right,' he said. 'You need to go north from here.' He pointed down the empty road. 'That way. Until you hit the A487, it's a major road, you can't miss it. When you get there, go left, towards Cardigan . . .'

He gave Terry precise directions and Terry made him repeat them several times, until he had a clear picture in his mind.

Basil would have been proud of him.

He generally felt a little better this morning. His headache had dimmed, although butting the businessman had brought it back with a vengeance. His knees were still very stiff and painful but he knew he had to keep them moving, keep them active, so they wouldn't seize up altogether.

He'd slept the night in the back of the Vauxhall. After pushing Basil off the cliff he'd driven around aimlessly for an hour or two, trying to get as far away from there as possible. He'd eventually found a quiet road and parked for the night.

He felt a bit sorry for Basil. After all, he'd helped him out quite a bit since Wandsworth, but it had to be done. A secret was a secret, and once one person found out it was no longer a secret. So he'd just have to cope without the child molester from now on.

As it was, he'd been making pretty good progress this morning. He'd asked a couple of people the way to Cardigan and it hadn't seemed that far. Then this fool had crashed into him.

Oh, well. It had worked out all right in the end. He knew exactly where he was going now.

He stood up, took all the pieces of paper back off the man and thanked him. He went back over to the Audi and opened the door.

No. What was he thinking of?

The businessman knew everything. Where he was going and everything. He'd maybe even guessed that Terry couldn't read. Terry sighed. What a nuisance.

He turned round and started back towards the man.

The man looked at him and must have understood. He leapt up with a little bleat and scrabbled over a stone wall into the field behind. Terry was after him as quick as his bruised legs would carry him. He vaulted the wall, but as he landed his knees buckled. He grunted and fell over.

The field was very muddy, slick with rain. Terry's legs hurt with a fierce ache, but he picked himself up and went after the man.

The man was over as well, sliding in the mud. Terry saw that he was wearing posh leather shoes with smooth soles. They were useless here. He was all over the place.

Terry picked up a long branch and followed. The man went down again and as he was getting up Terry clipped him with the branch. This time he stayed down.

Terry rolled him over and placed the branch across his neck, standing on either end of it. His weight squished the man down into the ground.

The man scrabbled about for a bit, clutching at the branch, wriggling like a snake, his white face turning red. He was looking right up into Terry's face and trying to say something.

Terry looked off across the field. They were on top of a hill and the view seemed to go on for ever.

There were some birds wheeling in the sky, calling out. In the distance some sheep.

He'd always liked the countryside. He remembered trips as a kid with his mum and dad. Up Epping Forest way, picnicking by the side of the road.

He filled his lungs with clean air.

He really should get out more.

The man had stopped moving now. Terry removed the branch and felt his neck for a pulse. It was all right.

He hid the body under the wall, cleaned himself up and got back into the Audi.

He started the engine. It sounded deeper than Basil's, quieter.

He put the car into gear. It leapt away from him and bounced down the road in a series of bunny hops before stalling. He re-started the engine and released the clutch more carefully this time, but it was still like the car was some kind of beast that wanted to tear loose. It was scary at first, if Terry relaxed for a moment it would all go wrong, but after a while he began to get the hang of it, he even began to enjoy the feeling of power.

Maybe it was for the best. Once they identified Basil's body they'd probably be on the look out for his car. It was a good idea to dump it. Only then, of course, when they found the second body, they'd be on the lookout for this car. No problem. He'd abandon it well before he got to the farm. Walk the last bit. As long as no one saw him, he'd be in the clear.

It was a good plan but things were getting unnecessarily complicated. Without Basil's help it was all that much more difficult.

Nevertheless, he was confident he'd find what he was looking for. He had right on his side.

He eased his foot down on the accelerator and risked changing gear. Holy cow he was moving, now! He smiled like a kid and looked at the speedometer. Forty miles an hour. His fastest yet.

THIRTY-TWO

Pike was washing at the small sink in his bedroom when he heard Noel calling his name and knocking on the door.

'It's open.'

Noel came in with a look on his face which said, 'You'll enjoy this.'

'They're here,' he said.

'Who?'

'Tweedledum and Tweedledee.'

Pike splashed water over his face. 'And?'

'And they're going to give us an armed escort out of town.'

'Yeah?' Pike towelled his face dry.

'They've given us five minutes to get ready.'

'Yeah?'

'Yeah. So what we gonna do?'

Pike pulled on his shirt.

'I'm gonna do what I should have done a long time ago.'

'What?'

'I'm gonna sort things out.'

'You mean . . .'

'First thing I want you to do, Noel, is make me the perfect Bloody Mary.'

'It'll be my pleasure.' Noel rubbed his hands together and left the room cackling.

Pike sat on the edge of the bed and pulled on his socks. He was clearing his mind now, shutting everything down, pulling the heat in from his skin, hardening the surface, focusing everything down into one hard cold spot.

First the compression, then the explosion.

He found his trainers, slipped them on and laced them up.

He took a long breath and held it till it was all used up then slowly let it out, and as he did so the years fell away and the fog in his mind cleared. He took a couple more deep lungfuls then steadied his breathing, slowed it right down. He could feel his heart settle too. He felt almost weightless. All the clutter in his head was drifting away. No distractions. Nothing mattered any more.

Noel came back in with two glasses full of thick, dark Bloody Marys. He handed one to Pike, they clinked.

'I figured it out, Noel,' said Pike. 'When you've got nothing to lose, you've got nothing to lose.' He drank, and the Bloody Mary burned down inside him and settled there.

'Well?' said Noel eagerly. 'What d'you think?'

'Perfect.' Pike stood up. 'I'm ready to face the new day, Noel.'

'You're gonna do it, aren't you? You're gonna go for it. Full diddly.'

'Full diddly, Noel.' He took another drink and closed his eyes, drawing in the last few loose ends. 'Full diddly.'

'Oh, happy day,' said Noel. 'Welcome back Pike.'

'It's good to be back.'

'Let's go.'

Pike opened his eyes. 'Let's go.'

They left the bedroom and went downstairs. Handsome was in the hallway, leaning against the wall next to a full-length mirror. He had a big hunting knife in one hand, pointing at the carpet. Pike didn't say anything, didn't stop. He strode across the hallway and got to Handsome before he realized what was going on.

And then Pike went off.

With one hand he grabbed Handsome by the throat, pinning

him to the wall. With the other hand he hit him full in the face. Handsome yelped. Pike hit him again then took the knife off him. He flung the weapon to one side and Noel picked it up.

Still holding Handsome by the throat, Pike marched him backwards through the dining room and pushed him through the glass door into the garden. Handsome stumbled backwards, broken glass falling from his leather jacket. Pike didn't stop moving, he picked Handsome up and threw him in the fish pond. Then he squatted down and held his head under for about half a minute. The water was freezing cold, but Pike didn't notice, it was like dreaming, like dancing, you just let your body run away with itself.

He pulled Handsome out. He was gasping and choking, weeds clogged his hair, one of the lenses of his dark glasses was missing. Pike flung him aside and left him puking on the damp grass.

He went back inside. Mrs Jones was there with Noel, looking at the broken door.

'Morning Mrs J.'

'Good morning Mr Pekinpah.'

'Mr Pekinpah's caught a burglar,' said Noel.

'Oh.'

Pike was out the front door now and still moving. Noddy was in the front seat of the Land Rover, smoking a fag, his legs sticking out the door, the shotgun at his side. He saw Pike coming, threw the cigarette away and tried to bring the gun up. Pike kicked the door and it slammed into the gun barrel and Noddy's legs. It gave Pike time to come around and pull him from the car. He shoved him into the flower bed, picked the gun up by the barrel and began to beat him with it. Noddy tried to shield himself from the rain of blows but it was no use.

'Please stop it. Stop it, please,' he repeated over and over again as Pike clubbed him, clubbed him until the gun broke in two.

Handsome appeared now, limping round from the back garden.

He took one look at Pike, standing over the Soldier with the broken gun, and bolted. Pike went for him but Handsome got past and ran out into the road.

A car swerved just in time to avoid him, blared its horn at him and continued on down the road.

Handsome had fallen over and Pike grabbed him by the hair. He dragged him back to the car park, kicking and squealing.

Noddy was on his hands and knees, groaning. Pike kicked him in the face and dumped Handsome next to him.

Then it was over.

Noel came out of the house with the knife. 'Holy shit,' he said. 'Mrs Jones all right?'

'Yeah. Told her not to bother with the police. Said we'd sort it.'

'Good. Now, let's get this finished.'

They bundled the two sorry cases into the Mercedes. Handsome in the driver's seat with Pike sat next to him, pressing the knife into his gut. Noel in the back with the Soldier, who was in too much pain to do anything more than curl up in a ball and whimper.

'Okay,' said Pike. 'Drive.'

'I can't,' said Handsome. 'I think you've broken something.'

'It's a bugger, isn't it?'

'Come on, man.'

Pike dug the point of the blade in and Handsome hissed.

'Take me to your leader,' Pike said and Handsome started the car. The Philip Glass tape came on quietly and Pike left it playing.

They drove towards the sea, down narrow winding roads. There were no trees here and what they could see of the country above the steep, overgrown banks looked bare and exposed and weather-beaten. Pike read the signs to odd, unfamiliar places, Mwnt, Gwbert, Felinwynt . . .

The road was only wide enough for one car and at one point they had to stop and reverse back to a passing place to let a tractor go by.

Nobody spoke, but the warmth and the breath from four sweaty bodies kept fogging the windows. Pike turned the screen heater on full.

After a few minutes they came over the crest of a hill and below them was the sea, big and grey and misty, merging at the edge with the sky, then they rounded a bend and the view disappeared behind the high sides.

They drove on for a couple more minutes then Handsome turned off the road onto a rutted dirt track which cut through a wide, muddy field.

The sun came out, breaking through the clouds, and the big sky was reflected on the bonnet, moving slowly back along it. The wind hummed and whistled around the car and otherwise there was no sound or movement in the whole landscape.

Inside the car the music went round and round.

Ahead of them there was an old farmhouse with a pointed slate roof. It looked like something from a child's farm set. There was a cobbled yard, barns and outhouses, a tractor. As they got nearer they could see that it was badly run-down, the woodwork was peeling and rotting, the pointing flakey. Machinery in the yard was rusting, tangled with weeds. There were holes in the roofs of the sheds.

A black jeep Cherokee with tinted windows was parked across the field next to a small, filthy caravan, which, like everything else, had seen better days. A mud-spattered Range Rover was parked next to the house.

Handsome stopped the Mercedes next to the Range Rover and they all got out. Pike bundled Handsome up to the door and pushed it open.

They went into a kitchen, it was dark and smelled of cabbage. There was a big oak table in the centre of the uneven stone floor with a couple of cardboard boxes full of cans on it next to a pile of vegetables. A large pot was bubbling on the gas stove, giving off the unpleasant stink. Hanging on the walls were a collection of dull, brass pans, some antique farm implements and a loaded crossbow.

'Where is everyone?' said Pike.

Handsome shrugged. 'Dunno.'

Pike prodded him with the knife.

'Maybe down in the lab.'

'Show me.'

Handsome led him out of the kitchen into the narrow hallway. There was a rotten wooden door under the stairs, he pulled it open and it scraped along the floor, creaking on its broken hinges.

'Down there,' said Handsome.

'Go on, then,' Pike shoved him and Handsome stumbled down a couple of steps before grabbing onto a railing and going down more slowly.

It didn't look like Pike's idea of a lab. It was more like a light engineering works crossed with a school science experiment. As well as two or three pieces of machinery whose function Pike couldn't even guess at, there were lots of plastic buckets and what appeared to be washing-up bowls, connected with lengths of dirty rubber tubing. There were jars of crystals and various paper sacks and canisters spilling chemicals and powder. There were some battered industrial scales, large and small, a calor-gas heater blasting out dry, smelly air and a cat curled up asleep on top of a plastic dustbin. Against one wall was a large fridge and what looked like a giant pressure cooker. It was all very ramshackle and unhygienic.

Noel and Noddy clattered down. Noel coughed and looked around.

'Hello,' Pike called out. 'Anyone home?'

'I'm afraid so,' came a deep, cultured voice and Pike turned to see someone at the top of the steps. A very tall, very thin man who looked to be somewhere between forty and fifty. He had wild, blond hair and a long scraggly beard which came to a point on his chest. He was wearing white overalls tied round the waist with string, and green wellington boots.

And he was holding a shotgun.

The shotgun was pointed at Pike's head.

'Fuck me,' said Noel. 'It's Gandalf with a shooter.'

Pike held Handsome round the neck. 'You shoot that,' he said to the tall man, 'you're liable to blow both our heads off.'

The tall man shrugged.

Pike couldn't tell. He didn't know people like this. Handsome and Noddy he understood – wimps pretending to be tough guys. You knew where you stood with someone like that, someone in a leather jacket. But this bloke? He didn't know how he might react, what he might be capable of. It was the wellington boots which did it. If he'd been wearing army boots, or DMs, then he was readable – but wellingtons . . .

Pike put the knife down and let Handsome go.

'Hello again, Noel,' said the tall man in his plummy Oxbridge accent, and he slowly came downstairs.

'Doctor Fun,' said Noel. 'Meet Dennis Pike.'

Pike nodded at the Doctor and the Doctor nodded back. He then looked at his two security guards and tutted.

'Oh dear, oh dear, what a mess.' His voice sounded like one of those old BBC announcers you sometimes heard on black and white stuff on the telly.

Handsome looked sheepish, he stared at the floor. 'We tried to get rid of them, but . . .'

'Oh, do shut up, Handsome.' The posh man looked at Pike and Noel. 'We'd better get you two upstairs. I don't want you down here.'

He jerked the gun barrel and they all climbed back up the steps and went into the kitchen.

Chas was sitting there at the table, looking slightly nervous.

'Surprise, surprise,' said Pike.

THIRTY-THREE

Chas held up his hands in surrender. 'What can I say?'

'You can say sorry for a start,' said Noel. 'You know what I've been through for you?'

'It had to be this way.'

'Why?'

'The deal of a lifetime.'

'How many times have I heard that, Chas?' said Noel, wearily.

'All of you, shut up,' said the Doc. 'The only thing to discuss, here, is what we're going to do with these two.'

'Kill 'em,' said Handsome, sullenly. He was still damp and shivering slightly in the cold kitchen.

'Thank you, Handsome,' said the Doc. 'That's a very helpful suggestion. What I propose is that for the time being we lock them in the pantry. Then we'll think about it.'

Handsome came over to Pike. He'd taken off his broken dark glasses, and without them his eyes looked small and weak.

'I'm going to kill you, asshole,' he said, pointing a nicotine-stained finger in Pike's face.

Pike brought his arm up like a piston, slamming the heel of his palm into Handsome's chin. His jaws clacked shut and he flew over backwards, cracking his head off the edge of the table. He lay still on the floor, either knocked out or dead. Pike didn't particularly care.

'Enough of that,' said the Doc. 'Noddy, open the pantry door.'

Clutching his side, Noddy limped over to a blue-painted door and unlocked it with a big rusty key. He pulled a string and a fluorescent striplight flickered on, lighting up a tall, windowless room lined with mostly empty shelves.

The Doc gestured towards the opening and Pike and Noel shuffled over.

'And you, Chas.'

'Eh? You what?' said Chas, his voice high-pitched and affronted.

'I've had enough of this palaver,' said the Doc. 'Get in there, I need to think.'

'But I'm on your side, Doc.'

'This isn't a game of cowboys and Indians. Get in there.'

So they all three went into the storage room and Noddy locked the door. The air was dusty and it stuck to your lungs. Pike buttoned his sheepskin jacket and shoved his hands in his pockets.

'Well,' said Noel to Chas. 'This is another fine mess you've gotten me into.'

'Jesus Christ,' said Chas bitterly. 'If you two jokers have screwed up this deal for me ...'

'Shut up, Chas,' said Pike and he sat down on a box of dried beans.

The room was freezing, it must at one time have been a kind of cold storage for food. There were a couple of iron hooks hanging from the high ceiling and the shelves were deep and solid.

'What's he making down there, then?' said Noel. 'Acid?'

'MDMA,' said Chas, brightening up. ' "E". Ecstasy. Methylene-doxy-N-methamphetamine, to be precise. Enough to keep the whole population of London happy for a month. They've been here all summer setting it up. It's for a very merry Christmas and new year. All I had to do was come up with enough dosh to buy my stake in it. Twenty-five grand grosses me two hundred and fifty thousand – a quarter of a million. Shit.

All my problems solved.' Chas looked at Pike. 'But I didn't have the cash, did I?'

'Why didn't you just tell me, Chas?' said Noel.

'Would you have let me rip off Pike?'

'Well . . .'

'Besides,' said Chas. 'It was all hush hush. They insisted on it, total secrecy. I turn up tonight with the money and I drive away with a lorry-load of "E".' He blew into his hands and turned to Pike. 'You understand, don't you? I'd have been able to give the money back after the new year. It's the party season, I could shift the lot in five minutes. I'm sorry, all right? But you've got to let me go through with it. I can't back out now.'

'All that shit with Herman? You being dead, etc?' said Noel.

'I needed time,' said Chas. 'I needed you off the scent.' He looked at Pike again. 'A quarter of a million, Dennis. Think about it.'

'Chas, you're the only person in the world who could lose money dealing drugs,' said Pike.

'Jesus, I knew that'd be your attitude. Soon as I saw you in your poxy flat, I thought, Pike's gone straight.'

'Going straight's got nothing to do with it.'

'Well, there's nothing you can do to stop me, anyway.'

'Chas,' Pike said very quietly. 'You give me my money and that's the end of it. I won't even hurt you. Those clowns can do what they want.'

'No, Pike,' said Chas, angrily. 'I'm not letting you. Jesus, I've come too far. I'm so fucking close.'

There were shouts from next door, the sound of furniture scraping, something heavy bumped.

'Look what you've started,' said Chas, gesturing at the locked door. 'I had it wrapped up, sweet . . .'

Pike wasn't listening any more. He felt tired, now. Right down to his core. The clarity had worn off and the Bloody Mary had given him indigestion. So he'd beaten up a couple of small-time

258

hard nuts. Sad fucks who'd watched too many American films. So what? What had that proved? That he could still kick the shit out of someone? It hadn't solved anything.

He was back where he started. He never would really change. Not inside.

He looked at Noel. Happy to have his brother back, but pissed off at him for being alive and causing them all this trouble. Things were simple in Noel's world.

You've got to belong, Noel had said. But what he'd meant was you've got to belong to me. Everything's got to be the same as it always was. Noel needed Pike to be Pike. To be what he'd always thought he was. Perhaps in the end you never could live for yourself. You made up a story, you put on your face and that was that.

Sarah had told him to come back when he had his shit together, and, last night, lying in Mrs Jones's soft bed staring at the flowers on the curtains, he had thought about returning. He couldn't go back to her like this, dried up and confused. He'd forgotten his new rule: never make plans at four in the morning. Maybe he should make it his only rule, simplify it.

Never make plans.

Never do anything.

Shit. Canada? What was Canada?

He shuddered and his teeth chattered. His arse was going numb. He stood up and stamped his feet. Chas and Noel carried on bickering, like a couple of little boys.

He thought about Kirsty and wondered what kind of life she could expect. Well, at least she was smarter than her dad.

Kids. They can know so much and so little at the same time. When he was young all he'd wanted to be was a tough guy. And he'd become one. A feared and respected man. A man who had worked out that the bloke who wins the fight isn't the one with the better punch, the one with the black belt and the most experience.

No, the guy who wins the fight is the guy who's prepared to go the furthest. The guy who's prepared to be the meanest, most degraded, most soulless fuck in the universe.

That was how Patterson had pulled it off. Patterson really hadn't cared about the scousers, and while Pike was snivelling in his bed, Patterson casually went about stealing his money, his woman and his life. Noel was right, that should have been Pike up there in the Belvedere. Maybe if he hadn't chosen the life he had, if he'd gone down the route that had been mapped out for him by his parents – A-levels, college, respectable job, wife, kids . . . Maybe then he would have become what Patterson wanted to be. Legitimate. A pillar of the community.

That was the way it went. The hard man wanted to be a respectable businessman, the nice boy wanted to be the hard man. And in the end nobody wound up happy.

He thought back over the last ten years. Ten years of complete fucking misery.

Well, Pike, it's time to wake up. Time to quit feeling sorry for yourself and get back into the real world.

And then a thought struck him.

Where was Patterson? If his jeep was outside, and Chas was here, then where was the Jock?

And why, if Chas wasn't meant to turn up till tonight, had he got here early?

'You topped him, didn't you?' he said, and two faces snapped round, as if they'd forgotten all about him being there. 'Patterson.'

Chas looked at his feet.

'It was an accident,' he said.

'Chas, you didn't?' said Noel.

'He arrived at Herman's,' said Chas. 'After you've so helpfully told him all about me. Cheers.' He rubbed his neck and stared down at the floor. 'Marti done it. We're fighting, arguing, and she shoves him down the stairs.'

'So, she's with you, then?' said Noel.

'When I've first gone to see Patterson, try to get the cash off him, he's not there, right? And Marti's pissed up at three o'clock in the afternoon, pissed off and all. Starts coming on to me – well, I've always fancied her, and ...'

'What the fuck did she ever see in you?' asked Pike.

'She was bored. Fed up with Patterson, fed up with being a businessman's wife. She missed the old days, you know? The wild times. Hell, you know what she's like, Pike. And I was still the same old Chas. I'm an adventurer, she saw that in me.'

Pike started laughing humourlessly.

'Plus, he was seeing someone else,' said Chas. 'Some posh business-woman type and Marti's found out about it.'

'What a fucking mess,' said Pike.

'The end was in sight for him, anyway. He was losing it. That fancy pad of his up Chelsea Harbour, he couldn't afford that. He's got property all over, dodgy mortgages, all based on lies. He's skint; overdrawn to the tune of about two million, keeps stringing the banks along, borrowing from one to pay off the other. Any day now the whole thing was going to collapse. He always was a bullshitter, a chancer. Marti knew it, knew he was finished. She wanted out.'

'So you topped him?' said Pike.

'It was an accident.'

'What did you do with the body?' said Noel. 'Where is he?'

'On the compost heap. They've got this huge, like, shredder in one of the sheds. You can bung anything through it, branches and everything, chews 'em up and spits 'em out.'

'Fucking hell,' said Noel. 'That's disgusting.'

'Yeah. The Doc's done it. None of the rest of us could face it. Made two sacks full. Put him on the compost.'

'Fucking hell,' Noel said again.

'This was the only place I knew to dump the body. I had to come up here with Marti. We had no choice.'

'Where's Marti, now?' Pike asked.

'Kipping out in the caravan. She don't like getting up in the mornings.'

'Never did,' said Pike.

'You imagine,' said Chas. 'Patterson started going to bed early, getting up at, like, six o'clock …'

There was another shout from the kitchen, then a woman's voice, low and insistent.

'The fucking trouble you've caused, Chas,' said Noel.

'Look, I really need that money. You don't know. There's someone I owe …'

'Terry Nugent,' said Pike. 'We know.'

'You know Terry Nugent?'

'He tried to boil me alive,' said Noel. 'We've been busting our bollocks trying to get rid of him.'

'Well, you see my predicament.'

'Do you want to hear about my predicament, Chas?' said Pike. 'For ten years I work like a fucking slave. I do nothing, I have no life, and I manage to scrape together twenty-five thousand pounds. Now, I know that's not much, not much to show for ten years of someone's life, but it's all I got. Then I get the chance to lend this money to a complete fuckwit who intends to make a thousand per cent profit with it, but I know that this said fuckwit will wind up robbed, nicked, or dead. So, what do I do? Take the money or open the box?'

'You're a bloody fool, Pike,' said Chas. 'Don't blame me for wasting your bloody life. I'm offering you a good deal. I'll double your fucking money. I'll triple it. Just give me the chance, for once in my life, to hit the big time. To sit behind the wheel of a flash motor, drive into town and have people say, "Look, there's Chas … There goes old Chas. What a geezer." '

There was a click and a creak and the door opened.

It was Marti, looking mightily pissed off.

'Welcome to the club,' said Pike. 'Join the party.'
'Hello, Dennis,' she said flatly and stepped to one side.
Terry Nugent stood there holding the shotgun.
'Oh, shit,' said Noel.

THIRTY-FOUR

'Out,' said Terry Nugent, and they trooped out of the storage room.

Chas put a hand on Marti's arm. 'Are you all right, love?'

She shrugged him off. 'Mr Big-shot. This what you call showing me a good time? Why is it that everything I touch turns to shit?'

'That's a good question,' said Pike and he looked around the room.

Handsome still lay where he'd fallen. The Doc and Noddy sat back to back at one corner of the table, they'd been wired to the leg with thin fencing wire. Their mouths had been taped with gaffer tape. One side of the Doc's face was badly cut and his head lolled forwards onto his chest. Noddy looked like he'd had enough and given up.

Terry nodded at Marti. 'Now do them two.'

'Which two?'

'The Bishops. Leave Pike.'

'Terry,' said Chas. 'I've got your money, man. Give me a day or two and I can double it.'

'I'll deal with you in a minute, Chas. First I've got to settle something with him.' He pointed at Pike with the gun.

'Do what you like with him,' said Chas. 'But just trust me. I can make you a rich man.'

'I don't want to be rich,' said Terry. 'I just want what's mine.'

'You and me both,' said Pike.

'Come on, do them!' Terry snapped at Marti.

'All right. All right.'

Chas and Noel dutifully sat at a second table leg and Marti began to wind wire round them from a big coil. Terry's eyes flicked backwards and forwards from her to Pike.

'Still got a taste for excitement, then, Marti?' Pike said, looking around for anything he might be able to use.

'If you hadn't fucked up all those years ago, Pike,' she said, grunting with the exertion. 'None of this would have happened.'

'You'd have made something else happen though, wouldn't you? You were never happier than when you were breaking things.'

'Get a move on,' said Terry.

'All right,' said Marti petulantly. 'I'm not a bloody labourer though, am I?'

'Terry,' said Pike. 'Why don't you give it a rest? Calm down. Enjoy life. You go charging about the place like a bull with a hot poker up its arse. Is that the best way to get things done?'

'I do things my way. The right way.'

'There,' said Marti, standing up. 'Satisfied?'

Terry checked that Chas and Noel couldn't move. 'Good,' he said, and Marti neatly cut off the end of the wire with a pair of pliers. Then she turned to Pike.

'You know what?' she said. 'My whole life's been lousy. I can't remember a single good time. Not with you, not with anyone. Even the good times were bad.'

'You, girl,' said Terry, pointing to the storage room. 'Go in there.'

'Go in there yourself,' she said. 'I've done what you asked. They're all yours.'

'No. I want you to go in there.'

'Bollocks. I'm going home. You can stay here and play your macho games with the other little boys. This is nothing to do with me.' She took a step towards the door.

'Don't,' said Terry,

'Ooh, hark at him.' She opened the door.

'Marti,' said Pike. 'Don't.'

'I can do what I like, Pike,' Marti yelled. 'I've always tagged along with bloody men, and where has it got me? From now on I'm on my own. I do what I want.' She hit her chest with a fist. 'What *I* want – me – Marti Stoddart. I mean, look at you.' She swept a hand round the room. 'What *do* you look like?' She shook her head, turned away, disgusted, and stepped out into the yard.

Terry shot her in the back. She fell down in the mud and one hand pawed at her back, like someone trying to get at a difficult-to-reach itch. Blood stained her white jacket. After a few pathetic attempts the hand fell still.

'Why did you do that?' Pike asked. 'You didn't have to do that.'

'I don't really like women,' said Terry. 'They don't understand.'

He raised the gun. Two barrels – two charges.

'Now you,' he said to Pike and he pulled the gun back and smacked Pike round the side of the head before he could do anything to defend himself.

'That's for my knees,' said Terry.

The force of the blow knocked Pike to the ground. He picked himself up, his head stinging badly, and Terry hit him again.

'That's for my head.'

Pike staggered back towards the kitchen wall.

Good, he thought, you just keep doing that. You just keep hitting me, you little cunt.

Whack. A gout of blood flew from the side of Pike's head and sprayed the stone floor.

'That's for the memories – the ones I don't have.'

Come on, come on, hit me again, push me over the edge, make me go berserk.

Whack.

'That's for Basil.'

Pike collapsed against the wall, knocking things off their hooks.

Good. It's coming now. Full whack. Full diddly.

Whack.

'That's for making me drive.'

Pike dropped to the floor and sprawled among the fallen objects.

Terry stood over him. He aimed the gun at Pike's face. 'This is for me,' he said.

Pike looked up at him – his thick, squat body, his pebble-like, no-neck head, his dead eyes – and the madness went out of him.

This wasn't the way to do it.

He didn't have to be a moron all his life.

'You're a tough guy, aren't you, Terry?' he said.

'Tougher than you, Pike.'

'So why not prove it? Shooting me doesn't prove anything. A girl could shoot me. Why not a fair fight, eh?'

'Like you gave me last time?'

'That's the point. That wasn't fair. I had a weapon. Like this isn't fair, now. No weapons. Just the two of us, eh? You and me and our bare hands. See who really is the hard man.'

Terry thought about this for a while.

'Well?'

'Come on, then,' said Terry, and he threw the gun to one side. 'Come on. Get up.'

Pike stretched out his hand and looked up at Terry. 'You're a hard man, Terry Nugent,' he said. 'But you're stupid.'

Pike picked up the fallen crossbow and shot the bolt straight through Terry's glass eye.

Terry went rigid, his arms and legs stuck out stiffly, like a dead frog. He took a couple of steps back on tiptoe, then crashed to the ground, the bolt pointing straight up at the ceiling.

'That was for Marti,' said Pike.

'Good shot,' said Noel.

'Lucky shot,' said Pike.

'Get us up from here.'

Pike got the pliers and cut the two brothers free.

'Thanks, Pike,' said Noel, looking down at Terry. 'He was one scary bastard.'

'Boy, am I glad that's over.' Chas sat down heavily at the table. 'What a day.'

Pike looked at Marti lying out in the yard. It had started to rain and the blood on her back was soaked to a pale pink. He went out and picked her up gently. She felt heavy in his arms. He kissed her on the forehead and carried her in out of the rain.

He laid her on the table in front of Chas. She looked like she was asleep. 'She'll never have to get up early again,' he said.

'What a shitty day,' said Chas.

'I'm off now,' said Pike. 'You can sort this mess out with the hippies.' He looked at the Doc, still wired to Noddy. 'Looks like you're gonna be busy with your compost shredder, mate.' He turned back to Chas. 'Now, Chas, where's my money?'

'Oh, no, Pike, please Pike.'

'Look, Chas, it's over. You had a little dream for a while. You kept yourself busy, filled up some empty moments, shone a light into the darkness, and four people have wound up dead. Isn't that enough for you? Aren't you satisfied yet? What more damage do you think you'll do if you carry this thing on?'

'I want to put things right . . .'

'Where's the money?' Pike advanced on Chas.

'All right, all right . . . It's in the back of the jeep. There's a compartment under the floor of the boot.'

'Thank you, Chas.'

'You're a bastard, Pike. You always were. I never liked you.'

'I don't care – give me the keys.'

Chas groped in his pocket and brought out the car keys.

'I'll go,' said Noel. He took the keys off Chas and went out into the rain.

'I'm sorry,' said Pike. 'But once a loser always a loser. See you, Chas. I'm going home.'

Pike took the keys for the Merc out of his own pocket and left the farmhouse. He turned his collar up against the wind and the rain, but he was still instantly cold and wet. He set off towards the car, splashing through puddles in the yard.

He hadn't taken ten paces, however, when he heard a shout behind him.

'Pike!'

He turned to see Chas with the shotgun. His heart sank.

'I can't let you go, Pike. I can't let you do it.' Chas was crying, like a kid who'd had his bike nicked. 'This is my one chance. My shot at the big time. I'm not letting you take that away from me.'

'Fuck it, Chas. Can't you ever accept anything?' he shouted. 'This is the way things are.'

'No. I do not intend to be Chas Bishop for ever. I want to be king for a day.'

'It doesn't work like that, Chas.'

'Well, fuck you.' Chas raised the gun.

They heard an engine start and both looked round to see Noel driving the Cherokee towards them across the field. As it picked up speed, it bounced and jolted over the bumpy, muddy ground, water and earth splashing into the air behind it.

At first Pike and Chas were so close together it was difficult to tell who Noel was aiming at. Then the car veered to the left and was bearing down on Pike. Pike stood his ground. The jeep hit a deep rut and slewed round, towards Chas.

'Noel!' Chas yelled, and the car twisted away, back towards Pike.

Forty, fifty, it was picking up speed.

Pike couldn't take his eyes off the great black shape hammering towards him.

What the fuck? Maybe it was in his stars.

Then at the last moment the jeep skidded round in a great flume of dirty water and broad-sided Chas, squashing him against the wall of the farmhouse. There was an explosion as the gun went off.

Noel jumped out of the jeep, slipped over, rolled back onto his feet and scrambled over the bonnet, catching his jacket and ripping the pocket.

'Chas!'

Chas was slumped against the side of the jeep, rain pouring off his silver-blond hair. He slightly raised his head and looked at Noel. The bottom half of his face was raw and bleeding.

'Noel . . .' he said, his eyes red from crying. 'Noel, it's me, Chas.'

'I know Chas, I'm sorry. I'm sorry. It's just . . .'

'I know. I ruined your life, didn't I, Noel? From the start.'

'No, that's not it . . .'

'I've shot myself, Noel.'

'Come on, you're all right.' Noel clambered back over the bonnet and got back into the driver's seat. He started the engine and steered the jeep away from the wall.

Chas fell to the ground and lay in the mud. When Noel got back to him he was dead. Now Noel began to cry.

Pike came over to him and put a hand on his shoulder. 'Thanks, Noel,' he said.

'Fuck off, Pike,' said Noel, bitterly. 'I was aiming for you.'

THIRTY-FIVE

'I'm a man of peace, Pike,' said the Doc, cradling his mug of tea.
'A spiritual man. This was a sacred place. Then you came here and
poisoned it.'

'What about that poison you're making in the cellar?'

'That's not poison. There's not a single recorded case of MDMA
ever directly harming anyone. Alcohol is poison, tobacco, sugar, fat,
the fumes from cars, factories . . .'

'I'm not gonna listen to a lecture from a hippie,' said Pike. 'Even
an educated one.'

'I was going to turn on London,' said the Doc. 'Like those celeb-
rities who turn on the Christmas lights on Regent Street. I was
going to make this a happy country.'

'Still can. I've not touched your gear.'

'You've soured the whole deal. You've pooped the party.'

'So? What? Are you not going to sell it now, then? Now that I've
fucked its karma?'

The Doc said nothing, just stared into his tea.

There were four of them sat round the big table, Pike, the Doc,
Handsome and Noddy. Noddy still looked sick. Handsome looked
like he'd just risen from the grave. Neither of them showed any
interest in joining in the conversation.

'You're making something that people want,' said Pike. 'You're making money, here. And once there's money involved you've got to take on all the shit that comes with it.'

'I'm not interested in money,' said the Doc, loftily, as only a man who's been brought up with the stuff can.

'Bollocks,' said Pike.

'I don't sell to make a profit, just enough to finance the next operation. These two . . .' He nodded at Handsome and the Soldier. 'They do what they like with their share. That's not my concern.'

'God save us from hippies with a mission,' said Pike.

'Why don't you fuck off?' said Handsome, lisping chronically.

'What happened to your voice?' Pike asked grinning.

'I bit the end of my tongue off.'

Pike laughed. The Doc looked at him for a few moments then joined in. Handsome got up from the table.

'Don't ever turn your back, asshole,' he said. 'I'll be waiting for you.'

'All right,' said Pike, and he, too, got up. 'Here you go.' He turned his back on Handsome and leant forwards. 'Kick my ass. Come on, kick my ass, motherfucker.'

He heard the door slam, and when he turned around Handsome was gone.

'What about you, then, Soldier-boy?' Pike asked Noddy. Noddy looked up from his tea, then looked down again.

'Jesus, young people these days,' said Pike. 'No backbone.'

The door banged open and Noel came in from the yard.

'It's done,' he said. 'I'm ready.' He was soaking wet and covered in mud.

Pike got up. 'Let's do it, then.'

'We should really have put him through the shredder like the others,' said the Doc.

'No way,' said Noel. 'He may have been a fool but he was my brother.'

'You'll have to clean up behind us,' said Pike. 'But then, I'm sure

272

you don't want anyone coming round asking awkward questions any more than we do.'

'Don't worry,' said the Doc. 'It's taken a great deal of time and money to set this up. A lot of organization. We'll just have to do a little bit more. But rest assured. Nobody will ever know what happened here.'

'See you, then,' said Pike and the Doc saluted.

Pike went out to the field with Noel. The Cherokee was there, surrounded by cardboard boxes and piles of newspapers. Noel picked up a petrol can and emptied it into the back seat. He stood away, lit a match and threw it in the door. Nothing happened. He threw another. On the third attempt the petrol caught, there was a whoomph and in a few seconds the jeep was shrouded by flames.

Noel, his face red and sweating, ran back to where Pike was standing. Pike offered him a cigarette, Noel took it and they watched the fire together.

One by one the windows popped. The last to go was the windscreen. Pike caught a brief glimpse of Chas sitting upright in the driver's seat, for all the world as if he was driving.

Finally he'd got what he wanted, to take the wheel of a flash motor and set the world alight.

Then the flames and the smoke took him and they didn't see him again.

Neither of them knew any prayers, so they just stood in silence, looking at the burning car and smoking, the wind whipping their hair, the rain falling off their noses.

A couple of minutes later the petrol tank must have gone, because there was a loud bang and parts of the jeep were thrown around the field.

'That's that, then,' said Noel. He started to walk back to the Mercedes.

'Wait a minute,' said Pike and he took a pile of papers from his pocket.

'What you got there?' Noel asked.

'Williams and Creen's stuff. I've been carrying it around for too long.'

He dropped the small pile of documents onto the fire and watched them briefly flare then curl up and turn to ash.

'We're the only two left, now,' said Noel.

'Yeah.'

'Fuck,' said Noel. 'What a way to spend Christmas.'

'Come on. Let's go home.'

They took Noddy into town and dropped him off at the guest house to pick up the Land Rover. Mrs Jones was inside with a glazier who was fixing the broken glass door. They settled up for their rooms and Pike gave Mrs Jones some money for the damage. She wouldn't take it at first – hadn't they seen off the burglars? Hadn't they protected her? – but Pike insisted and in the end she gave in.

She came out to the car park to wave them goodbye.

'So long, then, Mr Glass, drive carefully. If you're ever back down this way. Bye, bye, Mr Pekinpah, happy Christmas.'

'And a merry New Year,' Noel called out of the window.

They hardly spoke at all in the car. They didn't play any music. The journey felt long and dull. It rained all the way. Port Talbot steel works looked just like any other dreary industrial site in the daylight. Pike felt a strong sense of anti-climax. He had his money back, everything was just like it had been before the Bishops showed up.

Except it wasn't the same, was it?

The traffic got worse as they neared England, and by the time they got onto the Severn Bridge they were hardly moving at all. They crawled across the river through low cloud which hid the top of the suspension towers.

'Fuck this,' said Noel.

'Christmas, I suppose,' said Pike.

'Yeah. What d'you want to do now, then?'

'I dunno. Take me to your dad's, I guess,' said Pike. 'I'll pick up my car and go into Swindon, put this cash back where it belongs.'

'And then?'

'And then I go home.'

'And then?'

'Who knows?'

'When do you go to Canada?'

'Maybe never. What the fuck would I do in Canada?'

'I thought . . .'

'I've been wrong, Noel. There are worse things in the world than me. I belong here. What about you? What'll you do with Chas's car?'

'Leave it in dad's garage. He'll never remember how it got there. Jesus, Pike, how can I face him?'

Pike couldn't think of anything to say. So he said nothing. Neither of them did until they arrived on the estate in Swindon fifty minutes later.

Noel parked the car and they sat in silence for a while. Pike lit a cigarette.

God, it had been a long four days.

'Pike?' Noel said finally.

'What?'

'You never asked how Terry Nugent found us.'

'I figured you must have told him.'

'Yeah. Sorry.'

'It doesn't matter,' said Pike. 'I'd have done the same.'

'I should have told you.'

'Leave it, Noel. It doesn't matter. He's dead. He's on the shit heap.'

'You should have fought him,' said Noel. 'You should have gone up against him. I'd have liked to have seen that.'

'Are you kidding? He was the real thing,' said Pike. 'He'd have torn me limb from limb.'

Pike got out of the car. Saw his yellow Escort sitting where he'd left it.

Noel got out as well. Looked at his father's house. He sighed and shook his head. 'Poor old dad. Chas was always his favourite. I guess we could spend Christmas together. Least I can do. Maybe clean his place up.'

'Noel?' said Pike.

'What?'

'What happened back there? With Chas. What happened?'

Noel took in a deep breath then slowly let it out. 'All the way across the field,' he said, 'I wasn't sure what I was going to do. Should I stop Chas or help him? Was it going to be Chas or you? All the way, I didn't know. Then in the end I realized Chas was my brother. No matter what. Blood is thicker than water. In Chas's case, fucking thick. But I had to help him. So I steered towards you ... and then I went into a skid. The car was all over the place. I lost control, didn't know where I was heading. I closed my eyes. Fuck it, I thought, let God decide. I'm too much of a wanker to make a decision like that ... and when I opened my eyes, there was Chas.'

'I didn't know you believed in God, Noel.'

'I don't. You think if there was a God he'd have let me run over my own brother?'

'Well, thanks.'

'It's all right, Pikey,' said Noel. 'I don't blame you ... I just ...'

'Yeah,' said Pike. 'So long.'

'Maybe we could meet up sometime, for a Christmas drink, or something. Eh?' said Noel, forcing a smile.

'Maybe.' Pike looked up at Sarah's house. He couldn't face her now. Maybe one day. There was still hope. Maybe one day he could turn up on her doorstep with a big, genuine smile on his face and say, 'Can I come in? It's cold out here.' It was something to aim for at least.

He realized that Noel had said something.

'You what?'

'Stay for a bit,' said Noel.

'I don't think so.' Pike began to walk away towards his car.

'Stay for a bit,' said Noel, following Pike. 'Come with me to pick up Kirsty. She'd like to see you again. Stay for tea. We'll get a take-away . . .'

'So long.' Pike didn't turn round.

'Come on, Pikey. At least wish us a happy Christmas.' Noel caught up with him and trotted at his side. 'I mean, you've enjoyed it, haven't you?'

'I've got some money to put in the building society, Noel. I don't want to miss it. They won't be open again till after Christmas.'

'You'll keep in touch, though, eh? I mean, we're mates, yeah?'

Pike stopped at his car and looked at Noel, standing there like a little boy. His jacket ripped. An over-eager grin plastered across his round, egg face.

'See you, Noel.' Pike unlocked the Escort.

'Oh come on, Pikey. You've seen the films. You know the plot. Two blokes, thrown together, they start off hating each other, arguing all the time, then they share some adventures, they learn things, they grow as people, and at the end they're friends for life. Best mates. You've seen the films. You've seen 'em . . .'

'All right, Noel. We *were* thrown together, yes. And, yes, we did start off hating each other, I'll freely admit I thought you were a twat, but we certainly had some adventures, didn't we? We had some times.'

'Yeah. That's more like it. You went full diddly. I got to do a handbrake turn. Terry Nugent got what was coming to him . . .'

'And I guess we both learnt some things,' said Pike. 'I've changed my plans. I've changed my life thanks to you and your late brother.'

'That's right.'

'But it's not like the movies, Noel. There's a big difference.' Pike got into his car.

'What?'

'The difference is . . .' Pike smiled at Noel. 'I still think you're a twat.' He slammed the door and started the engine.

'What?'

'Happy Christmas, Noel.' Pike pulled away.

Noel called after him. 'Pike! Pikey! Dennis!'

But Pike didn't stop.